Praise for

SOMETHING I SAID

'Fantastically, gloriously funny. I loved this book; it gave me such joy at every single page'
Katherine Rundell

'All the star ingredients for a funny, touching read which will really resonate. I thoroughly recommend it!'
Jasbinder Bilan

'A hilarious and original story. Carmichael Taylor is the stuff of legends – he's my new favourite character'
Katya Balen

'An original concept, spot-on observations of family life and friendships, and snappy dialogue give this book a fresh feel. Best of all, it's very, very funny!'
Lesley Parr

SOMETHING I SAID

BEN BAILEY SMITH

BLOOMSBURY
CHILDREN'S BOOKS

LONDON   OXFORD   NEW YORK   NEW DELHI   SYDNEY

BLOOMSBURY CHILDREN'S BOOKS
Bloomsbury Publishing Plc
50 Bedford Square, London WC1B 3DP, UK
29 Earlsfort Terrace, Dublin 2, Ireland

BLOOMSBURY, BLOOMSBURY CHILDREN'S BOOKS and the Diana
logo are trademarks of Bloomsbury Publishing Plc

First published in Great Britain in 2021 by Bloomsbury Publishing Plc

A catalogue record for this book is available from the British Library

ISBN: PB: 978-1-5266-2868-8; Waterstones: 978-1-5266-4505-0;
eBook: 978-1-5266-2869-5

2 4 6 8 10 9 7 5 3 1

Typeset by RefineCatch Limited, Bungay, Suffolk

Printed and bound in Great Britain by CPI Group (UK) Ltd, Croydon CR0 4YY

To find out more about our authors and books visit www.bloomsbury.com
and sign up for our newsletters

For Luke, who knows funny

CHAPTER 1

Life's a Joke

'Is *everything* a joke to you, Carmichael?'

Ugh.

That question.

Again.

I don't know how to write a sigh but just know that I'm sighing as I write this.

Hearing it once more that afternoon at school, I felt like I'd been asked the same question my whole LIFE, or at least the majority of my near fourteen years on the planet.

And yet, for as long as I can remember I've found LIFE a bit of a laughable pastime.

LIFE:

- Wake up: why? Sleep is amazing.
- Go to school: put on a miniature suit (weird).

and travel through the rain (probably, because: London) to a building to find out about long division, split infinitives, how to bake rock cakes and other things you will NEVER NEED TO KNOW IN THE FUTURE.

- Come home: tell your parents about your day (yuck).
- Tomorrow: do the EXACT SAME THINGS AGAIN.

Pretty ridiculous. And you have to laugh at ridiculousness, don't you? I mean, if you don't laugh at it, how the actual heck do you live through it?

'Is *everything* a joke to you?'

I sometimes wonder if I was asked that as a toddler. I definitely remember Mum asking it when I was around five years old. My older brother, Malky, had dropped his ice cream into a pile of dog poo, and I laughed and said, 'Three-second rule?'

Three-second rule was something Mum often said when we'd drop a chip in the kitchen or a grape in a museum or something. She'd encourage us to pick it back up and eat it before the lurgies of the world descended on the morsel, so in my five-year-old brain I'd assumed it was a funny observational reference. She didn't think so. She said I was being *vindictive*.

Words are important.

Words can surprise you, hurt you, make you laugh.

Words are powerful.

In fact, words have the power to change your life, *forever*.

Considering how important words are, you'd think we'd know all the ones we need, wouldn't you? But if you keep your eyes and ears open, there are new ones to discover every single day.

Like *vindictive*.

In that moment, I had to ask my mum what *vindictive* meant. (I was *five years old*, guys, give me a break!) When she told me it meant that I was being cruel, I tried really hard to explain the events – unseen by her – in the build-up to me laughing at my brother's expense. Unfortunately I was missing a couple of crucial words in my pre-school vocabulary: *context* and *karma*.

Of course, now I know all too well that *context* is like a frame around a picture. It gives you all the elements that make up the whole story and helps you to focus on it clearly.

And *karma* describes the practice of *cause and effect*: do a good thing and good things might happen; do a bad a thing and bad things might happen.

So if I could go back to that day as a five-year-old outside the park, me and my seven-year-old brother licking

99s with Flakes and strawberry sauce in the crisp early September sun, I'd say to my mum, *'Hold your horses there, Mother, that was actually KARMA. Let me give you a little CONTEXT so you know I wasn't being VINDICTIVE.'*

And I'd go on to eloquently describe how Malky had kept nudging my shoulder, trying to make me drop *my* ice cream, exactly the type of meanness in which my brother would regularly – and gleefully – partake.

So when Malky nudged too hard and lost his grip on his own frozen trophy, sending it hurtling not just towards the earth but all the way into a putrid, fly-infested point of no return, YES, I laughed. I laughed heartily and delivered the most stinging of rebuttals – a recognised Taylor Family saying, fiendishly turned on its head for ultimate humour and justified revenge.

Oh, you better believe it – if I knew then what I knew now, I would've defended my corner like a debate team champion. Unfortunately, I was only five so I just cried, *'I'm NOT binvictive!'*

'Is *everything* a joke to you?'

Yep, I'd heard that one throughout most of the following years of primary school, like when I laughed in a Year 5 assembly because Magid was awarded a certificate for one hundred per cent attendance but missed the presentation due to a dental appointment. Or in Year

3 when we missed our tour slot at the London Transport Museum because of severe delays on the Central Line.

My laughter wasn't appreciated by my teachers, which was odd because I wasn't laughing at anyone's hardship or bad luck. I was laughing at the *irony* of the situation, which is actually an impressively mature form of humour, thank-you-very-much, and should, in my opinion, have been celebrated and encouraged.

The first two years of secondary school had been much like the last two years of primary school: life had become a series of events that I found funny in ways that the vast majority of adults around me just didn't.

Kids, on the other hand? I mean, I don't wanna blow my own trumpet (although, hygiene-wise, shouldn't we stick to blowing our own?), but I'm kind of a big deal when it comes to making other kids laugh. I'm the go-to guy for chuckles. Kids from all walks would invite me to parties and outings, sit with me at lunch, generally get me involved in stuff – I guess the thinking was, if I was there, something funny might happen. I was literally a funny sort of popular.

A big part of school is purely about survival. To survive, you need an identity and I had one. That identity was known and celebrated throughout Year 8.

My speciality is the ability to say what most kids want to say out loud but don't. Because when you're doing a practical science test, the act of holding up two flaming Bunsen burners whilst yelling 'I AM THE GOD OF HELLFIRE!' tends to get you a couple of detentions and an eye-wateringly boring one-hour safety course alone with Mr Clarkson, Head of Science.

It was worth it.

Look. I'm not going to pretend I'm the *Cool Kid*. I'm not the fastest. I'm below average in goal, defence and up front. I'm not the best looking. Girls never fancy me. I'm definitely bottom of the league in the Quality Trainers category. But in that exclusive league of Oh My Days, Remember That Time?, I'm top of the table every season. I mean my stats are through the roof.

I'm the undisputed champ in Unnecessary Outbursts in Double Maths ('Guys, I've nailed the algebra problem! Me plus Maths equals Y! *Why, why, WHY?*').

I'm number one in Witty Comebacks to Bullies ('Well, technically, Jack, if you're gonna "eat me for breakfast" we'll need to postpone this until tomorrow morning at the earliest. What's your schedule looking like?').

I'm also unparalleled in Sarcastic Comments to Teachers ('Sir, what does it feel like to achieve your life goal, live your dream and teach PE?').

Sarcasm's kind of a mean one, pretty low, so I try to save it only for those who deserve it. Sometimes it just pops out. I mean, when you're soaking up the pleasure

Mr Jenkins takes from making you do push-ups in the rain you just have to go with your instinct.

As much as I love playing with words, I will say I am a lifelong fan of slapstick. Actual, physical stuff happening at random, preferably involving muck, liquid or falling – ideally all three – to someone. Anyone. Even me.

Don't get it twisted. I have no issue with being the butt of a joke. When I'm not making stupid people look stupid, I'm all for looking stupid myself.

Anyway, slapstick was sort of the reason I was where I was at this very minute.

FOURTEEN MINUTES EARLIER:
You see, me and my Year 8 Geography class were outside on the playing field with the tightly wound Miss Stillman, trying to identify different types of cloud forma- tions. She was screaming *'Nimbus! Nimbus!'* at an uninterested Dion James when, out of the very blue which we were looking up at, A PIGEON FLEW DIRECTLY INTO HER FACE.

It was in the weird silence, after both the stifled laughter of the class and the wild yelping of Miss Stillman had subsided, that I said what I said.

THIS VERY MINUTE:
'Is *everything* a joke to you, Carmichael?'

Miss Stillman tilted her head down and her eyebrows up, hoping to coax a response from me by using my full, admittedly ridiculous, first name.

I did that thing of looking at my feet, partly to display that kind of *'I'm really sorry for everything, even existing'* body language, but mainly to avoid eye contact, both with her and Mr French, the Head of Year whose office she'd dragged me into.

'Well, is it?'

WHAT I WANTED TO SAY:

No, not everything. But lots of things are, and it's like no one else wants to admit they're funny. I mean, if you're genuinely asking me did I find it amusing that whilst you were unnecessarily screaming at a child, you were head-butted by a flying rat? Like, if you're actually questioning whether it felt like a joke when you panicked and then the pigeon panicked and pooed all over your clipboard? I'm sorry but the answer is yes. Life is full of really stupid jokes and I'm going to enjoy them. Is that so wrong? DOES THAT MAKE ME A MONSTER, MISS STILLMAN? DOES IT?

WHAT I ACTUALLY SAID:

'No.'

'I could have been *blinded*!' Miss Stillman squawked, appealing for similar levels of outrage from Mr French. 'Infected with *God knows* what kinds of germs. Most people would have rushed over – *"Are you OK, Miss*

Stillman?", "*Shall I get help, Miss Stillman?*" But no, not Carmichael. You know what his response was?'

She paused for dramatic effect and Mr French raised his eyebrows as if to say, 'No, what?'

'He said, "*See? Even nature hates Geography.*"'

The Head of Year performed an involuntary gulp-cough combination, took a sharp breath inwards, as if sucking on an invisible straw, then looked to his colleague.

'Thank you, Miss Stillman, I'll take it from here.'

She nodded, brushed past me, paused at the office door.

'Send him back when he's ready to take life seriously.'

I glared at the door as it closed behind her. Mr French let a moment of silence hang in her wake, then pulled a file from a cabinet behind his desk, opened it and tapped it as he spoke.

'There's a pupil in Miss Miller's English class – she came to me raving about him. *Attentive, confident, engaged, incredible ability* ... basically a joy to teach. Know what his name is? *Carmichael.* When I heard that, I thought what are the odds? *Two children born in the same year, in the same class, both with the unusual name Carmichael!* The other Carmichael? Grades slipping, attitude worsening, respect for almost all other subjects and their teachers at a worrying low.'

He turned a page of the file.

'So I pull out the contact details to send a commendation to the parents of Carmichael One and a *third* behaviour warning to the parents of Carmichael Two and *whaddaya know?*'

He waved a single Personal Information Sheet with a School ID photo of me in the top right corner, pulling a subtle goofy face – nostrils ever so slightly flared, eyes ever so slightly crossed. They said we shouldn't smile in the photos, but straight faces have never been my bag, so I'd improvised. I kept a straight face as Mr French held up the sheet, but my internal smile was beaming.

'Sir, can I—'

'We're an Academy with a strong focus on *respect*, Car. Something I'll have to reiterate to your parents yet again in the email home I'm about to write. In the meantime, why don't you spend some time with the other Carmichael? I hear he's a *fantastic* influence.'

Mr French did a smile that wasn't a smile and gestured to the door. I nodded and shuffled out.

Sarcasm.

Ugh.

The lowest form of wit.

CHAPTER 2

Car. YES, Like a Car

I stood in front of the mirror of Wainbridge Academy's ground-floor boys' toilets, nose slightly wrinkled, breathing through my mouth as I always did because: *boys.*

I stared at my reflection, pondering.

In adverts for perfume and hair gel, glamorous models look to the camera as if to say, *'Hey, I can't help being this gorgeous.'*

In selfies, taken and retaken, edited, deleted and reposted online, people pose as if to say, *'Yep, this is my AMAZING FACE, I think you'll find it's pretty darn pretty – enjoy it, world.'*

In movies, actors look past the camera as if to say, *'I already know how good I look, I don't even need to make eye contact with you – get a load of this beautiful right ear.'*

But when I looked at my own close-up in the

11

smudged and graffiti-spattered mirror, I patted my unruly nest of hair and shrugged as if to say, 'That'll have to do.'

OK, listen – I'm not a gargoyle. But I'm also no supermodel. How do I put this? My appearance is a lot like my humour – under-appreciated.

At thirteen and three quarters, I was shorter than average with a round, light-brown freckle-covered face, eyes with odd swirls of hazel and green, and a badly behaved ginger Afro.

This was my parents' fault.

If you ever wondered what happens when a black woman from Grenada and a white man from Aberdeen have kids, well, the answer is there's no answer.

Me and my fifteen-year-old brother, Malky, looked totally different. Almost weirdly different. Like *one-of-us-was-actually-found-in-a-bush-as-a-baby* different. Malky was darker skinned with deep brown eyes, wavy, tame-able black hair and the pointed, chiselled features of a young athlete. Which – annoyingly – was exactly what he was.

As much as I'd love it if it turned out that Malky really was a poor bush child, the simple explanation for our physical difference was that Malky looked like our mum and I looked like our dad. And while my mum, the pint-sized, youthful-looking Jocelyn Taylor, had smooth, blemish-free features, permanently kissed by an eternal

Caribbean sun, my dad, Stuart Taylor, reminded me of the rough granite blocks of Aberdeen's city centre, weather-beaten and starved of natural light, with silver-blue eyes topped by a shock of frizzy red hair. Lanky and awkward at six feet and four inches, he basically looked like a Scottish lamp post on fire.

And together, they looked like they weren't together.

I'd been handed down everything from my dad except the height. That blessing I was lucky enough to inherit from my mum, who was only an African headwrap taller than an Ewok. *Thanks, guys.*

Then there was the name.

The name, the name, the name.

Carmichael.

Ugh.

I was called Carmichael because my parents were idiots.

I've always suspected a lot of parents are. Forever searching for 'unique' and 'unusual' names with which to tarnish their offspring, when all any kid wants to do in their young life is FIT IN. Simple rules:

- Kids don't need a name that rhymes with a body part (Peter, who I play football with, is forever 'Tiny Feet Pete'. Rose in my RE class is 'Big Nose Rose' – her nose is actually smaller than average, but to be fair, she is super nosy. Isaiah in my form group probably thought he'd got away with it until we found out his surname was Cluttock).

- They don't need a name that is also a brand (I had a Dior *and* a Chanel in my primary school class. I mean, you might as well go all out and call your kid Reebok – at least it'd be funny).

- And they really, *really* don't need to be named after a great-great-great-Scottish-grandfather who, rumour had it, was the first to think of putting poppy seeds on a bun, although was never recognised for it, never got any money from it to pass down, and now his great-great-great-grandson was still wearing the same Pumas with the flappy sole on the right foot from last winter.

Yet ultimately I was ambivalent about all of these things. That's right – *ambivalent*. It's a versatile little word that means having mixed feelings about something. Ambivalence is neither one thing nor the other, which seemed a perfect way to describe someone who looked and felt like neither of his parents.

The name is a perfect example. I can see how, at this point, that was partly my fault. Let's be honest, I had the chance to reinvent myself in Year 7 – to use the more normal half of my name by becoming a 'Michael' or a 'Mike', but I didn't. Partly just an oversight, partly because the four or five friends – including my best mate, Alex Kember – who came with me to Wainbridge from primary school had always called me Car and I couldn't change that now. Plus my Uncle Lan always called me 'Carm', which I kind of liked, and which both of us felt was – enjoyably for word enthusiasts – something of an ironic nickname, considering how often my behaviour was the opposite of *calm*.

I remember telling him a story about a detention I'd got for surfing down the newly waxed corridor floor of the Science Block. Finding myself unable to stop, I'd continued my uncontrollable journey into an A-Level display of handmade helixes, destroying a term's worth of papier mâché DNA.

'You remind me of me at your age, Carm,' he'd said, 'A penchant for impetuousness.'

I screwed my face up.

'*Penchant*. It's like a strong tendency to do stuff. In your case it was to be *impetuous* – you made a slightly mad decision on the spur of the moment. Your grandad used to say it about me.'

Not 'Carm' enough, then.

Oh well.

So I'd grown ambivalent about my name. And my

15

appearance? Well I mean, *come on*, I lived in *London*, where everyone looked – and sounded – different, so … *So what?*

Yes – my height, my face, my name could all be described as weird and used against me by some new idiotic adversary at any given moment (*'Ha-ha! Car? What type of "car" are you? A Mini? Ha-ha-ha-ha-ha.'* Genius), but you know what? I *lived* for those moments. In my opinion, no one at Wainbridge had a smarter, quicker, sharper tongue than me. So if someone wanted to have a go, my default position was largely:

BRING.

IT.

ON.

CHAPTER 3
Get Me

I stepped out of the boys' toilets into a June afternoon sun that bathed Wainbridge Academy's playground in a warm glow, as if celebrating the arrival of 3.30 p.m. along with the rest of us.

Alex Kember stood waiting for me, leaning against the outer wall of the gym with sunglasses on, arms folded and one leg bent, foot flush against the wall, doing little nods and muttering 'Sup?' in a low, tough-guy voice to anyone that passed, like those dudes you see outside shops who seem to know everyone in the neighbourhood. Except most of the kids who passed Alex screwed up their faces in vague confusion. Berkan from our History class walked by. Alex nodded at him.

'Sup, Brian?'

'My name's Berkan.'

'Cool, cool. Sup, Mr Hargreaves?'

'Lose the sunglasses, Alex.'

'Yes, sir.'

I chuckled watching my old friend at work. Without the shades it was easy to see Alex had the plump, rosy cheeks of the well loved, blue eyes that bounced positivity back off their bright surface and the type of hair that did what it was told – a chin-length, smooth blond mop that nits could be evicted from within minutes. Back in our Reception days anyway. I tended to be up till midnight, my parents deep into a bottle of wine to ease the stress.

But ever since we were five years old, no nit infestation, no bully, no new friend group, no house move had ever kept us apart. We never argued.

In fact, one of our biggest differences was the very same thing that kept us close: Alex was an optimist and I was a cynic. In practice that meant Alex would celebrate a sunny morning for the additional joys it would undoubtedly bring; I would celebrate if the heavens broke at lunchtime to wash out the playground dance performance planned by those Year 9 girls who always 'joke' about my hair.

Alex thought the best of everyone whilst I expected people to disappoint me, either straight away or in the near future. We both had big mouths, and if you'd just met us, you might assume that I was the sharp one and

Alex was the daydreamer, but actually Alex could *feel* stuff better than me.

When we were being coached on creating our own self-portraits in an Art class early into Year 8, Miss Salter had urged us to 'define and express your own *attributes*: the qualities or features central to your characters'. My best mate always found tasks like this tricky because most of the obvious attributes that the casual observer might see in Alex would traditionally be seen as standard for a boy.

But Alex wasn't a boy.

Like me, Alex used an abbreviation of a birthname, in this case, Alexandra.

Her attributes included enjoying a well-timed public fart, chewed fingernails, what some considered a 'boyish' hairstyle, permanently grass-stained trousers from playing football, an eternal love of goofiness, and – despite the confusion sent through both her male and female school-mates – a tirelessly sunny demeanour. Loads of them assumed she wanted to be a boy or wanted to kiss girls. To Alex, it really wasn't that complicated. She loved being a girl, her best friend was a boy and she spent her days simply doing what felt good and what felt right.

It's fair to say that I found Alex's *attributes* pretty cool, and to each other we made perfect sense.

I ambled over, chuckling at Alex's performance.

'What you doing?'

Her voice returned to its normal pitch.

'Trying a new stance.'

'Why?'

'I saw a boy doing it in the hallway in some American high school movie and everyone who passed him gave him a high five.'

'How many'd you get so far?'

'None.'

We both laughed and I gave her a consolatory fist bump.

'Don't say I never do anything for you.'

We walked through the gates and crossed the road, settling at a crowded bus stop. Alex offered me a stick of bubblegum.

'What did Mr French say?'

'The usual.'

'Is he gonna write to your parents?'

'Already has.'

Alex blew a bubble until it popped.

'Peak.'

I shrugged.

'The way I see it, *school* … school is a process. It's a process of narrowing your interests.'

Alex furrowed a questioning brow, so I continued.

'You start off studying *everything*, yeah? You know,

pointless stuff – like Geography. Then you ditch all the dead weight and it's down to nine GCSEs. Then you choose three A Levels and finally you're down to one subject at University – the one thing you actually *wanted* to learn more about in the first place, true?'

'O-K ...'

'So what am I really in trouble for? I mean, *really*? I'm in trouble for basically being good at only one subject, and not showing enough respect for the rest, right? But if you look at it another way, I'm light years ahead of everyone else ... I just found my one thing earlier.'

I put my wrists together out in front of me, as if handcuffed, enjoying myself now. I did my best/lamest American accent.

'And if that makes me an outlaw, *Your Honour*, then maybe you should just go ahead and lock me up! But maybe, *maybe* I'm right, and your whole damn justice system is wrong!'

'Huh. Reckon your parents'll buy that?'

'Nah.'

We laughed and hopped on to the newly arrived 274.

'Check this out,' Alex said, pulling out her phone. She opened a link to a video and we both lit up and yelled in faux-American unison:

'Those Crazy Kids!'

21

'Those Crazy Kids' was a segment on an American talk show called *Missy*. It was only on British TV in the daytime but you could watch all the latest clips on YouTube, and Alex and I had been hooked for at least three years now. We huddled over the small screen to watch a five-year-old boy singing a seriously dramatic love song by Adele – seriously passionately and seriously out of tune. It was hilarious. *Missy* always was.

The eponymous Missy was a former comedian who now hosted her own fluffy, shiny-floored talk show, a large feature of which was kids from all over the world doing crazy stuff. I loved the chaos of it, the way anything could happen. Missy and her audience would often react with stunned silence or uncontrollable laughter at the unpredictable nature of their underage guests. Alex and I would battle to find clips one of us hadn't seen and we shared our favourites with other kids in our year.

'You can't write this stuff.' Alex chuckled.

I leaned forward and pressed the red button on the pole by my seat on the bus. Alex tightened her face with gentle concern.

'Scale of one to ten, how bad d'you reckon it'll be?'

''S'like a seven,' I replied with a shrug. 'Mum'll shout for a bit, Dad'll nod, I'll do my time. You think I can't handle a seven?'

Alex smiled.

'Some days I'll *want* a seven,' she said. 'Just cos I'm bored. Remember when I found that massive sheet of plastic on the street?'

'And you put it over the doorway to the kitchen.'

We both started snickering.

'I've still got the video of my dad …'

'When you were crouched behind the fridge …'

'The way he's whistling, then – WHAM!'

We both whistled the tune from memory and creased up.

'Some things are worth a seven!'

'Yep.' I chuckled, heading to the door. The bus slowed to halt at my stop and I stepped off and turned to give Alex a nod. She was up on her feet, walking to the door whistling, aping her dad in the video. As she reached the door it closed and she feigned whacking her nose on the glass. The bus pulled away with the other passengers staring at her curiously before leaving my sight. Although I couldn't hear or see her, I knew Alex would be laughing too.

CHAPTER 4

Reality Check

I hit the High Street and pondered the Seven, but my thoughts were muddied by:

'Road's for cars, mate! Pavement's for walking!'

BEEEEEP!!!

'Strawberries a pound now! Come on! 'Ave a look! Oi oi! 'Ave a word!'

WOOWOOWOOWOO!!!

'Are you dizzy, bruv?!'

'Salaam, Brother!'

BRRRRRURRR-EEEEEEK!

''Scuse me! EXCUSE ME!!'

Camden Town was never quiet.

It's a traditionally raucous borough towards the north of London, famous for its legendary musicians, legendary punks and legendary mad people. It's the kind of crazy place the powers that be are always trying to tidy up, but it just seems to stay grimy and chaotic.

Camden was annoying and irresistible at the same time and it was never, ever quiet – a fact I knew all too well.

I was born in University College Hospital in the London Borough of Camden; lived in a three-bedroomed flat in Queen's Crescent in the London Borough of Camden; went to Bright Futures Nursery in the London Borough of Camden; attended Messina Primary in the London Borough of Camden, and was now a student at Wainbridge Academy, lights years away in the London Borough of Camden.

Yep, I'd certainly been a man of the world.

I was used to noise, dreamed of quiet and yet, whenever quiet surprised me by its presence, felt weirdly uncomfortable without noise.

That same feeling struck me as I left the High Street behind and felt the volume drift down to a hum; a sudden cautiousness.

I paused briefly as I turned into our street.

Malky.

I frowned and slowed my pace.

The sibling thing is weird. In every other walk of life, you hang with kids around your age until you've had enough, then you leave. Or if they're annoying or mean or whatever, you don't bother hanging at all. But with siblings, there's just this other kid who's always *there*. Nothing you can do about it. They can tease you, push you around, and perhaps you do the same to them. Steady, mutual torment, with no escape until you're an adult and you can get the hell out of there. And the worst part, the undisputedly grossest element is – *ugh* – you *love each other*. But of course this will never be said aloud, nor demonstrated with any regularity.

Why would it? On the surface, Malky and me were pretty different. He was sporty, I was nerdy. He was tall, I was short. He was an idiot, I was brilliant. *Like chalk and cheese*, as the saying goes. He was definitely the cheese.

Side note: Why is it *Chalk and Cheese*? Why isn't it *Trousers and Turkey*? Or *Doorknobs and Donuts*? Like, who was eating chalk and thought: *You know what this really doesn't taste like? Cheese.*

There *were* little crossover points of interest though. Like music. My taste was more varied than Malky's, but we both loved British rap and grime. To be fair, pretty much all of the rap and grime stuff I listened to was whatever I heard and liked from my brother's collection. But unlike Malky, the songs that caught my ear from Malky's playlists also contained couplets that made me laugh.

It always brought a smile to my face when I heard Stormzy aggressively claim that '*I take care when I water my plants*'. I'd asked Uncle Lan – an actual real-life musician – why I found the lyric so funny and he explained it was because it was *incongruous*, meaning it wasn't like the rest of the song. In amongst boasting about his physical strength and street credibility you didn't expect Stormzy to discuss tending foliage.

And whilst Malky enjoyed the posturing, the bravado and the fashion, I liked how economic these guys were with their words; they told stories, got right to the point and it felt like their performances came from the heart. Plus, swearing. *Brilliant.*

So even rap, the thing we had in common, was kind of a point of contention. Another thing to bicker about.

And there he stood, big sarcastic grin on his face, watching me approach our flat, hanging outside with Tweedledum and Tweedledumber, Dane and TJ, his ever present 'die-hards' as he irritatingly called them.

This tended to be a worst-case scenario to come home to, because Malky was always that little bit meaner in front of his friends – more dismissive, showing off his assumed superiority. And Dane and TJ were always happy to goad. Classic goaders, the pair of them.

For as long as I'd known the Tweedle Twins they'd left me out of their games – unless they could somehow belittle me with my involvement. They'd laughed at me and my books and encouraged some verbal jousting between me and Malky, purely for their own entertainment. I always gave as good as I got, but that usually tended to stoke more goading.

For now, I got my head down, fished out my keys and approached our building. Out of the corner of my eye I saw Malky elbow TJ and nod in my direction.

'Ey! It's the Ginger Ninja!'

The three older boys cracked up as I reached the gate. I nodded back and mimicked his tone.

'Ey! It's the Poet Laureate!'

All three boys screwed up their faces. Malky looked suspicious.

'Who's she?'

Dane elbowed Malky in the ribs.

'He's tryina say you're a *girl*, fam!'

'*Laureate* innit,' added TJ. 'That's a girl's name.'

Malky's features shrunk into a glare. I chuckled to myself. Older, better looking, but not the sharpest. I shrugged.

'I did tell you not to call me Ginger Ninja.'

Malky straightened up, bouncing off the wall he'd been leaning on with an air of menace.

'Oh, *you* told *me*? You don't tell me nothing, bro.'

'Yeah, you're probably right,' I responded with mock understanding, 'I'm better off sticking to my intellectual equals.'

'Ooooh!' TJ covered his mouth and widened his eyes, nudging Malky.

'That's a burn!' Dane added gleefully.

'Shut up, man, go inside and play with Sylvanian Families or whatever.'

I beamed at him, feigning excitement.

'Ah, thanks, bro! You never normally let me touch them!'

I slid past the clique with a satisfied smirk, leaving Malky to the cheers and jeers of Dane and TJ.

'Nah, he got you, bruv! You got done by the red Teletubby!'

'Ha-ha-ha! Man like Po! The boy's sharp though, still!'

'Yeah, yeah, whatever,' Malky mumbled, then shouted after me, 'Oh yeah, Mum's home. Dad just showed her some email or something?'

Without turning back, I paused as I inserted the front door key and took a second to close my eyes and perform a tiny wince of pain, hidden from Malky.

'They was saying something about "*Wait till he gets home*" … Enjoy!'

I turned the key and entered the house like my Afro: gingerly.

My family lives on the first floor of a terraced house split into two parts. 'Terraced house' had always struck me as weird when I'd heard my parents say it. This was mainly because 'terraced' sounded a bit like *terrorist*, or like a mix between *terror* and *harassed*, so it always gave me the image of houses with horrific backstories, rather than a row of identical buildings.

The house had been built about 120 years before

I was born and sometimes I wondered about the 113 years we *hadn't* been there. Had there been other thirteen-year-old residents, fighting for their freedom of speech like me? Battling bully brothers and close-minded parents? Bringing the fluid watercolour of a sharp and illuminating wit to an otherwise grey and uninspired canvas?

Maybe. Maybe not.

Assorted carrier bags lined the steps from the ground-floor hallway up to our interior front door. They were assorted because if either Mum or Dad came home from the supermarket with new, non-recyclable plastic bags, they were due an earful from the other. To me, this was less about supporting the environment and more about the little victories married people seemed to enjoy scoring over one another.

And so there was a rainbow of supermarket brands, 'Bags for Life', old cotton shoulder bags, even a wicker basket, all full of the Big Shop. At the top, on the threshold of the open door, was a bright green string bag that looked like a fluorescent fisherman's net.

I poked my head into the hallway and spotted Dad at the kitchen table, on his laptop. Another small wince. I edged inside as Mum appeared from behind the fridge door and brushed past me to collect more shopping.

'Hi, Ma.'

'Just sidestepping the shopping, Car?'

Classic Mum. Already on my case.

'Huh? No, I—'

'Bit like you're sidestepping Geography according to *another* email from Mr French.' She raised her eyebrows at me whilst hoisting two heavy bags in another classic Mum move: small but powerful.

'OK,' I began. 'Let me give you some context on that—'

Mum interrupted again, halfway to the kitchen already. 'You know what?'

She dropped the bags heavily on the kitchen table, startling Dad and calling back to me where I remained teetering awkwardly on the threshold.

'I'm off the back of two night shifts and I'm not in the mood for one of your articulate speeches about how misunderstood you are. Keep your context and do me a favour. *Study*. OK? Just study. And when you're a big man with all your qualifications you can bang on to me about all the context you want. Deal?'

'Dad!'

'She's right, mate,' he offered. *Typical.*

'Seriously, Car, what is this behaviour about? Is it Alex again? Did she put you up to this?'

'What's that supposed to mean?'

'I asked Mr French if she was involved in this ridiculous pigeon thing. He said you two are partners in crime.'

'Sure that's not what *you* told *him*?'

'I didn't need to! Ever since you were in Reception, if I heard about or saw you doing something dumb, it was with that girl.'

'So a pigeon flew into a teacher's face, I made a joke about it and it's Alex's fault?'

'Maybe not directly this time, but I bet she egged you on.'

'I don't need egging, Mum, I can egg myself!' (Weird thing to say but my temper was rising.)

'OK. Year One, spring term. You and Alex scooped sand from the nursery sandpit into all the teachers' coat pockets hanging up outside the staffroom.'

'I remember that,' Dad offered with a nostalgic chuckle.

'It wasn't funny, Stuart! That was a lack of respect for authority! You know what I think? I think you do these things to impress her.'

I scoffed at this but didn't say anything. No point. Mum was on a roll.

'Just because she's headed ... wherever she's headed, you don't need to go down with her.'

OK, hold on.

'Mum, what are you talking about? You make it sound as if she's joined a biker gang or something.'

'You don't think all this mucking around affects your grades?'

'Did you see my English commendation? How did

I get that when I've been sitting next to Alex all year?'

'Yep, your dad showed me that too, and I'm glad you're doing well there, I really am, but there's more to school than your best friend, and there's *definitely* more to school than one subject! And even if you only like one, you *don't* go out of your way to disrespect the others and their teachers!'

I could feel my face getting hot. I wasn't someone you could describe as aggressive, but I had a temper – I mean, everyone has one, don't they? I guess the thing was, I generally only lost it at home. I rarely got upset at school, even when I was actually upset.

When Mr French ranted about underachieving, I'd just focus on his moustache and think, *Who has a moustache these days? Like, a stand-alone, no-beard, check-me-out MOUSTACHE?*

But anything involving my family? It was like too much popcorn in the pan – I just couldn't keep a lid on it.

And now here it was: as sudden as a matchstick's head turning orange with flame, I found myself shouting.

'How is it disrespectful to focus on what I'm actually good at? Maybe I'm gifted and talented! Maybe I'm a *G and T*! Ever think of that?'

'Are you raising your voice at me, Carmichael?'

FULL NAME ALERT.

'I could use a G and T,' Dad lamented.

'There's a difference between being Gifted and

33

Talented and being arrogant, Car,' Mum shot back, as Malky appeared on the threshold sporting the soft expression of a volunteer charity worker, carrying four bags of shopping. FOUR. *Ugh.*

'Don't want the frozen stuff to melt,' he chirped. I cut my eyes with disgust at this calculatedly well-timed performance.

'Thanks, love,' Mum said. Malky smiled and trotted past us, turning back to beam at me behind Mum's back. *What a fraud.*

'You're not "above" school.'

'I never said that!'

'Just bring the last few bags in, OK? Or are you above that as well?'

That stung. Dad noticed.

'Joss ...'

And that's when it happened. I wasn't proud of it. I just didn't see it coming. But the temperature in my body had skyrocketed and, as sometimes happened to me at home, I was lost for words. *Words.* My only superpower. *This house was like my kryptonite.* I was left with nothing but raw anger.

So it just *happened.*

That's right.

I kicked a chicken.

CHAPTER 5

Don't Kick Chickens

As you've probably guessed, there wasn't literally a defenceless live chicken having an afternoon stroll through the Taylor residence, minding its own business, only to find itself mercilessly punted down the hallway by a malevolent, fowl-hating, red-headed boy.

But it *was* literally a chicken. A plucked and very much already deceased chicken, presumably for Sunday's roast, sat in the green string bag on the threshold, not so much minding its own business as having no business to mind, seeing as its mind was undoubtedly a victim in the unfortunate business of losing its head.

This literal chicken barely moved upon impact.

It made a satisfying thud, but also caused a sharp pain in the big toe of my right foot. It was heavier than I'd thought and I can't lie: I regretted the physical pain pretty much instantly.

But the dramatic effect was strong.

Mum's eyes widened.

'Car!'

She called back to the kitchen.

'Stu, he's just kicked the chicken!'

Dad finally gave up on attempting to work from home and ambled over, placing his hands on the hips of his lanky frame.

'Not cool, mate. Not cool.'

'Go and cool down in your room. *Now!*'

'Fine!'

I stomped to my room and slammed the door, much to Malky's amusement. I flopped on to my bed and listened, furious, to the aftermath outside.

Mum's voice first. 'Who kicks a chicken?'

'Hormones. A lot going on.' Dad, semi-supportive.

'I know, but …'

PAUSE FOR TACTICAL MALKY INTER-VENTION.

'*I don't remember ever kicking a family dinner.*'

No, Malky, you've always been perfect, haven't you?

'Y'know, some types of meat actually react quite well to a bit of pummelling. If anything, he's tenderised it a bit.'

Thanks, Dad … I think.

'It's not funny, Stu. This happens too often. He's

gonna end up in *real* trouble before the end of the year if this keeps up. He needs to focus.'

I heard a gleeful click of the fingers.

'Boarding school! Send him to boarding school. Like in … Scotland or something.'

Shut up, Malky.

A sigh from Dad.

'Not helpful, Malcolm. Look, maybe he just needs something academic to work towards?'

'I don't know. Maybe.' Mum sounded tired, then tetchy. 'Isn't that what GCSEs are?'

'Sure, but something *more*. Something that brings the … *enjoyment* back to school.'

'I'll speak to his English teacher. She seems to get the best out of him …'

'Or his PE teacher,' Dad offered, 'I mean, he's clearly got a great right foot – look at that bird's wing!'

'Ha-ha, nice one, Dad.'

'Ugh! Clowns! I'm surrounded by boy clowns!'

I'd heard enough. I plugged earphones into my phone. Too angry to select a song, but wanting to block the world out, I hit shuffle on my whole library, awaiting a livid rapper or a screaming rock frontman to bombard me.

So when the summeriest, sweetest, friendliest *You go, girl* sounds of Calvin Harris suddenly had Katy Perry telling me not to be 'afraid to catch feels', I yanked my earphones out in disgust and texted Alex.

THE MIGHTY CAR:

Y R families SO ANNOYING?

TOP GAL AL:

IKR?

Guess it's cos you can't pick 'em like you can with friends

THE MIGHTY CAR:

So why the heck did I pick u? Lol

TOP GAL AL:

Looool

Double English tomoz *DEADFACE EMOJI*

THE MIGHTY CAR:

My Happy Place *HEARTFACE EMOJI*

TOP GAL AL:

GTG dinner ready

THE MIGHTY CAR:

What u havin?

TOP GAL AL:

Toad in da hole

Sounds gross

Isn't

YUMFACE EMOJI

You?

THE MIGHTY CAR:

Maybe nothing

I kicked a chicken

TOP GAL AL:

Hahahahahaha

Wait

What?

THE MIGHTY CAR:

[Typing ...]

[Not typing]

[Typing ...]

[Not typing]

TOP GAL AL:

?

THE MIGHTY CAR:

Chat tomoz

TOP GAL AL:

GIF OF SAD CARTOON-MONSTER-THING WAVING GOODBYE BEFORE RANDOMLY EXPLODING

CHAPTER 6

Still That Guy

'That is literally so peak,' Alex said, shaking her head as we turned on to Wainbridge Road the next morning, after hearing the story of last night in full.

'Mm-hmm.' I nodded, despite a vague annoyance at the general overuse of the word 'literally'.

Technically, it was tricky to argue with Alex's usage, considering it was in the same sentence as a slang term – 'peak', meaning *intensely troubling*. Were the events of the previous evening literally troubling? You could argue yes. In general, do kids use the word 'literally' too much? You could literally argue yes. They literally all do it every minute. Well, maybe not literally all of the kids in the literal world and not literally every minute, but very often. You get the picture.

The point is, I was irritable. Hungry too – never a good combination.

I hadn't come out of my room for dinner the night before, and that morning I'd left without breakfast to avoid further confrontation.

'Could be worse,' offered Alex.

'Yeah?'

'Yeah. Like, what if your foot actually got stuck in the chicken?'

'What?'

'When you kicked it. It would've been worse if your foot got stuck inside the chicken's body and you're there trying to make a serious point in the argument but you're stomping around with a raw chicken attached to one foot. Totally takes away your authority.'

'I mean, I guess that would be … slightly worse?'

'And it could get worse than that.'

'OK …'

'Say they can't get it off. And the flesh is too raw and tough to cut through. So then you have to lie on your back and put the foot in the oven to cook the chicken. Your foot doesn't burn because it's insulated within the carcass, but does it get hot? Oh, it gets hot. It gets *crazy* hot, my friend. Nature of an oven.'

'What?'

'Exactly. Now you're panicking. Sweat pouring into your eyes – if something goes wrong here you could lose the foot. You get through the cooking process, but you still have to suffer the indignity of sitting on a chair with your foot on the table while your dad carefully carves your foot out of there.'

'And my whole family is sat around the table saying Grace?'

I couldn't help sniggering. It set Alex off too.

'Lord, we thank you for this bountiful foot we are about to receive.'

Full-blown laughter.

Good job, Alex.

'Three Moes, wha blow?' Alex called as we met with Tyler, Mo and Mehmet at the gates and all bumped fists.

We called them the *Three Moes* because Mo was short for Mohamed, Mehmet means Mohamed in Turkish and, outside school hours, Tyler religiously wore a Liverpool shirt with *Salah* on the back – a footballer whose first name was Mohamed, better known as Mo – Tyler's hero.

'Nada,' said Mo.

'What's happening with you lot?' Mehmet asked.

'Car kicked a chicken,' Alex said matter-of-factly. I knew that wouldn't be a secret for more than thirty seconds.

'What?' Tyler snorted.

'Fam, why you abusing animals though?'

'Wait, wait – there's context …' I began as we turned into the playground.

'This guy,' said Mo, creasing up and slapping me on the shoulder. 'He will never stop killing me, y'know!'

'Legend,' Mehmet added, shaking his head with a quiet awe.

'Car!'

Two girls from my form group, Natalie and Hani, stepped across our path.

'Can you do the thing you did for Nat on my phone?' Hani asked excitedly.

I'd made a side hustle of recording funny voicemail messages for kids with different impersonations. 'This is Kermit *the* Frog, I'm afraid Millie can't come to the phone right now –' You know, goofy stuff. I would take pretty much any snacks as payment, apart from Twiglets and Reese's Pieces. Hani held out a Snickers. Boom. *Breakfast.* I shrugged, as if I wasn't thrilled to stem the noise from my aching belly.

'Mr French's voice?' I asked, taking and unwrapping the Snickers in one move.

'Nah, the Draco Malfoy one?'

The buzzer went and hordes of kids started meandering with a little more purpose towards their various entrances. I put on the sneering tone of Tom Felton.

'I'll do it after school, *Potter*.' I spat out the *Potter* bit with maximum disdain. Hani squealed.

'I told you he was sick!' Natalie smiled as they turned towards our entrance.

'My father shall hear about this!' I shouted after them for good measure and took a huge bite out of the chocolate bar.

'This guy!' Mo repeated, chuckling.

'Share the taste!'

'Chill, bro, this is my money!'

'Back to this chicken though.' Mehmet jutted his chin out at me. 'Was it halal, or … ?'

'I'll tell you after English.'

'Ah, man,' Mehmet lamented. 'Now we gotta wait. You ever notice how my man would probably get his bum out in Geography but he won't even *whisper* to you in English?'

'What?' I shrugged. 'I like English.'

'*Double English*, bruv? Long!' Mo elongated the word 'long'.

'Hey, don't ever dis English, man!' I nudged him. 'I'll get my bum out now if I have to!'

My first group laugh of the day.

I almost felt normal again.

CHAPTER 7

It's Lit, Fam! (English Lit)

Aaaah.
Double English.
English Language ...
AND ...
English Literature.
I was home.

With a passion equal to how much I hate fractions, hypotenuses and carrying the three, I love the idiosyncrasies of grammar, the oddities of words that should rhyme but stubbornly refuse to (don't get me started on *cough*, *bough*, *enough* and *although*) and, of course, all the etymology.

In fact, I became such an instant geek when it came to Year 8 English Language classes that I enjoyed the irony of loving etymology when many of my classmates didn't know the meaning of the word. This was beautiful to me because the meaning of the word 'etymology' is basically The Very Meaning of Words – defining the origin and development of words themselves. *Satisfying*. I explained it to the Three Moes once. 'Satisfying' wasn't the word any of them used in response. In fact, one of the words Tyler used was preceded by an adjective that I don't think I'm allowed to use in this book.

I get it though.

With my reputation, I was only a sharp haircut, a new pair of trainers and some slick-fringed, car-driving Sixth-Former's endorsement away from being considered officially Cool with a capital C. Unfortunately I never could quite shake the Nerd with a capital N out of my system. Being a teenaged boy, in Camden, in the 2020s, I understood and accepted my social standing: Well-Loved Popular Oddity, rather than simply Da Man.

I did hold aspirations of one day being Da Man, but I was never willing to give up or hide my love of English Language to do it. I wanted both.

And then there was English Literature.

Again, I get it.

In this era of smartphones, advertising, YouTube videos, online news and gossip, it's tempting to only read the bare minimum. Tiny bite-sized chunks of prose that tell you all you feel you need to know. It's hard to appreciate reading something as long as a novel unless you're forced to, but I guess I just never needed pushing. I *read*. *A lot.* *Love* a book – writing one now. *Enjoy.*

That said, I will read anything and everything.

I'll eat my breakfast and read the boasts on the backs of cereal boxes about how natural everything is, then chuckle inwardly at how the mass of artificial ingredients listed in the nutritional information reads like a comical appendix.

I love the great effort that highway maintenance people take in manufacturing, writing and printing a road sign that says nothing other than the words *Temporary Sign*. Why not just wait to write the final sign?

I enjoy grammatical errors in pamphlets, poorly conceived posters and even problematic pizza boxes (my current favourite being one that proudly declared '*Delicious Freshly*' in big bold letters).

I read comics, newspapers, old letters, funny poems, song lyrics, pompous emails … Sometimes I even read the *Terms and Conditions* on websites. To me it's mad that a company selling novelty socks or AA batteries wants to follow you around the internet after your visit like some creepy stalker, trying to find out what other stuff you're interested in.

But I really love books.

Books take you on a journey – their words stay with you like a travelling companion for weeks, months, even years if it's part of some epic series. Books provide a funny sort of power as well: being seen with them could be cause for ridicule from certain cave-dwelling types in the playground, yet it's books that have provided me with the vocabulary to scythe down my tormentors with the swift and incisive lashes of a razor-sharp tongue.

Like early in the Winter Term with classic meathead Tosun Kendall outside the school library.

'*Oooh* look, it's *Mini* Taylor! Got yourself a little picture book for bedtime?'

'Yeah, it's a good one actually, based on a true story. It's called *Tosun, The Boy Who Lived in a Bin.*'

On the unfortunate occasions when my verbal take-downs incited mild violence, I was impressed by the shielding qualities of books – an oversized hardback is a surprisingly effective forcefield of protection. Aside from words, a hardback and a thick skin are the only weapons a nerd really needs.

And, although I never admitted it, this love of words extended to my English teacher, Miss Miller, who delivered distinction after distinction for my comprehension work, my creative writing and all-round engagement. She was a lot younger and less stuffy than the other teachers and, like Alex, she seemed to 'get' me.

Also like Alex, Miss Miller and I complemented each other: me being respected by my troublemaking peers proved to be Miss Miller's key to getting them to concentrate in English. If I read aloud, if I delivered homework on time, if I answered questions in class, it was easier to encourage her trickier customers to follow suit.

In short, we got on like a dry book on fire.

'Hold on a second, Car.' Miss Miller stopped me as the class filed out for lunch. I jutted a chin at Alex, who jutted back and left with the rest of the group.

'Miss?'

'I got an email from your parents last night.'

Oh great, now they're gonna ruin English too? Can't I just have English? PLEASE?

'Oh.'

'They think you need an extra challenge—'

'I'll die before I go to Maths Club.'

Miss Miller laughed.

'Something English-related.'

I raised a questioning eyebrow as she continued.

'And I have to say I agree. Your marks are way above average, why not push you a little further?'

She reached into her desk drawer and pulled out a printed sheet of A4. I'd seen this print in various sizes around the school: a poster for next Friday's Annual Wainbridge Talent Night, a charity event to raise money for the school that featured both students and teachers doing turns onstage that, in any other theatre in the world, really couldn't have commanded an entrance fee. In fact, a better way to raise money would have been for the poor audience members to be sponsored for their breathtaking feats of endurance.

'Uh, miss? I'm not—'

'I know what you're going to say, Car – the performances make you cringe, the teachers make you wince, right?'

I held up my hands with a sheepish smile.

'Not my words!'

'A bit amateurish, yeah?'

'Mr French's Shakespeare monologue last year … I mean, why was he dressed as a donkey?'

Miss Miller suppressed a snigger.

'You need to read *A Midsummer Night's Dream*. He was Bottom.'

'Oh, that makes sense now. I remember Tyler calling him something similar.'

'Uh … OK, I didn't hear that. Look, your creative writing is exceptional, Car. I mean it.'

'But no one wants to hear a short story I wrote in English class!'

'I agree.'

'Huh?'

'But what if you put those creative writing skills to

use in a more … *contemporary* way? I see you and Mo and Mehmet reciting rap lyrics all the time. What about some kind of performance poetry?'

I squished my face like I'd tasted something sour, but the truth was I hated to disappoint Miss Miller.

'I dunno … Seems corny.'

'Only if you make it corny! And I don't think you do "corny", do you?'

I looked around the classroom as Miss Miller continued the hard sell.

'It can be as funny or as serious, as light or as heavy as you want it to be. Short and snappy, or epic! But it could be really … *real*. Something you feel. It could be *sick*! Your mum thinks it's a great idea. I spoke to Miss Choudhary, there's still a couple of spots open, I can just give her the word.'

Now, I wasn't completely comfortable with my English teacher conspiring with my mum, or with my Form Tutor and event organiser Miss Choudhary – or saying '*sick*', for that matter – but I had to admit, she'd got my brain whirring. She held out the poster, hopefully.

'Can I think about it?'

'Of course! And I can help with any edits. Or not. Whatever you want. I just think it'd be great to see you really shine.'

I took the poster, folded it and nodded.

'I'll think about it. Thanks, miss. See ya.'

And I did think about it.

Instead of going straight to the lunch hall I paced empty corridors for at least twenty hungry minutes, pondering the pros and cons of a live performance in front of everyone I knew:

PROS	CONS
• Could look like a legend	• Could look like a fool
• Girls will be there	• Girls will be there
• Could get parents off back	• Could get parents back on to back
• Show Malky a thing or two about rhymes	• Show Malky nothing he doesn't already know
• Could wear that hoodie	• Drip snotty tears over that hoodie

Hmmm.

I'd been hoping there'd be way more in one column than the other: so many negatives that I'd be mad to go for it, or so many positives that I'd be mad not to.

What I really needed was further advice. I defined my requirements for the perfect advisor with an imaginary, non-specific national anthem playing along in my head:

DER DER DA DERR DA DER DERRRRR ...

A true visionary ... a mountain of wisdom and guidance!

DER-DER-DA-DUM-DUM-DAHHH ...

I wandered through the lunch hall, grabbed a sandwich and some crisps, then continued through the glass doors at the back, out into the early afternoon sunshine, where waves of kids were either queueing up to go in to eat, or flying out after finishing.

Blessed with invaluable experience ...

DEE-DE-DEE DIDDLY DUM DUN DERRR ...

Gifted with supreme intellect and a devastating sense of authority!

DRUM ROLL BUDADA-BUDADA-BUDADA ...

Presently the waves parted, biblical-style, to reveal Alex Kember, sat back on her heels, looking at a mound of grass through a piece of cling film she held taut between both hands, through which she appeared to be chanting, 'Fry and die! Fry and die!'

DER DER DERRRRRRRRR!

...

Or I could just ask Alex.

CHAPTER 8

Let's Not and Say We Did

On closer inspection, Alex was knelt over a small swarm of ants at the edge of the playing field. I took a big bite of my sandwich, then nudged her. She turned to see my face full of questions.

'I'm not sure if I *wanna* know? But I'm gonna ask.'

'Apparently you can burn stuff with a magnifying glass in the sun.'

'Buuuut you don't have one, sooooo …'

We both said the next three words in unison but in opposite tones, mine flat and knowing, Alex's high and excitable:

'Next best thing.'

'Sure.' I nodded. 'Hey, what if you came back as an ant in the next life? Ever think about that?'

Alex screwed up her face.

'Well, first I'd need to believe reincarnation was, like, a real thing.'

'It is real, in a way. I mean, who knows where your soul goes – your spirit or whatever. Heaven, space, down the toilet ... But your body will be in the earth somehow, right? Eventually it's just gonna break down into minerals that will get absorbed into something – a plant, a tree, a river ... or eaten by an ant.'

Alex looked down at the bustling creatures.

'So, wait ... are you saying ... one of these ants could be my grandad?'

'Could be. At least some essence of him.'

Alex scrunched the cling film into a ball and stood up.

'Sorry, Gramps.'

'I don't think he would've suffered much. Cling film really isn't a great conductor of, like, anything.'

Alex nodded and chucked the ball towards a nearby bin, into which it bounced neatly off the rim.

'Three-pointer!' Alex celebrated.

'Nice.'

Alex jutted her chin towards the Three Moes and a bunch of other kids laying out jumpers for goalposts on the grass.

'You playing?'

I nodded and we walked and talked.

'Hey, what did Miss Miller want you for? She give you another lifetime achievement award or something?'

'Doofus.'

'What then?'

I paused.

'Well, actually I was thinking … now that I've given you some food for thought on the circle of life and that, maybe you could return the favour. Bit of advice.'

'Oh my days, she wants to marry you?'

'Shut up! She wants me to write a poem to perform at the Talent Night.'

We stopped at the edge of the makeshift football pitch.

'Ah man, those nights are kinda cringe.'

'I know!'

'Remember those girls doing the a cappella pop song mash-up last year?'

'And they got everyone to stand up and clap and chant *Ooh baby baby*.'

Alex shook her head with disdain.

'Crowd participation.'

We both shuddered.

'But you're a whatchacallit.'

'What?'

'A wordsmith. You're good with words. You could probably make it decent.'

I put on a goofy voice.

'Hey, you says right thing, I *am* bit good word guy!'

'Lolz. So I guess the real question is – are you a performer?'

I frowned. 'I mean, my head says no, but my heart says a lot of teachers have given me detentions for basically being one.'

Mo shouted over from the group of players, who had now split into two and were picking teams.

'Yo, Al! Car! You in?'

'In!' I called back.

In or out. If only life were as simple as football.

CHAPTER 9

Nah

By the time I reached home, I'd made my decision. *Nah*.

No way was I going to stand up in front of everyone and perform. What if it was so amazing, so sprinkled in literary magic from the mighty pen of a child prodigy, that it just went over everyone's heads? OK, an unlikely scenario, granted, but I don't do indifference. I wasn't interested in it being 'fine'. Either it'd be rubbish and I'd be ridiculed, or amazing and under-appreciated.

So in short, nah.

It felt good to have decided my position, and I felt a bounce return to my step as I made a beeline for the fridge to get some juice.

'Good day?'

I jumped at the sight of Dad sat at his laptop on the kitchen table.

'Didn't realise you were in.'

'Did you speak to your English teacher?'

'Huh? Oh … Kinda. Yeah.'

'Great! Mum'll be pleased.'

I did an awkward half-smile and shuffled out towards my bedroom as Dad turned his attention back to his laptop.

In the sanctity of my room, I hopped on to my bed and plugged in my earphones. With the flat's WiFi connection I could use my phone to listen to as much music as I wanted and I was definitely in a rap mood. So much so that after half an hour I was so immersed in these rhythmical stories of men and women not much older than me that I didn't even notice Malky standing in my room, gesturing at me wildly.

Until he pulled the earphones from my ears, that is.

'I said, go on YouTube!'

'Huh? Why?'

'Cos you know I can't stream songs at the same time as you!'

This was annoyingly true: being old, my parents saw no reason to spend the extra money required to buy a music app that allowed different family members to listen to different music simultaneously.

'How's that my problem?' I countered.

'Cos I wanna listen now.'

'So *you* go on YouTube!'

'Such a little brat!'

'Hey, I learned from the best!'

The sound of the front door opening and closing brought a brief pause to the debate. Mum was home.

'Hiya!' Her sing-song greeting rang through the hallway.

Malky broke into one of those smiles that wasn't a smile and, with his eyes trained on me, pulled open the bedroom door.

'Mum, Car's hogging music!'

'Wha—?'

'For goodness sake, I've only just – *Car, can you time-share please!?*'

Malky shrugged.

'You heard the lady.'

I shook my head in disgust and yanked the earphones out.

'Wow,' I said flatly.

Malky swaggered out and I pulled a face at his back. As he pulled the door shut behind him, I heard Mum call from the kitchen.

'Car! A word!'

I sighed deeply and sloped out.

* * *

In the kitchen, the scene was pretty much as I'd predicted in my mental checklist on the slow walk I'd taken along the hallway:

DAD AT TABLE, SLOWLY CLOSING		
LAPTOP AND SIGHING:	**CHECK.**	☑
MUM STOOD, BACK AGAINST		
SINK, ARMS FOLDED:	**CHECK.**	☑
MALKY ON EARPHONES,		
GENERALLY LOVING LIFE:	**CHECK.**	☑

In fact, Malky was bopping his head, rapping along to some unheard track, eating salami straight from the fridge, apparently oblivious to the drama that was clearly about to unfold. But he wasn't oblivious at all – he was only in the kitchen to see his nemesis get an entertaining dressing-down.

For the tone of my opening response I attempted 'breezy' – unfortunately not my strong point.

'Yeah?'

Mum lowered her head and raised her eyebrows. Never a great combination.

'We need to talk about yesterday.'

'What about yesterday?' ('Feigned Innocence' – also not a strong point.)

'You kicked a chicken, Car.'

'Not cool,' Dad offered.

'You said that yesterday, Dad. What *would* be cool?'

'Car ...' Mum tried to interrupt while Dad took a shot at brevity.

'*Not* kicking a chicken?'

'Ah! Well, you know "cool", Dad. Really got your ear to the streets.'

'Car!' The spike in Mum's tone stopped me in my tracks. 'Don't get sarky! We want an apology.'

'Sorry,' I said, in that classic thirteen-year-old way that sounds remarkably like '*So what?*'

'OK, well that's a start,' Dad began in a conciliatory tone, causing Mum's lower back to lurch violently from the edge of the sink.

'No it's not! I won't have *violence* in this house!'

I opened my mouth to question whether a chicken could technically still be a victim of violence, post death, but seeing her daggered look, closed it again.

'I want an apology that actually *sounds* like an apology!'

Malky watched the entertainment with thinly concealed glee, stuffing circles of meat in his mouth like popcorn at the movies. I threw out my hands, pleadingly.

'I'm sorry!'

'Thank you. I don't wanna have to confiscate your comics or your phone, but I will, Car. You know I will.'

Dad picked up the slack.

'So, let's get back to good vibes, yeah?'

I winced at 'vibes'.

Satisfied, Mum's focus switched.

'Now, can we talk about the Talent Night? Dad said you'd spoken to Miss Miller?'

Pause.

'Yeah.'

'And you're going to perform a spoken word piece?'

'Well … To be honest, I dunno if – um …'

Malky pulled his earphones out of his ears.

'You doing poetry, yeah? Ha! Car crash!'

'You can't even spell poetry!'

'Boys …'

'I don't *wanna* spell it. It's like you – lame!'

'BOYS!'

Mum's no-nonsense tone returned with interest to silence us both. She turned to me and softened a little.

'What's your *plan*, Car? Because your father and I are worried that you're turning into a kid who doesn't have one. I know Malky plays the fool, but you know what? He gets his grades, he grafts where it's needed, he knows what he wants to be.'

Malky nodded and added smugly, 'Sports psychologist.'

Great. Thanks, Malk.

'You wanna be like *your* brother or *my* brother, Car? Cos one of those is a very slippery slope.'

She always used Uncle Lan as a byword for *Loser*. In her opinion that was because he was in his forties, living alone and playing music for a living. I'd say *Legend* rather than *Loser*, but that's opinions for you.

I watched my brother pull a face at me and felt my blood bubbling like a kettle close to the boil.

I watched my mother refold her arms and look at me with that '*Come on, Car*' face.

I watched my father do a shrug and eyebrow-raise as if to say, '*Hey, I'm on your side, mate, but your mum's right. Also I'm actually on her side.*'

This was the Taylor Family dynamic in full flow. Mum was too pushy. Dad wasn't pushy enough to be pushy himself and was scared of being a pushover pushed by his wife, so generally pushed himself to support her pushiness. And Malky was just a butthead.

I clenched my fists and gritted my teeth.

How many more days of my life was I going to put up with being belittled by my brother?

How many more days were my own parents going to make me feel like I couldn't do anything right at school?

How many more days was I going to be told I didn't know what I was good at, when I knew all too well it was **words**?

HOW MANY MORE DAYS?

None.

'None more days!' I suddenly blurted.

Everyone looked confused. Dad narrowed his eyes. 'What?'

Whoa. I really hadn't meant to say that last thought out loud. Weird. Time for some improvisation.

'That's the … name of the piece I'm writing.'

Malky screwed up his face.

'That don't even make sense, bruv.'

'It's abstract, Malky. You wouldn't understand.'

Malky went to open his mouth but Dad shook his head with his eyes closed as if to say, *'Best not.'*

Mum slowly nodded.

'So … you *are* gonna perform?'

'Yeah,' I said, narrowing a glare at Malky, 'I am.'

'Great! Well, let's look at this as the start of a new chapter, eh?'

'Mm.' I nodded, unsure exactly what had just happened.

Great.

CHAPTER 10

A New Chapter

'*S*ame old street
    Same old bus
    Be on time
    Don't make a fuss
    Everybody wants to know
    Go against?
    Or with the flow?
    Reach the locker
    Grab your stuff …

'Grab your stuff … Stuff. Stuff?'

'Pick your bellybutton fluff!'

'Oh that's perfect, Al, I should just let you write it.'

'Hey, what can I say? I got those Shakespearean skills. I'm Skilliam Shakespeare.'

We chuckled, but then I looked back down at the

disappointingly small amount of rhymes I'd written into my phone since last week's kitchen showdown. I'd had a whole weekend and had deleted way more words than I'd kept. Now it was Wednesday, and Talent Night was feeling worryingly close.

'This is gonna be terrible, isn't it?'

'So why bother?'

'Because my family thinks that's exactly what I'm gonna do! Not bother. I need to take a stand.'

Alex adopted a cheesy American accent.

'*And at that moment I knew. There was something different about Carmichael. From then on, everything changed.*'

'You're such an idiot.'

'Seriously! This is gonna be like one of those high school movies where you have this moment in the gym and all the cheerleaders go crazy and the basketball team lift you on their shoulders in slow motion and some song plays like "*Der-der-ner-ner, you da champ*". I'm telling you.'

'Yeah, or like one of those horror movies where the guy tries to be a hero but the zombies just surround him and eat his face.'

Alex shrugged.

'Both strong endings. Hey – I'll tell you one good thing about all this: Talent Night rehearsals are the same time as Double Science!'

'Boom!'

We fist-bumped.

'Nothing's worse than Double Science.'

Of that, I was certain.

That afternoon, I pushed open the doors to the school hall and realised I was wrong.

Year 7 girls in tutus and baseball caps doing Hip Hop ballet, that snobby kid Justin Armfield in a leotard practising a gymnastic routine, Bahir Nandy with sock puppets made to look like world leaders, Mr French on roller skates, for some horrific unknown reason, another a cappella troupe, and the Kings and Queens of all Nerds at Wainbridge Academy: The Year 10 String Orchestra.

Miss Miller and Miss Choudhary both beamed at me.

I had a sudden yearning for a hypothesis, a method, conclusive findings and a Petri dish.

Bahir finished up his run-through onstage.

'Great, Bahir,' said Miss Choudhary. 'Maybe lose the accent for the German Chancellor. It sounds a bit Welsh and I feel like both countries might be offended.'

Bahir nodded with slight disappointment and sat on the edge of the stage, adding more hair spray to his American Sock President. The Hip Hop ballet girls took the stage and Miss Choudhary made a beeline for me.

'Carmichael! Miss Miller said you were interested!

I'm so glad. So exciting to have a bit of the *grime rapping*. We need to engage more boys.'

I stood momentarily speechless, in awe at how my Form Tutor was able to make the phrase *'grime rapping'* sound like *'garden centre'*.

'Well, it's really more just, like, spoken word. I guess.'

'Amazing. Shall we take a look?' She pointed to the stage, then did a sort of pointy *I'm-a-rapper* thing with her fingers that I wished I could un-see. 'Jump up and break it down!'

'Well, I don't have – I mean it's not finished yet ...'

Miss Miller came over.

'That's fine, Car, we've still got two whole days and you don't have to memorise it. It'd be fine to just read it.'

I nodded and pulled a folded piece of A4 from my pocket on to which I'd copied what I'd written on my phone before handing it into reception that morning. I made my way to the stage and paused to look questioningly at the four Hip Hop ballet girls attempting *pliés* with attitude. Miss Choudhary motioned for me to carry on.

'Oh, never mind the girls, you do your thing!'

So up I got and unfolded the paper, cleared my throat.

'Same old street
Same old bus

Be on time
Don't make a fuss
Everybody ...'

I paused. Something caught my eye through the big windows of the hall that looked out on to the playground. Malky's class were walking to the Maths Block and TJ stopped, squinted through the window, then nudged Malky and Dane. The three of them stared at what to them was a silent scene of Malky's pathetic little brother surrounded by girls in pink tutus and baseball caps, with a boy at his feet brushing a wig on a sock.

I stared back at what was an equally silent scene of my three tormentors, bent double with laughter, pointing through the glass, slapping and shoving each other with glee.

'Car?'

Miss Miller looked at me questioningly and spun to see who I was looking at, but they were too quick for her, already hotfooting it to the Maths Block. When Miss Choudhary looked over at me, the concern on her face meant I didn't need a mirror to know how angry I must have looked. I was going out on a limb here, trying for the first time to say something in public that wasn't just for laughs. Something with meaning. Something from the heart. As much as I'd grown accustomed to people laughing *with* me, if they were going to laugh *at* me when I was doing something serious, sorry, but I didn't want to do it at all.

'Everything OK?' Miss Choudhary asked tentatively.

I'll be honest, I didn't hear what either teacher said after that. My ears were ringing. My chest rattled as my heart pounded like drumsticks against my ribs. I could feel each freckle slowly becoming camouflaged by the burning redness in my cheeks. I'd never fully lost it at school before but I felt volcanic, ready to blow.

In fact, I was so suddenly and absolutely consumed by anger that as I stormed off the stage, banged through the double doors, flew across the playground and out through the school gates, I didn't even register Bahir's wails or notice the Prime Minister of New Zealand stuck to my shoe.

CHAPTER 11

Wait, What?

It was really only after the third ring on the doorbell of Uncle Lan's flat, as I slumped down and sat on the stoop with my back against the door, that I fully understood the weight of what I'd just done.

I'd left school without permission – I was a truant, a fugitive on the run. My phone was at the school reception and no one knew where I was or how to reach me. This was actually pretty bad. No wonder I'd run to the place where I knew I wouldn't be judged. But now my uncle wasn't even around to not judge me.

Great job, Car, you donut.

I put my head in my folded arms over my lap and blocked out the world.

It was a deep baritone that snapped me back to reality.

'He was a sweet little homeless boy
Who couldn't find any joy,
And he slept on the ground in a doorway
Till policemen shouted "Oi!"'

I looked up to see my uncle, Landon Benjamin, stood over me with an armful of shopping, looking how you'd always find him, particularly in the summer months: baggy linen drawstring trousers and sandals, some kind of South American multicoloured poncho-looking thing on top. His neat dreadlocks tied back, showing off the same blemish-free, dark hazelnut skin as my mum's, with the same perfectly round nose except with added piercing on the left nostril, same big warm eyes except with added piercing on the right eyebrow.

'Guess who wrote that?'

I shrugged.

'Me. Just now.'

I nodded. Lan frowned.

'School finish early today?'

I shook my head. Lan tilted his.

'Huh. Guess you better get inside before the feds ID you.'

Lan's flat looked smaller than it actually was because of *stuff*.

So much stuff. I never failed to wonder at the sheer volume of knick-knacks, bric-a-brac, books, souvenirs, arts and crafts, rugs, cushions, speakers, cables and endless instruments that closed in on every room from the walls inwards – even the bathroom. It was the flat of a man who spent most of his time elsewhere, but it still felt homely to me. Reggae music poured soothingly out of the kitchen where Lan sang along, stirring two teas.

'You know they woulda called Jocelyn, like, already,' Lan said, appearing in the front room and handing me a cup, having heard the full story as the kettle boiled.

'I guess.'

Lan's phone rang from his pocket. He pulled it out.

'Speak of the devil.'

He turned the screen to me and I winced at the sight of my mum's name.

'Joss. Yeah … Yeah he's here … Hey, I know. Don't worry … Yeah … I'm on it … OK. Cool.'

He hung up and returned the phone to his pocket.

'So what's going on with you?'

We linked eyes, then I sighed and looked at my feet.

'Nothing.'

Lan smiled.

'Nothing, yeah? That means *something* … Did I ever tell you I can speak Teenage?'

I looked back at him with a sheepish smile.

'I'm fluent, mate,' Lan continued, warming to his theme. 'Like … "Ugh". That means "*Sure, why not?*" And "Thanks, I'm full" just means "*I hate vegetables*" …'

I snorted a laugh. Lan's look softened.

'And "nothing" means "*something*". No one runs out of school for nothing.'

I shrugged.

'Mum's pressuring me. My teachers … and Malky – I dunno, it feels like everyone's on my case,' I mumbled.

'Well, look, first off – I know my sister. She's like our mum. Hated it if she thought we weren't working hard enough. Thought I was an underachiever, but look at me now!'

He stood, in those trousers that looked suspiciously like pyjamas, stretched out his arms and motioned first to himself, then to his chaotic surroundings.

'Winning.'

We both laughed.

'I was never an academic, Carm. Your parents, your teachers expect a lot from you. You know why?'

'Why?'

'Cos you're smart, you idiot!'

A playful shove, a playful shove back.

'They know you can do *anything*. Me, I dunno how smart I was, but all I wanted to do was make music. Your grandma still thinks I'm a loser, but I make enough from playing to rent this place and do the one thing I love, so I'm winning. The real question in life is always, *Am I happy?* If the answer is yes, continue past Go, collect two hundred pounds, keep playing the game. If the answer is no, something needs to change.'

I began hesitantly.

'I *am* happy. 'S'just … I dunno. Mum and Dad are so … demanding, y'know? And Malky's always giving me grief for no reason, teasing me or whatever, and they think he's so perfect! And I hate Maths. And Geography. And Science.'

'Huh. Sounds joyous! But look at it another way – you got a family that actually care, you got loads of friends … That reminds me, tell Alex I'm good for back-gammon on Thursday.'

'I will.' I smiled. I liked how he and Alex had their little after-school backgammon club at his flat. He was right – I had friends. Good friends … *'And* I got a commendation for English, so …'

'There ya go! I had Music, you got English. Hey – you know one good thing about music?'

'What?'

Lan sang the answer. *'When it hits you …'*

A family favourite by Bob Marley. I joined in.

'You feel no pain!'

'Unlike Maths,' I added, 'which properly hurts.'

Lan laughed. 'You remind me of me, but not as handsome. Come on, you need to get home and face the music. I'll tag along. Be your emotional support animal.'

Twenty minutes later, we stepped off the 274 and headed towards my street.

'I entered a talent contest one time. 'Bout your age as well.'

'Bet you smashed it,' I said glumly. Lan laughed.

'I was rubbish. Proper rubbish. I mean it was 1994, I'm in a church hall in Cricklewood doing a bass solo, trying to win a hundred pounds.'

'Who was in your band?'

'No band. I thought I was such a hotshot, I could just play a five-minute bass guitar solo on my own and people would go nuts.'

'But they didn't?'

'Well they kinda did. I mean, if you're forced to listen to an untrained fifteen-year-old play improvised experimental funk on a bass guitar for that long you might actually go nuts.'

I laughed for the first time since that morning as we stopped outside the front door.

'I still look back and think that horror show was one of the best things that ever happened to me.'

'Really?'

'Really. I never ever wanted to be rubbish again. Didn't wanna feel that feeling again. So for the first time in my life, I practised. I actually tried. And surprise, surprise – I got better. Not rocket science.'

'But I don't even wanna be a poet.'

'OK, but you wanna be *something*, right? To *be* something you gotta *try* something. Try everything if you have to. That way, even if you're not clear on what you wanna do, at least you start to learn what you *don't* wanna do. I thought I wanted to be a solo space-funk bass freak. But with trial and error – mainly error – I realised I wanted to be in bands. So I just … let it happen.'

A net curtain twitched on the first floor above us. I put my key in the lock and was about to turn it, but Lan hadn't finished.

'It's a weird thing. You work so hard to control everything, right? What you see as your destiny or whatever. You don't wanna look like a loser, so you try to manufacture everything you do to *look* like you know all the answers. Then one day you just let go and let the universe decide. And life just kinda … I dunno … *simplifies*.'

I nodded, turned the key and went to push the door, but it suddenly opened from the inside.

'Big problem, matey. *Big* problem.'

Dad stood in the doorway, folding his arms in his best Mum impression. He nodded at his brother-in-law.

'Lan.'

Lan nodded back.

'Awright, Stu.'

He turned back to me.

'Your mum's gone ballistic. I'm not best pleased either.'

Lan tapped my shoulder.

'I'm gonna scoot.'

'Thanks for getting him back, Landon.'

'No drama ...' Lan smiled at Dad, made to leave, then turned back. 'Hey ... He's had a rough one.'

Stuart ushered me into the building.

'It might get rougher.'

I watched over my shoulder through the gap of the closing door as my uncle disappeared from view.

CHAPTER 12

Small Mercies

It did get rougher, but with small mercies.

'Small mercies' was another phrase I'd inherited from my uncle. Lan often referred to clouds with silver linings; little positives to pull out from difficult situations, tiny but significant bits of relief – *small mercies*.

Two small mercies for me were:

1. Mum was working a late shift so I wouldn't have to face her until tomorrow.
2. Malky was staying at Dane's, having a 'heavy session of revision', earning yet more of the kind of Brownie points that made me want to vomit, but at least I didn't have to deal with his gloating face all evening.

It was a strange, lonely sort of night with the family temporarily split. I sat in my room, feeling Dad's disappointment emanating through the walls. I had no phone and couldn't text Al. All there was left to do was count down the hours until the dreaded morning, when me AND BOTH MY PARENTS would meet with Mr French to discuss 'next steps'.

In school language, 'next steps' meant 'appropriate punishment', and with my recent track record, it was likely to be a little harsher than writing out '*I will not be a donut*' one hundred times.

It took way longer than usual, but eventually I fell asleep.

A third small mercy arrived the following morning, which was a real blessing as everything else felt about as comfortable as sitting on a traffic cone.

Waking up to a mother so angry she had nothing to say was an excruciating start.

Walking with both parents to the bus stop felt like a silent journey to a prison cell flanked by two heartless guards.

And simply sitting in a seat in front of them, feeling their frustration needling the back of my neck, contained the same levels of joy a baby antelope might experience when bumping into a pride of lionesses at the local watering hole.

So when Alex hopped on board and greeted Mr and

Mrs Taylor with a level of effervescent pleasantry that they were forced to match, it really was some small mercy having all that tension broken, if only for a few measly bus stops.

We fist-bumped, and Alex plopped down next to me. There was a brief pause, then she furrowed her brow and spun sideways to address all three Taylors at once.

'Wait – was I supposed to bring my parents to school today?'

'I hope not,' said Mum. 'That'd mean you were in the same amount of trouble this young man is in.'

I winced. Alex exhaled with realisation.

'Ah, this is about yesterday. The Great Escape.'

I nodded and muttered guiltily, 'Gotta see Mr French.'

'Eesh.'

'You ever run out of school, Alex?'

Mum asked the question in a way that was framed as a kind of performance for me. I burrowed my face deep into the collar of my jacket. Alex shook her head.

'No ...'

'You see, Car? Most kids don't—'

'I mean I've fantasised about it loads. This one time? I had a full-on daydream about creeping out of a window in the Science Block and climbing up the drainpipe to the roof where there's this long electrical cable that runs right over the gates to a telegraph pole on the street, and I was thinking, like, I could use my tie like one of those … those things? What are they called? The ring things?'

'Karabiners,' Dad offered.

Mum, whose face was already in a state of some confusion, shook her head at him as if to say, *'Don't encourage her!'*

'Right! Use it like a karabiner and, like, slide down the cable to freedom.'

Dad did a small nod and raised his eyebrows.

'Right.'

Mum slowly closed her eyes and opened them again, as if she were doing an invisible sigh inside.

Nothing Alex said ever came as a surprise to me so I just tried to enjoy the deflected attention for however many seconds it might last.

Not long.

'Anyway –' Mum picked up the slack – 'the point is, Car's lack of focus is affecting his behaviour now and I'm just not having it.' She glared down at me. 'Not a bit of it.'

It was shaping up to be a long day.

I picked up my phone at reception and Mum yanked it straight out of my hand before I could even turn it on. Being on school premises with other kids in earshot now, I whispered my protest.

'Mum!'

'I warned you.'

'Oooh!' I heard a collective chorus from behind me. The Three Moes were watching my mum's public fury like fans watching their favourite player get a horrible injury. All three faces screwed up in different winces.

'Can I just check my messages?'

'What do you think?' Mum tucked the phone into her pocket.

'Cold,' I heard Mehmet whisper. I wasn't in the mood for an audience and shot the Moes a look to let them know. They pretended not to watch, clearly anticipating some further drama.

I heaved a sigh as Dad looked around reception.

'Which way's Mr French's office?'

'Oooh!' the Moes chimed again.

'Peak!'

'Frenchy time!'

Alex piped up again. (Why was she so enthusiastic this morning? Scratch that – *every* morning?) 'I know – follow me!'

The four of us went up the stairs to the first floor, Alex leading the pack, me dragging my heels at the rear. The Moes followed in a separate group, still hungry for more spectacle. At the third door along the corridor, Alex did a sort of *'Ta-dah!'* presentation with her arms.

As my parents went to knock, Alex slipped round to where I stood and held out her fist for a bump. 'Good luck, bro! See you on the other side.'

I nodded sagely, a man condemned.

Alex scuttled off towards our tutor room, then suddenly reappeared, looking as if she'd just remembered something important.

'If you don't make it out alive, can I have your earphones?'

Off my glare, she darted back the other way and the door to Mr French's office creaked open.

CHAPTER 13

Lucky for Some

Was *this a good thing or a bad thing?* I wondered as I watched Mr French take a seat behind his desk next to Miss Choudhary and Miss Miller. I'd kind of expected Mrs Craig, the Head, to be there, but she wasn't – which was good, right? But having *all three* of the teachers I answer to most regularly felt like a firing squad, locked and loaded. I sat uneasily between Mum and Dad, with no idea which way this thing was going to go.

The only thing I knew was that this didn't feel nearly as funny as other times I'd been in that office. As I sat amongst all the grown-up seriousness, I found myself anxiously willing something absurd to happen: Mr French absent-mindedly pouring his goldfish bowl water – with goldfish – into the kettle; two window cleaners having a silent punch-up through the glass behind the teachers; all the chairs spontaneously collapsing as each adult sat down …

Instead:

'Mr and Mrs Taylor,' Mr French began.

'Jocelyn, please,' Mum said warmly, 'and Stuart.'

Dad nodded lamely. Mr French smiled in appreciation.

'OK, well, we all know why we're here, so this shouldn't take long. Now, I'll be honest – I've spoken to the Head and she has advised a two-day suspension for Carmichael for leaving school premises without authorisation.'

Mum slumped in disappointment. *Ugh. Worse than anger.*

'That said, I've also spoken to Miss Miller here, who says there were some mitigating factors. Miss Miller?'

My English teacher sat forward.

'That's right. Car didn't run just because he wanted to. He was being teased by some Year Ten students and was clearly upset.'

Mum looked to me, anger returning, but in a more defensive form.

'Who?'

I looked at my feet. Miss Choudhary chimed in.

'If I may, we're trying to identify the students, but neither I nor Miss Miller saw their faces. We were wondering if you might clear that up, Car?'

I looked up and scanned all five adults. I'm not sure how my face appeared exactly – I'm guessing red. The memory of Malky and his goons laughing at me burned painfully.

It was Malcolm Taylor, Your Honour! And his hapless minions! They're the true criminals here! I was but a lowly artist, trying to make my way in the world when I was set upon by three vindictive morons, like rabid foxes on a beautiful hare. Spare me the cells, Your Honour! Take them! Take them! Oh, the injustice!

'I ... didn't recognise them.'

There are all sorts of ridiculous codes, practices and unwritten rules made for teenagers, by teenagers. Ancient commandments embedded in huge stone tablets that no one has ever seen:

- Thou shalt never wear Adidas joggers with Nike trainers.
- When thou hearest about the latest trend for the first time, thou shalt immediately pretend to have known about it for weeks.
- Thou must constantly be wary of accidentally calling a teacher Mummy or Daddy, lest thou wishest to burn in Embarrassment Hell.
- THOU SHALT NOT SNITCH.

It makes no sense at all. So even with this opportunity to land my brother in it, I was more afraid of the *telltale* label that would knock my popularity down more notches than I could face.

A pause. Looks were shared around the room. Miss Miller picked up the slack.

'But … they *were* teasing you?'

I nodded.

Another pause.

'Right then,' said Mr French, turning to me. 'Due to the seriousness of Car's actions, I'm suggesting upholding the suspension, *but* … the Head and I are willing to downgrade it to one day and will wipe the record at the end of the school year in return for good behaviour and completion of your commitment to the school Talent Night on Friday.'

'That's … *good*,' Dad chipped in. 'Isn't it?'

'We're very grateful.' Mum sighed. 'Aren't we, Car?'

All eyes on me. Mum leaned her head towards mine and repeated the question, but not as a question.

'*Aren't we, Car.*'

'Yes.'

'And nothing like this will ever happen again.'

'I hope not.' Mr French closed my file and shuffled it like a newsreader at the end of the programme. 'Suspension will take place immediately, give you a bit of time to reflect and also rehearse your piece, no? Back tomorrow, hopefully for a fresh start.'

'Yes, sir.'

'Thanks,' said Dad.

We all got up and the adults shook hands. I felt weird: timid, uncertain and – worst of all – lost for words. No matter what space I was in at school, I'd always felt I had a trick up my sleeve – a witty comeback or a funny thought that would calm my nerves. But with my parents there, suddenly it was like I was back in the kitchen. I felt Malky smirking from some unseen vantage point and already resented letting him off the hook. Then there was the frustration of knowing how annoying the next few days would be at home … My mouth felt dry and my throat was a blocked road – no words could make it through.

Words had deserted me. Old Faithful, my Trusty Sidekick. *How could you, Words? I thought we were friends!*

I exchanged a look with Miss Miller and shuffled back out with my parents, speechless, and on route back to the lions' den.

CHAPTER 14
Time Out

OK, pause.

Let's get a few things straight here. We're fourteen chapters in, so I'm pretty sure you guys know by now that I'm not perfect. But I'm also sure you aren't either, so don't bother playing Charlie Big Potatoes with me.

In case you're still wondering, here's a little Q and A on my life so far:

	HAVE I ...	
	YES	NO
LIED?	☑	☐
CHEATED?	☑	☐
STOLEN?	☑	☐
BEEN SELFISH?	☑	☐

See how bad that chart makes me look? Even when I look at it now I'm like, *This guy sounds pure evil*. But before you mosey on into your courtroom and take your seat as the newly crowned Judge Judgy McJudgerson, you should flick back to Chapter 1, where you'll remember when I was talking about the word 'context' – the details behind the facts.

I've lied, sure. I've lied to my parents about finishing my homework, to my teachers about why I've been late for classes, in Year 6 to Stacey Norman about how I once climbed Mount Everest. (She was pretty and into adventure holidays: leave me alone.) But I've never done ones like 'No one told *me* he was allergic to nuts' or 'Your hamster was dead when I got here'.

Have I cheated? Have you ever played Uno? You have? Then you've cheated, just like me. As if you've never once seen the next guy's cards … I also may have copied one or two Geography homework exercises from the internet, but COME ON, GUYS, IT'S GEOGRAPHY.

Stolen stuff? I'm not proud of it, but I took a stormtrooper from my friend Irfan's house when I was six. He had, like, twelve and I had none, so in my six-year-old head it felt fair game. My parents made me give it back and I hated them for it, but really I hated myself. And I'm still sorry about it.

Been selfish? *Hello?* Young teenage boy over

here! Find me a kid my age travelling around the world in an air balloon, healing sick animals and building houses for homeless people, and then you can call me a monster.

What I'm saying is, I'm not getting any awards from the Queen or anything, but I know right from wrong, I'm not Voldemort.

So if I'm sounding bitter it's because that's exactly how I felt in that moment, riding the bus back home with my mum and dad in angry silence. I felt a deep, cutting resentment that wouldn't seem to lift.

The bus slowed and Dad got up.

'Right – more meetings for me, hooray. I'm gonna jump on the tube. See you tonight, love.'

He kissed Mum on her icy cheek and turned to me.

'Just … listen to your mother, OK?'

I nodded. *Good dadding, Dad.*

He hopped off, and Mum and I continued in that awkward silence.

I decided to break it when we reached the doorstep.

'Ma?'

She fished through her handbag for her keys.

'Mm?'

Before she could find them, I whipped mine out instead and turned the lock.

'You still mad?'

She looked briefly grateful as I opened the door, then a text on her phone made her frown.

'On call, I've gotta go in. Lemme grab my pass.'

She headed past me and I followed up the stairs, my question still lingering.

'More sad than mad, Car. I just want you to do well.'

'I'm actually doing OK.'

'Not *OK*. *Well*.'

That annoyed me.

'What, like Malky?'

'Don't do that, Car.'

She stopped at the interior door and I caught up and faced her.

'What?'

'You know what. Make out that we have favourites.'

I opened the door and she made a beeline for her room. I followed.

'Do you?'

I stood stationary in the hall as she called back over her shoulder without turning.

'That question doesn't even deserve an answer.'

She reappeared with her NHS pass and white plimsolls.

'And you know it doesn't.'

I knew.

'Like Mr French said, spend the day reflecting.

Work on your piece. Blow 'em away on Friday, and by Saturday you'll be celebrating. At the very least about getting your phone back.'

I nodded without smiling, but I can't lie: I appreciated the attempt at humour, however tiny. She patted my chest.

'See you tonight.'

'Yeah.'

Damn you, Words.

CHAPTER 15

Things to Do in Camden When You're Dead

As the door closed behind me I leaned against it and weighed up my one option:

I was alone for at least the next six hours. No mobile, no interruptions – plenty of time to finish this stupid poem, I guess. It had never felt like more of a chore than it did at that moment.

I sat at the kitchen table with a ballpoint pen and stared at the blank side of an old phone bill for at least an hour. Or maybe ten minutes. Either way it seemed to last forever.

I pushed my chair back in frustration and opened the fridge, staring blankly at cold food instead of paper, then I flung the refrigerator door shut again and stared blankly at the wall.

If there was one thing I was really nailing that morning, it was staring blankly. If there were some kind of Olympic recognition for Blank Staring, I was surely in the medal positions.

Then, of all my blank stares, the wall-based one bore fruit. *The landline phone!* Thanks to smartphones being too smart and essentially replacing human brains, of all the contacts in my device, I knew precisely three numbers by heart. I could never seem to remember Dad's and never bothered learning Malky's. That left Alex, Mum and Lan.

With Alex at school, there was only one person who could save me from entering the Blank Staring World Championships.

'Perfect timing,' Lan chirped down the line. 'I'm on my way to the Heath. Meet me at the station, we'll get our nature on.'

Hampstead Heath is to London what I guessed Central Park was to New York City or a watering hole was to the Sahara Desert: a kind of oasis, a place to get refreshed and shut out the surrounding madness. Whenever my parents suggested a wander round the Heath I always complained, but whenever I got there I always enjoyed it. Unless it was cold or wet or both, which was at least half the year.

Fortunately, as I greeted my uncle outside the station, this was the other half of the year – the bit where it only rains for half of every week and the odd day is actually approaching warm. Lan shifted an old acoustic guitar on its strap over his shoulder so it rested on his back, and initiated our old handshake: *slap, slap, fist bump, finger wave*.

'Nice day for it!'

He was right. The sky hosted only a smattering of wispy woollen clouds and the sun was doing its best to beat back any Scandinavian breezes. As ever with my uncle, there was a knowing glint in his eye; this time, it seemed to say, '*Let's not forget why you're here.*'

'Kinda ironic, isn't it?'

'What?'

'Everyone comes up here to escape the madness of the city, get to this place of peace, and whadda we do? Spend most of our time admiring the madness of the city.'

'Huh. Yeah, I s'pose,' I said, staring out over the famous skyline from the bench we shared at the peak of Parliament Hill.

'Who do you hate most in your class?'

'Mmm … Probably Tosun Kendall.'

'Somewhere down there, Tosun Kendall is doing star jumps in PE.'

We both chuckled, then I checked my watch.

'Actually, it's RS right now.'

'What's that?'

'Religious Studies.'

'OK, so he's making menorahs or writing an essay on monkey gods. Still works. Either way, that's why I never understood suspension.'

'It's basically a day off.'

'Right. Which is why you're gonna finish this spoken word piece before we leave. Otherwise Jocelyn'll smell a rat and I'll be the one choking on the pesticides.'

I nodded an agreement.

'I'm just ... kinda struggling to come up with stuff.'

'Even the greatest minds struggle to come up with stuff.' Lan waved a hand out towards the city, 'I mean, look at these buildings. Think of the architectural genius it must've took to build one that looks like a walkie-talkie and one that looks like a gherkin. Then some Great Mind nicknames them *The Walkie-Talkie* and *The Gherkin*. You telling me they weren't having an off day?'

'Hm.'

'It's about emotion. Like ... How do you feel right now?'

'Actually pretty chill.'

'I mean about your life in general. Everything's perfect?'

'Ha. No!'

'So tap into the frustration of that. Like, how did you feel when you left school this morning?'

'Oh man, I was on the bus with Mum and Dad and it was ...' I pulled a face.

'Excruciating?'

'Yeah. It was like, I was with them, but I was alone.'

Lan's face lit up.

'You see! That's emotive!'

He strummed a chord on his guitar, then stopped. I furrowed a question into my brow.

'*Emotive*. Something that makes people *feel* something. *I was with them, but I was alone*. Now that moves me!'

He strummed again and did a sort of chant:

'*Nine million people in this city I call home, Everyone together yet everybody alone.*'

'What's that from?'

Lan laughed.

'You ain't heard that before? That's from the brain of Carm Taylor! You brought a pen, right? OK, line two. What else you been feeling?'

And on we went. For the next twenty minutes we entertained a few nearby tourists, but then started annoying quite a few others, so we wandered off with no set destination; up and down pathways, through trees and around lakes, throwing rhymed phrases at each other, laughing at the rubbish ones, surprising each other with the better ones. Every now and again I'd stop to write the best couplets down and Lan would suggest different rhythms and tones I could use to perform them.

Maybe it was being out of the house, being out of

the school, having all this physical space or just hanging with Lan, but I could feel the right words coming back to me. Suddenly I was saying what I wanted to say.

It felt like no time had passed when we were sat on a fallen tree, reciting the whole thing. I couldn't believe it.

'You got it!' Lan grinned. I nodded, quietly stunned.

'I got it.'

A late lunchtime beam of sunshine filtered through the leaves above, warming selective spots on both of us. Lan looked at me.

'Ice cream?'

'Yeah!'

We wandered towards Gospel Oak station, where in front of an athletics track an ice-cream van was doing steady business with under-fives, out from nursery or not yet at school. After we got to the front, made our order and were handed two cones, Lan gently tapped his against mine and smiled.

'Cheers. Good job, man.'

'Cheers!'

'Five pounds, please.'

Lan looked back to the ice-cream man, tapped his pockets, then looked back at me, sucking air in through gritted teeth.

'Got a fiver?'

CHAPTER 16

The Fine Art of Spirit Dampening

I strongly recommend everyone reading this to ditch your phone for a few days.

It's mad how much your brain is forced to work when you don't have a tiny computer in your pocket doing all your thinking for you. Don't get me wrong, I would never have actually *chosen* to get rid of it, and I missed that little guy like a dead relative, but I was impressed by how much I was getting done in these gaps in the day which would normally be filled watching videos of people falling off/in/on/out of things.

Instead, I'd spent the short trip home from the Heath memorising this spoken word piece, reciting it in my head all the way to the front door, then out loud in my room. Then I typed up the whole thing and it was printing out at Dad's little desk in the hallway when he walked in that afternoon. All in all, I was feeling pretty darn good about myself.

I was in what they call *high spirits*. High and, for the moment, dry.

'Finished it!' I chirped as he closed the door behind him.

'Hah!' Dad smiled. 'Mum'll be stoked.'

I felt a tiny pang of disappointment. *What about you, Dad?* I thought. *Are you only stoked if Mum's stoked? Jeez, Dad, how about an opinion of your own sometime?*

I shrugged it off and took the two sheets of paper back to my room.

My spirit would not be dampened.

I would no longer use cynical jokes to hide my emotions. This was the new Car. Car 2.0. The guy who can write serious creative pieces with no need to laugh at everyone and everything. The guy who doesn't need to trawl the internet for comic inspiration. This was a guy with something meaningful to say.

I stood holding the papers in the centre of my bedroom, closed my eyes and tried to recite the piece from memory. Halfway through, I heard a slow clap and spun to see Malky stood in his uniform at the doorway. He sniggered.

'Whoa, you a rapper now, yeah?'

'It's spoken word.'

'Oh yeah, my bad. Spoken word – that thing people do when they're too lame to rap.'

'I wouldn't expect you to get it, Malky. The most intellectual thing you've ever done is a sit-up.'

'Yeah? Well I reckon this was a smart move.' He waved five strips of paper like a fan to his face. 'Tickets for tomorrow night.'

'You're coming?'

'With Dane and TJ. As if we're gonna miss the car crash of the year! I wanna see that sock guy – he looks like he's got problems – and of course, give you some … whatchacallit? *Moral support*.'

We glared at each other for a few seconds before he turned and walked out. I didn't like the way he made the words 'moral support' sound like 'verbal abuse'. His was the last face I needed to catch in the audience. But hey, this was Car 2.0 – I wasn't going to get upset, I wasn't going to retaliate, I wasn't going to get distracted from my work. My spirit had a few droplets on it, but I had my spirit umbrella up; I was still largely dry.

When Mum came home, I heard her usual greeting, followed, this time, by a knock on my door. I was lounging on the bed reading comics as she peeked in.

'Hope you haven't been doing that all day.'

'I'm on downtime.' I smiled proudly, waving my printed papers at her. 'Now that I'm all prepped for tomorrow!'

She held out a flat palm of refusal.

'Don't show me,' she said, then smiled. 'I wanna be surprised on the night.'

I nodded and laid the sheets back on the desk, turning them face down as she sat next to me on the edge of the bed.

'Well done, Car. I mean that. You could've wasted the day sulking. I'm proud of you. Tomorrow's a fresh start, agreed?'

'Agreed.'

'And on that, I was thinking – starting afresh and all – maybe we should be looking at how you spend your downtime in general.'

'What do you mean?'

'Well, just – what you get up to, who you get up to it with …'

'I don't *get up* to anything. With anyone.'

'What about Alex?'

'Oh, here we go again. She's my best friend, Mum.'

'And best friends are often the biggest influence.'

'I do have a brain of my own, you know. Why do we keep coming back to this?'

'That's the question, isn't it? Why are we still concerned about Alex after all these years?'

'*We* aren't concerned. You are!'

'It's a recurring issue. I'm just saying is she the best person for you to be around? I mean, she's a little …'

'What?'

'Eccentric.'

'Right. So you're saying ditch her because she's interesting.'

'I'm saying the next year is going to be one of the most important of your life. I just don't want it jeopardised.'

'What, by my *best friend* making me *happy* through *friendship*?'

'You're making it sound worse than it is.'

I did one of those laughs that isn't a laugh.

'No, that's what *you're* doing.'

Dad's voice rang from the kitchen.

'Car! Can you set the table please?'

Thankful for the interruption, I got up and headed for the door.

'Car ...'

'When do I get my phone back?'

'Like we agreed – after the show. Car, listen—'

'Great. Be good to be in touch with my *friends* again.'

I walked out, my sarcastic tone ringing in the air behind me.

My spirit umbrella caught an upward gust of wind and snapped backwards, leaving me somewhere between dampened and soaked.

CHAPTER 17

Nice Day for It

'Wait. Why are they coming if they don't wanna come?'

'It's not that they don't wanna come, it's like they wanna come for the wrong reasons.'

Alex screwed her face into a question just as our morning bus paused for an old lady to shuffle on to the pedestrian crossing with her equally shuffly and old-looking dog. I looked down at the two sheets of paper that had barely left my hands since the Heath.

'Malky just wants to see me crash and burn, my mum wants me to get the Nobel Prize, and my dad … Actually I have no idea what Dad wants. I'm not sure he knows.'

'But are you doing it for them?'

'I … I mean, kinda. But I guess more just to *prove* I can do it.'

'Well, there ya go. You're like a male sea horse.'

'What?'

'Well, male sea horses are the ones—'

'That actually get pregnant, yeah I know, but how does that—'

'*Because!* You …' Alex frowned, then quickly widened her eyes in surprise satisfaction at her choice of metaphor. 'You don't need anyone else to *give birth* to your *ideas!*'

'But they still need the female to get pregnant in the first place.'

'OK. So … your uncle helped you write the poem, right?'

'Spoken word.'

'Spoken word. So I guess … he's the female one?'

'I'm … not sure this works.'

Alex shrugged.

'Hey, just giving you the positives.'

'Right. Well … thanks. I guess.'

The tiniest speck of hurt flashed across her eyes, then disappeared as soon as she blinked.

'Anyway, *I'll* be there. Bigging you up. I'm like your hype man. Your cheerleader. I'm the sardine to your sea horse. With my sardine fam all, like, *A-yo! Whoo! Go, Car, go, Car!*'

I cracked a smile.

'That the scientific term, is it? A *fam* of sardines?'

'That's the legit zoological term.'

We both cracked up as we rose from our seats with a bunch of other kids at the stop nearest Wainbridge.

I paused as we reached the gates, wondering if I'd be stood back out here tonight as a hit or a failure. Another pang of nerves ran through me.

I thought of Bahir and his sock puppets, and calmed down again.

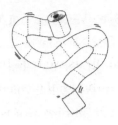

CHAPTER 18

And ... *Breathe*

I t was a weird day from that point on.

Like I was there, but I wasn't there. Does that make sense? I guess I mean I was *doing* one thing (school), but my *mind* was in a whole other place (show time). I could only think forwards, basically.

It was a bit like when you need a poo so bad that everything else kind of becomes irrelevant. All life simply melts away and your entire existence is simplified; narrowed and filed down like a sculpture to one simple goal: *poo*.

You must poo. Just poo. Nothing else matters until that fateful plop.

In that scenario I'm pretty sure there isn't a human being on the planet who can fully relax until they've finally dropped off their little brown kids at the pool.

And that basically summed up my Friday. I normally

like Fridays, for obvious reasons, but this one was a blur: ICT, History, Break, Double Maths, Lunch, French, Art … They all sort of washed over me. Teachers spoke words in broken pieces, interrupted by the voice in my head reciting my spoken word piece, jabbing words at random into my brain like some bully poking me in the side of my head.

At one point that afternoon, as Miss Salter was discussing the iconic ceiling painting of the Sistine Chapel during Art, I literally said, 'Oh, shut *up!*' in a loud whisper to the cluttered noise in my mind.

'Excuse me? Something to add, Car?'

'Hm? Oh! No. No, sorry, miss. Just got a … um … some kind of ringing in my ears.' I clapped once, pointed at the whiteboard with both hands and did my best *'I'm listening'* smile. 'Sixteen chapels. I was with you from Chapel One.'

Miss Salter rolled her eyes and the class chuckled. I exhaled.

Normality.

Well, *partial* normality.

You see, normally I would watch the second hand on the big clock above Miss Salter's head tick all the way from around 3.28 p.m. Then, from 3.29 and fifty seconds, Alex and I would tap our feet in time with a ten-second countdown to the best two and a bit days of school: the weekend.

Alex tapped, but my feet remained leaden blocks. My stomach felt tight, as if it were stretched around all my other organs. I watched as two of the Hip Hop ballet girls excitedly pulled matching pairs of pumps from their bags with added fake stick-on diamonds and pointless phrases like *YO* plastered on with permanent markers, itching to get out and head to their dress rehearsal.

Our dress rehearsal.

'Assessment week next Friday, folks!' Miss Salter called above the thunderous din of thirty impatient kids packing up and racing for the door. I sat staring into space. Alex turned back.

'You staying?'

I stared out into nothing. Trance-like.

'Maybe. Maybe I'll sleep here tonight. Maybe I'll just live here, under the desk.'

Alex shook her head, smiling sympathetically as the classroom emptied. Miss Salter stopped packing her satchel and looked up.

'Can I help you, Car?'

'He's sleeping here tonight,' said Alex, throwing me out of my hypnosis just as Mehmet and Mo filed past me behind the others.

'Rah, you homeless now, yeah?' Mehmet asked with a chuckle.

'Is that a chicken-kicking consequence?' Mo threw in.

'Sorry, miss,' I said, jumping up and following the others to the door. We turned as Miss Salter spoke again.

'Looking forward to seeing your performance later.'

I did a weird smile, said 'Ha' and spun on my heels.

Alex and I sat in a takeaway chicken shop on the High Street near the school. The full trio of Moes were squished on to a neighbouring table, out of earshot.

'It's actually really good.'

'Really?' I asked hopefully, after finishing the last whispered phrase of my piece across our little table and folding the two sheets of A4 into my back pocket.

'Yeah,' said Alex, holding up a half-chewed chicken wing, 'I think they're using a new recipe. Something in the coating.'

'Idiot.'

She cracked up and I couldn't help a small snigger.

'Seriously, it's good, man. Just perform it like you mean it, I guess, and in two minutes it's over, right?'

'I've never felt this nervous about anything. I can't understand it. Like proper nerves. In my stomach.'

'You should poo.'

'What?'

'Might help.'

'I'm eating.'

'Not right now, but soon. Big one. Like a five- or six-wiper.'

I chucked my own half-chewed wing back in the box.

'Thanks.'

'Any time.'

Alex stared at her phone and I stared out of the window at all the busy Londoners, racing back and forth, living their non-public-speaking, no-performance, un-embarrassing lives.

'Speaking of time –' Alex turned her phone to face me, the clock on the screen front and centre – 'shouldn't you be in Dress Rehearsal?'

'Nope.'

'Huh? Why not?'

'I just wanna do it in the moment. I don't want Miss Choudhary or Miss Miller telling me I should do it like this or do it like that. I'm just gonna do it. Do it once. Then bounce.'

'No practice run?'

I held up a fresh wing and smiled.

'Nah.' I took a big bite, chewed and swallowed.

'I'm gonna wing it.'

CHAPTER 19

Winging It

I t's way handier than you think, not having a phone. Dress Rehearsal was 4.30 to 6.30 and doors opened to the audience at 7 p.m. By my judgement, that meant Alex and I could go to the cinema, enjoy a movie and still be back in good time for the show. And without a phone, no one could try and stop me.

Apart from Alex.

'You sure about this?'

I pulled out my allowance card and paid for two tickets on a machine in the foyer of the Camden Odeon.

'Al, I can't do a single minute more freaking out about performing. I need to do something totally different.'

Alex's phone rang. She froze as the caller's digits flashed up on the screen and turned it to face me. The School Office.

'Decline!'

'Really?'

'Really!'

Alex swiped the call from existence, went to put it back in her pocket and it rang again. Same number. She looked at me questioningly. I shook my head warningly.

We both stood there, frozen by the ringtone, until Alex's face changed suddenly from confusion to determination and she swiped in the other direction and answered the call. My eyes widened.

'Hello?'

I dived for the phone but Alex was too quick. She sidestepped me like a kung fu master and held her finger up, mouthing, *'Trust me.'*

'... Yes ...'

PAUSE.

'Yes, I'm with him now.'

I launched at her again, but this time she spun so quickly out of my reach I nearly fell face first on the sticky carpet.

'Yeah ...'

PAUSE.

'No, he was on his way to rehearsal but realised he'd left his costume at home so we ...'

PAUSE.

'Well, it's quite elaborate ... There's a lot going on with the ... with the hat and the ... the ...'

I winced and mouthed, *'What the HECK?'*

'The feathers …'

FEATHERS.

'Yeah … he didn't wanna perform without it. He'll be back for the show.'

PAUSE.

'Can you *speak* to him?'

Alex looked at me. I shook my head as vigorously as I could.

'Sure, hold on.' She held the phone out to me, covered the mic and whispered, 'Miss Choudhary. Don't worry. *We got this!'*

I thought for a second. Alex was right. If they'd called her, they'd probably already have called my parents. Best not to let this thing escalate any further. I didn't have to work too hard to put on a flustered voice.

'Miss Choudhary? Hi … Sorry, sorry.'

'Car? We never spoke about a costume. You really don't need a—'

'It'll really add to the performance, miss. Give me the confidence I need, y'know?'

A resigned sigh made its way back through Alex's phone.

'Fine. Just … don't be late. I'm serious, Car.'

'Yes, miss. So am I. Those feathers are no joke.'

I hung up and gave the phone back to Alex, who

was doubled over in silent laughter. I frowned at her in disbelief.

'Feathers? Really?'

'Saved *your* butt.'

I shook my head with a smile and handed her a ticket.

We left the cinema hyped up.

The movie was about this teenage soldier in the First World War who had to deliver a vital message to another unit across enemy lines. It made me feel heroic. Inspired. Like a younger, lamer, much less life-threatened version of that kid, with my own message to get across enemy lines. The only life at risk onstage at Wainbridge was my social one.

The stakes are still kind of high, I thought, shrugging to myself on the bus back to school. *But you know what?*

I'm ready.

CHAPTER 20

Watershed

One of the best things about words is that they don't stay still.

They're like living organisms – like us, like animals, they grow and change and eventually evolve. Some words start off meaning one thing, but somehow end up meaning something totally different. Sometimes they're weird words you rarely hear, other times you hear them every day – you maybe even use them regularly.

I know this because I look stuff up when I don't know what it means. Now that might sound like doing homework for fun, but trust me, I would never do that, because I'm not a freak of nature. I just need to know what someone's talking about so that *I* know what *I'm* talking about.

In a metaphorical nutshell, all of this means I'm the type of guy who goes down metaphorical rabbit holes when it comes to the meaning of words. So now I know stuff I probably don't really need to know, but I'm not keeping it all in my head – you're gonna have to share the burden.

And hey, if that bugs you or bores you? By all means, skip this chapter – but just know that if you do, you'll miss the build-up to one of the craziest things that ever happened to me. Your choice.

I'll wait.

We good?

Cool.

It all started when I was about eight years old and read the word 'feisty' in a comic book. I wanted to know what it meant (*generally aggressive and overenthusiastic, like a pop singer's backing dancers*), but underneath the dictionary description I found a short history of the word itself.

Bear with me here.

In *Ye Olde English Sack-Wearing Rat-Eating Disease* times, a *fist* was slang for a *fart*, right? I know – lolz – but true. OK?

SO:

Over time, *fist* morphed into *fice*, which was once described as '*a small windy escape backwards, more obvious to the nose than the ears*'. Classic. Then, a smelly dog became known as a *fisting cur*. (Don't know why – you'll have to look that one up yourself. I can't do everything.) And soon enough, any yappy little dog was called a *feist*.

Long story short – next time you want to show off for being *feisty*, remember: you're basically calling yourself a *farty little dog* and we can smell you from a mile off.

Sometimes words start their lives describing what they mean very literally, then become a *metaphor* for something else. I'll give you an example:

As an innocent little baby-word, 'tenterhooks' used to literally mean *hooks* on a *tenter*. That was back in the fourteenth century – that's like seven hundred years BC (Before Cat-memes) – when craftspeople used to stretch out newly woven cotton to get the oil and dirt out. The *tenter* was a wooden frame, and the hooks were … well, hooks, and these guys would stretch the cotton out between them. Being stretched out and tense like that, somehow along the way people started saying they felt like they were on *tenters* when they felt stressed or anxious, as if they were hanging on *tenter hooks*.

Same deal with the word 'watershed'. As a cheeky young onesie-wearing nipper of a word in the early 1800s, *watershed* described any patch of earth that separated a river into two, so the *shed* was the patch and the *water* was the river. But now it's used to describe a moment where everything changes – things go a different way – and just like the river, they can't go backwards.

They're changed forever.

OK, for all the bored guys, or you lot who prefer to just pretend they know what words mean, start your Chapter 20 **HERE:**

So there I stood, on the side of the stage in the school hall.

On tenterhooks, but feeling feisty – waiting for my watershed moment.

I was hidden from the crowd, tucked behind a curtain, but felt the presence of every single audience member, their eyes boring through the fabric somehow. Miss Choudhary stood as close as she could, very deliberately not letting me out of her sight, partly perhaps because she was scared I'd do a third runner in a week, partly because she was probably wondering when I was going to pull out this *Carmichael and His Amazing Technicolor Dreamhat* she'd heard so much about.

I zipped up my lucky hoodie. I hadn't been lying to Alex in the chicken shop – with no rehearsal I was winging it. Literally. Like actors from two hundred years ago, onstage and underprepared, prompted by helpers in the 'wings' – the sides of the stage. *Winging it. On a wing and a prayer*.

I was better prepared than those guys, I thought. Under-rehearsed perhaps, but over-energised and – all of a sudden – *ready to rock*.

I looked out on to the stage. Polite laughter accompanied Bahir's increasingly desperate attempts at delivering a funny look at world politics through the medium of used footwear. He would be the perfect act to follow – no gimmicks from me, just a short, sharp dose of hard-hitting real talk, poetic and from the heart. I nodded to myself. *This could actually be great.* I stretched out my neck by swinging my head from side to side, ear to shoulder, left and right, in a way I'd seen professional athletes do on TV. Definitely didn't help physically in the slightest, but it looked and felt cool. Miss Choudhary picked up on my readiness.

'Couple of minutes left. Good to go?'

I nodded back.

On my third neck stretch I noticed a narrow break in the curtain and took the opportunity to peek out over enemy lines.

Miss Miller sat at the foot of the stage, in front of the front row, all smiles and nodded encouragement, a silent cheerleader for each act.

Mr French sat at the side of the hall on a gym bench, tying up the laces on his roller skates. He also seemed to be wearing a tutu. *Lord help us.*

A bunch of other staff lined the walls, all three of

which featured kid-designed posters saying TURN OFF YOUR PHONES.

Scanning to stage left, I spotted Malky, Dane and TJ, bent double with laughter and slapping each other, pointing at Bahir and imitating him with their hands. My parents sat behind them, Mum sporadically shushing them, and Dad nodding and folding his arms.

The only electronic device I could see was held aloft by my favourite Geography teacher, Miss Stillman, who stood with her back to the far wall, watching the performance through a school iPad, occasionally throwing a glare towards my brother and his goons.

I looked back at Bahir and felt both a little sorry for him and a little scared for myself.

'This is it,' Miss Choudhary whispered, and I spun around from the curtain as she gestured with her head towards Bahir, hands poised for applause.

'I guess the world really is run by … PUPPETS!' Bahir threw out his last line with such gusto and self-belief, you kind of had to take your hat off to him. Speaking of which …

'Where's your hat?'

Miss Choudhary stared wide-eyed at me as she and the rest of the audience applauded. Bahir came happily bouncing past us and Miss Miller hopped on to the stage to resume hosting duties.

'Thank you, Bahir, that was genuinely unforgettable. Now time for some spoken word! A bit of street poetry from a very talented student – I know because I teach him, so he learned from the best, ahem …'

After a small wince at the term *'street poetry'*, I whispered back to Miss Choudhary, surprised at the steel in my own voice.

'You were right. Didn't need it. Let the words speak for themselves.'

'… Ladies and gentlemen, give a whopping, warm, Wainbridge welcome to … *Carmichael Taylor!*'

CHAPTER 21

Carmageddon

Have you ever woken up, looked out of your window and realised it snowed overnight? You step outside and the street you've known for most, if not all, of your life, suddenly looks completely unrecognisable. Foreign, like you might get lost in it.

That's sort of how it felt when I reached the microphone at the centre of the stage.

The world had changed.

The hall wasn't for lunch any more. The stage wasn't for stacking chairs, and these people staring at me felt as cold as any blizzard. Miss Miller returned to her cheerleading spot and gave me two thumbs-up as the applause died down.

Suddenly there was silence.

Deafening in its lack of noise.

I shifted my weight slightly and heard a floorboard

creak under my foot, as loud as the bombs in that war movie.

I opened my mouth and heard – maybe for the first time in my life – every tiny sound made by the parting of my own lips.

Super weird.

Space had changed, sound had changed … Time had changed.

It already felt like I'd been standing there for an age. I saw my expectant parents, then Malky raising his eyebrows in a look that said, *'Come on then, Doofus.'* I saw Miss Stillman focusing her iPad, then, down in the third row, Alex smiling and nodding, mouthing something:

YOU GOT THIS.

'Hi,' I said, a bit too close to the microphone.

Strong opener. My voice croaked and echoed back at me. I backed off a little and pulled the crumpled sheets from my back pocket.

'This is called, *Alone, With Everyone.'*

Malky snorted.

Idiot.

Mum shoved him from behind. I cleared my throat.

'Same old street
Same old bus …'

I paused, hearing some sniggers. Malky was moving his head and mouth like a ventriloquist's dummy, in some dumb impersonation of me. I caught his eye and he did a *'Who, ME?'* face and waved at me to continue. I did, but watched him as I recited.

> *'You.*
> *Me.*
> *This is us ...'*

He was doing it again, flapping his mouth open and shut, crossing his eyes. My stomach did a somersault and my free hand made a fist so tight I could feel my nails digging into my palm. I went on, through gritted teeth.

> *'Everyone together yet everybody alone.*
> *Millions of people and—'*

'And I wish I could go home!' chimed Dane. TJ and Malky creased up in silent laughter.

What I would've done with a First World War grenade at that moment.

Whilst the adults grumbled and tutted, the kids laughed along with my idiot brother and his stupid sidekicks. Even more so when my mum walloped him on the head with her handbag. *Even more again* when

Mr French shouted '*RIGHT, YOU LOT!*' and made an angry beeline for the trio, forgetting he was in a tutu and roller skates, creating an impromptu slapstick routine right through the centre of the audience. Miss Stillman slowly lowered the iPad, a look of horror contorting the lines of her face into a picture I wish she could have accidentally taken of herself in that moment and somehow sent to me.

All attention was gone now.

Broken.

Alex looked up at me, super awkward.

Miss Miller pleaded for calm.

Mum scowled.

Mr French roller-frogmarched Malky, Dane and TJ to the wall, where all the staff sat or leaned, with help from my dad, who I could hear apologising on Malky's behalf. *Malky's behalf? Why's he apologising for that donut?* At one point I thought he was going to say something *really* lame, like '*Boys will be boys*', and the temperature behind my cheeks went up another notch.

I stood behind the microphone, surveying the chaos.

To this day I'm not sure why I didn't just walk off.

I guess the world really had changed and I was just frozen, watching the snowfall transforming it all.

Miss Choudhary was onstage now as well, looking worried for her event and for me, I think. Mr French steadied himself and shouted, aiming at the largely youth-endorsed mayhem from the side.

'OK, thank you! THANK YOU! Quieten down now. Miss Miller?'

He looked pleadingly to the bubbly host, who dutifully jumped up alongside Miss Choudhary and held out both arms, doing a fanning motion with her palms faced down, both women shushing the rowdy hordes.

Miss Miller leaned in front of me and spoke loudly into the mic.

'Let's try again, shall we? Round of applause?'

She clapped, and encouraged everyone else to do the same as she hopped back down off the front of the stage. It produced what might generously be called a *smattering*. My face must've been the same colour as my hair by now, surely.

I reluctantly held up my two sorry sheets of cursed paper and approached the microphone. Again.

Miss Stillman raised the iPad once more.

I looked down at the opening lines as if I didn't know them.

I looked up at the unsettled crowd as if I didn't know them either.

Loads of kids were still laughing and pointing, either at me or Malky or Mr French.

I lowered the two sheets of paper so they were hanging at waist height.

'Apologies for my brother's crew over there. It's not always easy for them to take intellectual content on board. I mean, Dane still thinks Mona Lisa is a nickname for a nagging woman.'

Alex snorted. A couple of younger kids gasped at the burn.

'Least I don't write lame poems!' More gasps at Dane's retort.

'OK, right, that's enough of that,' Mr French said as he and Dad began to shuffle him to the door.

'True,' I said calmly into the mic. 'You'd need to know how to read and write first.'

A bigger reaction of *oohs*, *aahs* and laughs rose from the crowd.

Miss Stillman lowered the iPad once more.

Out of the corner of my eye, I spotted Alex sneaking her phone out and sitting it covertly on her belly, camera towards the stage.

'Right, er – thank you … Carmichael Taylor, everyone!' Miss Choudhary began, trying to wrap things up, stepping towards me, but something new in me had taken over.

Watching my dad bowing to whoever was making decisions, watching my mum watching me, shaking her head with bitter disappointment, seeing Malky and co. through the window, getting a dressing-down from a man in a tutu,

still somehow getting all the attention ... an age-old frustra-
tion stewing inside like a big casserole, but over years – not
hours or days – perhaps dating all the way back to that ice
cream in the poo when I was five ...

I pulled the microphone out of its clip on the stand and sidestepped away from the approaching teacher.

'Don't you want to hear some spoken word?' I put the question directly to Miss Choudhary, but in a pointed, pantomime tone into the microphone so the crowd could hear me. A few kids cheered, a handful of *whoops*, a couple of *yeahs*.

Miss Choudhary looked desperately to Miss Miller, who shrugged and nodded, then turned from her spot in front of the stage to face the audience.

'Carmichael Taylor!' she said once more.

Some kids whooped and whistled. Parents and staff shifted awkwardly in their seats.

Carmichael Taylor.

CARMICHAEL TAYLOR, EVERYONE.

CARMICHAEL TAYLOR.

My stupid name echoed in my burning-hot ears as I lifted the papers back up to my face.

'That's right,' I said, for some reason, into the mic. 'My name is Carmichael Taylor. You know why? Because my parents are idiots.'

Somehow, beyond what now felt like an impenetrable

circle of fire around me, I spotted Alex's eyes dart from left to right and back again, doing that thing cartoon characters do when they're in a haunted house and not sure if they're alone or not.

I blocked everyone out and kept going, sensing people were unsure whether this was some kind of rebellious protest poetry or ...

'Yeah. They named me after some old guy who reckoned he invented poppy seeds. I'll tell you who invented poppy seeds ... POPPIES.'

Pure confusion from every chair in front of me.

'So they invented a name for me after an inventor who didn't invent anything. It'd be tragic if it wasn't ironic.'

Silence.

Miss Choudhary had shuffled back to the wings, where Miss Miller met her and the pair went into whispered discussion. I placed the mic back in the stand.

'I know you lot think I'm a clown. You probably find this –' I waved a hand over my hair, head and body – 'funny. But this ... this was also my parents' fault.'

Heads turned to face my mum as my dad peered in nervously from outside the glass doors at the back of the hall.

'What did you expect from the lovechild of a Scottish lamp post and a Caribbean Ewok?'

Shocked gasps from the adults and nervous giggles from the kids. A 'Rah' from somewhere – definitely Mehmet.

To heck with it, I thought, *if I'm going down – let's make it memorable.*

'Hey. You don't have to tell me. *I know*. Short, brown, ginger on top. I know I look like half an HB pencil.'

Friendlier chuckles.

'I know I look like candyfloss on a stick, I'm self-aware like that.'

Laughter. Definite laughter.

I caught a small smile from Miss Miller in the wings; she seemed to be reassuring Miss Choudhary now. I think she assumed this was still just an intro to my actual performance piece.

Maybe it was, at some point.

But then it wasn't.

'Hey, it's spoken word so I'll just speak some words,' I said innocently, taking one of my sheets of paper and folding it into a paper aeroplane.

'They're only words, right? Yeah. Hey, listen, I really hope we do Talent Night every year. Maybe next year we could even do it with some talent.'

Back to gasps and nervous giggles. A 'He went there, bro!' from Mo.

'Relax, I count myself in that. I'm not talented. I

mean seriously, you know what I'm good at? Eating Jaffa Cakes without breaking the orange bit and sucking on it till it's the size of a penny. Anyone ever make a career out of that?'

Knowing nods and smiles.

'You know what? I actually feel like I've learned a lot at this school. I learned the best school day of the week is Saturday.'

Laughter.

'I learned that the phrase *"It's your own time you're wasting"* really isn't a threat.'

More laughter, more recognition.

'Anything to make the day go quicker, right? Hey, did you know the word "school" was originally an acronym? It's true. S. C. H. O. O. L. Six. Cruel. Hours. Of. Our. Lives. See?'

Even some parents liked that one.

'Mad. Who knew you could *learn* stuff at a *school*?'

Loud laughter. Clear whoops.

Some mad part of me started to enjoy this car crash. I pointed to the back of the room, where Miss Stillman looked on aghast, her iPad by her side.

'And you're right to not be filming this, Miss Stillman.' I nodded sympathetically, then bent my body towards the kids in the front row. 'Imagine a Geography teacher having content on their computer that was a thousand times more interesting than Geography. *Awkward!'*

Belly laughs.

I finessed the last fold in the paper and fired my plane out over the crowd.

I glanced to my right. Miss Choudhary and Miss Miller were in a full-blown battle now. Was Miss Miller … *wanting* me to continue? Was this some heroic fight for my freedom of speech? Or were they both just working out the best way to have me forcibly removed? I mean, probably the latter.

In that moment – I'll be completely honest with you – I just didn't care. I felt like I was floating. I was a helium balloon pumped full of bitterness … *and they were gonna have to come pop me*, because I was *flying*.

Miss Stillman marched out to get Mr French, who rolled back in with Dad and Malky.

'Uh-oh!' I nodded theatrically to them as they entered, and everyone turned to the back door.

'It's the Three Wise Men!'

The kids were losing it now. Parents were trying to calm them, getting their coats. It was pure, delicious pandemonium.

'What gifts dost thou bear for Little Lord Carmichael?'

From left to right, I pointed at Mr French, Malky and Dad in turn.

'Rolled, *Notmuchsense* and *Meh*.'

At least thirty parent-less young teens howled; their younger counterparts stared, clapped and cheered in awe at this disaster-bound Firestarter.

'I don't remember any of the Three Kings wearing skates. Guess that's just how he rolls …'

Good-natured moans.

'Hey, I'd call that a "Dad Joke" but it'd give my dad way too much credit. I'd like to say he had an opinion on that one, but original ideas aren't really his strongpoint. I mean, look at him.'

Heads turned to stare at my lanky, red-faced father.

'His main talent is nibbling leaves from the tops of trees.'

Back to proper laughter.

I pointed at Mr French and shook my head theatrically.

'Can we talk about the tutu?' I had to raise my voice over the roaring guffaws now. 'I mean, pardon my *Mr* French, but he looks like a total—'

A crackle and a squeak and the mic went dead. Just in time, I guess: I was totally about to swear.

I looked to the right, where Miss Choudhary stood with the other end of the cable in her hand, glaring at me. Miss Miller ran onstage.

I quickly yelled, '*GOODNIGHT, WAINBRIDGE,*'

dropped the mic to the floorboards, and the hall went bananas.

Mr French was gliding ominously down the aisle towards me, Mum and Dad following in his wake. Alex tucked her phone in her pocket and looked around at the hall in wonder. Miss Miller put a hand on my shoulder.

'Let's go, Car. I think you're done.'

And she was right.

I was.

CHAPTER 22

Mumzilla, Part 1

So yep, that happened.

And now I had a new audience: Mr French, Miss Miller, Mum and Dad all facing me in a Year 7 classroom across the corridor from the hall, where Miss Choudhary was presumably working pretty hard to get the Talent Night back on track.

Less performance from me this time though – it was really more a chorus of opinions and questions and pointy-judgy fingers coming at me at speed, with barely time for me to say 'Um', let alone make any real response. That may have been a good thing. I felt weird and not myself. My time onstage had left me feeling electric – my ears were ringing and I felt energised, shivery, indestructible and vulnerable all at the same time. The room was spinning.

I snapped into reality when I heard my mum's question: 'But you wouldn't consider *permanent* exclusion?'

'Insulting the staff? Bringing the school into disrepute? I think we'd have to at least consider it,' said Mr French. Miss Miller jumped in, off the back of the horror that had suddenly arrived on my mum's face.

'Except, that would be a decision for the Head, and she's not here this evening, so …'

Mr French picked up where she left off.

'So it would be based on our recommendations, a thorough report of the incident and our opinions on the pupil himself.'

They all turned to me. I looked up at each of them in turn.

'What?'

'*Remorse*, Carmichael,' said my mum. 'Starting with an apology.'

'What about Malky and his stupid friends? They started it!'

'They're outside with Miss Stillman and their Head of Year. They'll be dealt with accordingly,' said Mr French. 'So let's focus on you, Car. What on earth were you *thinking*?'

I looked at my feet.

'I wasn't thinking.'

Dad tried to catch my eye.

'*And?*'

'And …' My voice went tiny. 'I'm … sorry.'

Mr French awkwardly bunched up his tutu by

thrusting his hands on to his hips.

'Go home, Car,' he said, before looking up to my parents. 'And don't bother sending him in on Monday unless you've heard from us.'

The teachers filed past us back to the hall, Mr French as stompily as you can stomp on skates, Miss Miller with a pained, almost apologetic shrug.

The three of us were left in silence. I couldn't look at either of my parents. Mum broke it first – not shouting, but with that horrible soft tone that smacks of exhausted disappointment.

'Did you mean all that stuff?'

'What stuff?'

'Onstage. About me and Dad? Your brother? Your teachers?'

'I was joking.'

'I didn't find it very funny.'

Everyone else did, I thought, but was probably wise not to say it.

Just then, the classroom door opened and Malky's Head of Year ushered him in, pausing on the threshold to announce:

'Mr and Mrs Taylor? Malcolm has apologised for his behaviour, but will get a suspension for Monday and detention Tuesday and Wednesday. Call the School Office if you'd like to discuss it further. Goodnight.'

And there we all stood, reunited. *The Family Who Ruined Talent Night*.

'I guess pizza's out of the question,' offered Dad.

'Surprisingly I'm not in the mood for more jokes, Stu,' Mum snapped. 'Look at these two. You've let yourselves and each other down. *Badly*. Malcolm – I'm surprised. Carmichael – I don't know where to start.'

What's that supposed to mean? I wondered. It already sounded like my brother was going to get off more lightly than me. I glared at Malky, who glared right back.

'Everything I said to you, Car. About knuckling down, focusing, having a plan … You didn't listen to a *word*, did you?'

I shrugged. There was no point trying to argue with Mum when she got into her '*What-I-Expect-from-my-Children*'-type speeches.

'You know how hard it'll be to get you into anything like a decent school if you get permanently excluded? You might end up having to go to a PRU!'

Dad looked questioningly at her.

'What's … ?'

'A *Pupil Referral Unit*! With all the hardcore crazy kids who attack their teachers with homemade weapons and smoke cigarettes in the toilets!'

I looked back at my feet. That didn't sound good. But it also didn't sound like the kind of place a clown should be sent to. No teacher was physically attacked tonight. No cigarettes were smoked. It was just words. I mean, whatever happened to that 'Sticks and Stones' phrase?

A couple of teachers walked by the door and glared through the window before heading back into the hall.

'We should probably leave,' Dad mumbled. 'I get the feeling we might have outstayed our welcome.'

He gently went to guide Mum out by the elbow, but she flinched hard, grimaced and threw both her hands up in the air.

'Don't touch me. *Please.*'

Uh-oh.

We watched as she pushed through the classroom door and set off down the corridor. The three of us exchanged a brief glance, then filed out like prisoners on their way to court. I watched my mum from the safe distance we held. She was a new kind of angry. As bulletproof as I'd felt twenty minutes ago, I was now genuinely worried.

I glanced to my right as we passed the double doors to the hall. I could hear music playing from the stage. The show was back under way. Through the glass I could make out Alex in the front row, and paused. She looked up and spotted me. The look she gave me was so strange, like a sad smile. I'll never forget it. Maybe I totally misread it, but that smile to me felt like it was saying something along the lines of: *What a hero. Such a shame you're dead.*

CHAPTER 23

Mumzilla, Part 2

*B*OOM, BOOM, BOOM!

I shot up in my bed, startled by three loud bangs on my door that had initially invaded my dreams in the form of some hidden enemy firing a cannon. I rubbed my eyes and looked at my clock. Six a.m.

Six a.m.? On a Saturday?

This was not good.

The time between leaving school and going to bed had already been pretty horrific. For starters, Mum had picked up such a pace stomping away from school that she'd reached the bus stop way before us, a bus came and she'd got on it, leaving us behind to wait for another.

That had been my second kind of *Uh-oh* moment, when I realised there was no smoothing this one over.

Mum was next-level livid. Even Dad looked scared, and he wasn't technically in trouble for anything.

'Maybe best to give her some space, eh?' he offered. Malky and I just stared at the bus as it disappeared round the corner.

Yep.

When we'd arrived home, she was already locked away in her room and I think both Malky and I were grateful we didn't have to face her again, but rightfully concerned about what might be coming our way at sunrise.

And here we had it: literally at sunrise, three aggressive thumps on my door, followed by my mum's voice: eerily calm and bright.

'Rise and shine! To the kitchen please!'

I heard her footsteps retreat, then the same across the hall outside Malky's door. *What the heck … ?*

Five minutes later, we were stood – me, bare-chested with pyjama bottoms, Malky in vest and under-pants – bleary-eyed in the kitchen opposite both parents. Mum had a big, weird smile on her face.

'First, we're going to talk about value and respect. Last night both of you proved to me you have a very low value and lack of respect for your school, for your teachers, for your family. So let's start with a basic lesson: valuing and respecting the home.'

She gestured to the dining table, which was covered

in cleaning products. She stuffed a rag in my hand and a mop into Malky's chest.

'If you have to really work for something, you'll respect it more. You have the weekend to clean every room in this flat, top to bottom. I'm not talking about washing up and doing the hoovering. I'm talking *TOP. TO. BOT. TOM.* Dusting the ceilings and light fittings, removing every book and cleaning the bookshelves, windows polished, doors wiped down – one side each. Floors mopped, carpets shampooed. Malky, you look confused. Questions?'

'It just feels like we're getting the same punishment, and I just wanna say I didn't do nothing as bad as him so—'

'Really?' I scoffed. 'Sabotaging my performance—'

'Boys …'

'That was Dane!'

'Yeah, right. And you were so supportive of your baby brother.'

'BOYS!' Mum spoke loudly, but also laughed – a worrying development. 'This isn't punishment. This is just Lesson One. *Value and Respect.* You two think the world revolves around you – I've clearly given you way too much of an easy ride up to now.'

No, I thought bitterly, *just Malcolm.*

'So this weekend,' she continued, 'is an introduction to a new way of being under my roof. You show me you value your home, you respect this family – then we'll talk *actual* punishment.'

We both instinctively looked with pleading eyes to our father, who predictably offered a *'Don't look at me!'* shrug and folded his arms.

Yay.

CHAPTER 24

Cute Puppies from Hell

I'm not built for child labour. Or any kind of physical labour really. I'm a man of words. Not that I shared many with my brother that Saturday as we scrubbed, wiped, polished, mopped, swept and vacuumed, tensing whenever we crossed each other's paths.

The only time we really spoke was in the living room when our parents finally went out shopping and we both took the opportunity to collapse in two teenage heaps, me to the floor, Malky to the sofa.

'This is madness,' Malky offered. I shuffled in reverse on my butt until my back met the wall and wiped my forehead with my forearm.

'Yeah, well, it is what it is. Let's just hope it isn't every weekend.'

'This is all your fault. You know that.'

I did a humourless laugh.

'*My* fault! I just reacted to you! I woulda finished that poem and we'd be off enjoying our Saturday if you hadn't decided to be an idiot!'

'That was Dane, man! I was—'

'Oh, *whatever*, Malky. You're just upset Mum and Dad have finally seen the *Golden Boy Mask* slip off.'

'That what you think, yeah?'

'No, it's what I *know*.'

Malky stared at me for a moment.

'You think I'm the *favourite* or something?'

'Don't *you*?'

Malky's turn to laugh without joy, his words laced with sarcasm:

'You get a lot of attention for a second favourite …'

'Huh?'

'Forget it.'

He shook his head, got back up, put his earphones in and started wiping down the bookshelves. I stayed in my spot on the floor, watching him, wondering what he meant by that.

Or, in truth, maybe just trying not to wonder too deeply what he meant by that.

Mum and Dad arrived home that afternoon with a military air about them. Malky and I had been working away in separate rooms as much as possible and had not spoken since the *'Golden Boy'* exchange. I heard the boom of Sergeant Major Jocelyn Taylor seconds after hearing the key turn in the front door.

'Kitchen!'

I came face to face with my brother in the hallway as I exited my bedroom and he came out of the bathroom. Sweaty and achy, we trudged to whatever fresh horrors awaited us.

Mum and Dad stood in the kitchen, waiting.

'Right,' said Mum. 'We've had a good few hours to go through this and I think we're settled on next steps. No going out, obviously. No friends' houses, no phones or video games for the next two weeks. You can use the family computer for schoolwork, but there'll be no internet whenever we're out of the house.'

Malky screwed his face up.

'That's not even possible …'

Dad chipped in, waving his phone.

'Actually there's an app for that, so it kind of is.'

Mum continued. 'We've got a calendar for you to chart your schoolwork progress, household chores and when your punishment time is up.'

Dad pulled out a garish pink-and-yellow calendar covered in cute puppies.

'It was the only one they had. June's not a great time for calendar shopping.'

He handed it to Mum and she clipped it to the fridge in a magnetic holder.

I watched as Mum marked out the end of our enforced quarantine and found myself troubled by the four joyous golden Labradors frolicking in a field of daffodils above the grid of dates. As Mum stepped back from the fridge and replaced the lid on her angry red marker, the angelic puppies' carefree approach to life seemed to take on a sarcastic, heartless tone.

They're mocking me, I thought. *Those tongues aren't panting, they're razzing me. They're enjoying this! THOSE ADORABLE LITTLE BALLS OF FUZZ ARE PURE EVIL!*

Damn you, irresistible baby dogs. Damn you all to Hell.

I glanced back at Mum's red timeline. It was Day One and I was already losing my mind.

CHAPTER 25

Hello?

That weekend was pretty painful.

Mum was off-call and Dad – well, Dad was often kind of *there* anyway, so both parents were around all day Saturday and Sunday. There was no slacking on the chores, no way around the internet ban. It was like being in prison (based on what I've seen in movies, obviously). As Malky and I silently scrubbed the pans after our Sunday roast, I did something I never saw me ever doing in the history of Carmichael Taylor: I prayed for Monday.

Mum and Dad would be at work. Malky and I would (at least) be able to sit down when we wanted to, staring out of the window, dreaming of freedom. Just a few more wretched hours to get through …

That evening I sat at the little bureau in the hallway on the shared computer, very visibly checking my online classroom assignments whenever a member of my family passed by. Whenever there was a window of solitude, I skipped across the on-screen tabs to my email account. This was a risky but justifiable pastime if caught, as – although it was my only means of communication with my friends – it was also the same email account my Form Tutor sent schoolwork to.

My inbox was full of messages from Alex with random subject lines like 'WHY?', 'I'm soooo lonely', 'R U DEAD?' and 'What even is LIFE?'

As I scrolled down they became a little more focused, with titles like 'HELLO?', 'Thoughts?', 'What do you think?' and 'Should I share?'

The first message was from Sunday morning:

SUBJECT: BRO. Check it out!!!
FROM: topgalal@me.com
TO: cardaman2006@me.com
ATTACHMENT: 1 VIDEO FILE – carspeaks.mov
MESSAGE:
Yep, I filmed it. Caught almost all of it. Thinking of uploading. Go viral. We could be millionaires. I mean, mainly you, but as your director and principal camera operator I've spoken with my lawyers and they feel strongly that I deserve a sizeable chunk of said millions. Lolz. But seriously. What do you reckon?????

Al

Just then, my mum wandered into the hallway and I swiftly clicked on to my homework page and calmly studied the screen. She peered briefly over my shoulder en route to the kitchen. As she disappeared again, I clicked back on to Alex's message.

My little arrow hovered over the attached file. I sat like that for at least a minute.

Then Mum called me and I closed the email account completely.

I went to bed that night with a small army of emotions buzzing around my head.

Look at me: what did I have to look forward to? Total lockdown. No phone. More chores, more parental tension and only my mortal enemy – Malky – for companionship. The only tidy thought in my mind was what a mess things had become.

And yet …

Alex seemed pretty excited. Maybe the video came across kind of … cool? Funny? Maybe it was heroic? Maybe, in context, it could be the justification for me NOT to get expelled, or even suspended! Maybe that video would confirm me as the victim in all of this!

Maybe it was gold dust we were sitting on!

I flicked the bedside lamp on and checked the clock on the dresser: 11.23 p.m. Mum and Dad could easily still be awake. So could Malky. Supreme stealth was required. I grabbed my earphones from the floor and put them on the dresser, then set the alarm for 3 a.m. and tucked the clock under my pillow.

It was time to take extreme measures.

CHAPTER 26

Journey to the Centre of the Hall

At 3 a.m. I bolted upright and reached under my pillow to shut off the alarm.

I held my breath and sat with my back to the wall in the darkness for at least a minute.

Stage One of my plan had gone without a hitch – the alarm hadn't woken anyone else.

I replayed Friday night in my mind again.

How long was I on that stage before they pulled the plug?

If I was going to watch the full duration of Alex's video right now, at three in the morning, *IN THE DARK, WITH EARPHONES IN, WITHIN CENTIMETRES OF MY PARENTS' BEDROOM*, it would've been good to know exactly how long I'd be sat in that hallway …

I eased my body out of bed and hung the earphones from the dresser round my neck, stuffing the loose cable in the waist of my pyjama bottoms.

If there's anything sensible about sneaking out of your room in the middle of the night while you're grounded to watch a video of yourself doing what got you grounded in the first place, I would say it might be best to get the whole thing over and done with as soon as humanly possible.

Instead I moved at a snail's pace – terrified of making any noise. It felt like ten minutes just getting out of my bedroom door. I tiptoed across the hallway, lowered myself into the chair at the bureau and plugged my earphones into the computer, leaving one ear free to listen out for rogue family members.

I clicked on Alex's first email, scrolled down and downloaded *carspeaks.mov.*

Fifteen seconds later the little attachment opened. A huge close-up of a thumb – presumably Alex's – accompanied by the unmistakeable sound of a baffled audience. *This was it.* I spun around to double check the flat was still dead, then returned to the screen, my heart suddenly beating hard against my ribcage. *Maybe Mum was right. Maybe I'd misjudged things horribly. Maybe I was a mean-spirited, cocky, selfish …*

GENIUS!

Ha! Listen to that! That is Full-Blown Laughter – so much louder from Alex's position than it felt from my own. *Bam!* Another laugh. *Wham!* Another. *Wow. I was killing it!*

I was about to place the loose earphone into my right ear when I heard a loud cough.

I paused the video and froze.

A second cough and a loud yawn.

Mum.

I heard her bed creak.

Oh my days ... Was she ... getting up?

I couldn't take any chances. I held down the POWER button and watched the screen go black, then sat stone-still for a second, listening.

Footsteps.

God, Allah, Buddah, Jehovah, Krishna, Aliens, Stephen Hawking, David Attenborough – HELP ME!

I jumped up on to my tiptoes and made a break for my bedroom.

BRAK-KACK!

The earphones were still plugged in and flew out of my ear and on to the floor!

Noooo!

I leaped through my doorway and eased the door to an almost closed position, breathing as if I'd run a marathon.

Too late to worry about the noise. Maybe she wouldn't have heard it ... ?

I listened as my parents' bedroom door opened.

Would she switch on the hallway light ... ?

No.

Good.

Through the crack I squinted into the darkness, holding my breath as the shape of my mother shuffled past and carried on towards the bathroom.

Just wait this out now, that's all you have to do …

I listened.

- A door opening
- A light switch
- A sound no one needs to really hear coming from their mum
- A toilet flush
- A tap
- Another light switch

I held my position and counted her footsteps as a kind of exercise in keeping calm. I nearly did a little wee of my own when I heard her slow outside my door …

And stop.

WHY HAS SHE STOPPED???!

Then I heard another yawn – a big one that sounded as if it was part of a stretch.

And the footsteps continued, all the way to their bedroom door.

Give her time to fall asleep, I thought, *then it's back out on the front line.*

At 3.42 a.m., I took a deep breath, returned to the computer and watched the video in full.

Yup. There was no doubt about it. *Legendary.*

When the screen turned black as Alex was shoving her phone up her jumper and all that remained was the muffled sound of shock, shouting, and raucous laughter before cutting out completely, I said to myself exactly what I emailed back to Alex, under the subject title 'LET'S POST THIS THING!!!':

That, my friend …

… Was one HECK of a show.

Now let's show the world.

CHAPTER 27

Priorities

With Mum and Dad both at work, Monday was a breeze. Malky and I stayed out of each other's way, did our chores and I even made a start on some schoolwork.

But considering the weight of family feuds, medieval punishments and a potential school expulsion hanging over my head, it was telling that I only had one thing on my mind all day:

Maybe I'm a star!

As well as emailing Alex back with pride at nearly four in the morning, I'd forwarded the video to Lan and the Three Moes, telling all four to hang tight for the YouTube link and subsequent spamathon. I couldn't *wait* for the return of WiFi so I could see what they said.

* * *

Mum and Dad were less frosty on their return from work. I guess it's hard for anyone to stay at boiling point for long, it gets kind of silly – especially when you've got jobs and stuff, working with friendly people who have nothing to do with your home life. Plus, my mum was a nurse – I'm thinking she had bigger issues at work anyway.

That's not to say she'd completely mellowed.

When she checked the punishment schedule on the puppy calendar, when she inspected the toilet, when she looked over our homework … each completed chore was acknowledged with a short 'Mm' or 'OK' or 'Yep'. There was no joy in her tone whatsoever, but those monosyllables felt like joyous praise compared to the last couple of days.

And Dad?

He just sort of shuffled around behind Mum, doing his best to mirror her emotions towards me. I felt like, deep down, he maybe found some of my Talent Night performance funny, but of course he'd never risk saying how he really felt. What was he so afraid of? I watched him as he came home from what he described as an 'intense meeting' and wondered how intense a meeting with my dad could ever really be …

MEETING WITH STUART TAYLOR:

A MINI-PLAY

by Carmichael Taylor

BOSS	So, Stuart, what do you think?
DAD	Hmm. (*Pause.*) What do *you* think?
BOSS	I'm asking *you*, Stuart.
DAD	Yes. Well. *Maybe* ...
BOSS	Maybe what?
DAD	Exactly. I agree. (*Pause.*) What do you think?

BOSS *looks at ceiling and shakes head.*

Fade to black.

As soon as Mum had finished her Prison Warden Inspections and given him the nod, Dad pulled out his phone, opened some unseen app and, after a couple of seconds, looked up at his two sons, who were practically salivating at the prospect of reconnection to WiFi and the outside world.

'Bingo.'

My brother and I raced to the hallway computer. Obviously Malky beat me to it.

'Work-related activity only! *One hour each!*' Mum called after us, as if we needed reminding.

I conceded first dibs to Malky and stomped off to my room.

I felt jittery and restless. My lack of communication with actual friends was starting to get to me. I'd waited all day, but this additional hour felt unbearable. I kept wondering what I would do if I could travel back in time to Friday night. *The same, but better, with tidier hair, a sparkly suit and devastating, perfectly constructed turns of phrase*, I concluded. *Then again*, I thought, *maybe the very fact that it was so unpolished and unrehearsed would make the video legendary.*

I checked my watch for what felt like the hundredth time.

6.14 p.m. Malky's hour was nearly up. Maybe Alex had already uploaded the video to a bunch of different sites before she went to school ... By the time I got back online this evening, I could already be an international phenomenon. My moment of truth was just a few footsteps across the hallway.

Twelve manic, fantasy-filled minutes passed until I heard Mum call, 'Time, Malky!'

I swung open my bedroom door and stood tall, hands on hips. I puffed out my chest, feeling like this was the last time anyone would see the *old* Carmichael Taylor. I felt bigger, tougher – a new man. *Da* Man. I raised a manly eyebrow.

Yup.

Cinderella was going to the ball.

CHAPTER 28

That Middle Bit with the Music

Guys – let's take another time-out from the story. I know what you're thinking.

If this was a movie, this would be that Middle Bit with the upbeat music, where I check my email and Alex has put the video on YouTube and we see the views on the video go up into the hundreds of millions and the comments all say stuff like 'FUNNIEST KID ALIVE' and 'NGL THIS DUDE IS A GENIUS' and 'SO FUNNY I'M DEAD', and I go outside and everyone recognises me and high-fives me and the music continues and me and Alex sign business contracts with some massive clothing company and make millions of pounds and get to wear all the clothes and the music keeps playing as all the money is being counted by our servants in the mansion and the toilets are made of gold so the seats are cold on your bum but it's worth it because they're gold and we're by the pool and as the music builds to a crescendo we laugh and jump up in slow motion and high-five and we freeze in that position and the music finishes.

That actually sounds like the kind of movie I'd watch.

But here's what really happened.

CHAPTER 29

What Really Happened

U nder the guise of checking my school assignments, I read Alex's reply, which just said:
'DONE!'

I shut the volume off on the keyboard, ensured the coast was clear and clicked the first link: YouTube.

Video Title: War of Wainbridge: Kid Destroys EVERYONE in EIGHT MINS!!!!
POSTED: THIS MORNING
VIEWS: 1

Unless you include this one, which technically made it two. Then again, it had only been around nine hours since Alex posted it, and things could take a long time to go viral, right? I'd check it tomorrow. *Unread email from Lan, subject title: LITTLE …*

Little vague is what that is, I thought. *I'll check that tomorrow as well.* First and foremost, this was a case of charting the progress of history. It was time to start a diary. That wouldn't seem needy at all.

DAYS SINCE POSTING: 1

Three views. But still very early days. With no online promotion, three views is understandable. We're not at the crest of the wave yet.

DAYS SINCE POSTING: 2

Three views. Hey, doesn't this count as a view?

DAYS SINCE POSTING: 3

Three views. OK, so me viewing again doesn't count as a view.

DAYS SINCE POSTING: 4

Four views! Averaging one a day. That's what the internet people call 'positive traffic'.

DAYS SINCE POSTING: 5

Four views. Negative.

DAYS SINCE POSTING: 6

Four views. This doesn't mean I'm not a star. No one becomes a star overnight. I mean, look at … look at the *sun*. The sun is the biggest star there is right now. You think the sun just popped up and suddenly went, *'That's right, universe! I'm the hottest thing out right now'*? No. Four and a half billion years the sun has been going. Grafting. Getting its name out there. Consistently performing. Course it's a legend. I've been going six days. Give me a chance!

It was Sunday evening, post chores. Half of my two-week suspension had been served. I'd barely left the house, hadn't spoken to a soul outside my family and still hadn't replied to Lan's email, which – when finally clicking on it – I realised wasn't a 'little vague' after all. It was a

LITTLE ...
... *Warning for you, man. Not to rain on your parade – I think you could be a great performer with some of those skills. Just saying though – isn't the school trying to decide whether or not you should be permanently excluded for this? Feels to me like if they saw you'd put it online, that'd kinda be the nail in the coffin, no? I mean I'm not your dad, just giving out freebies here, bro.*
Take it easy
Lan

I closed the window and stared at the desktop screensaver. An old picture of Mum and Dad with little versions of Malky and me, arms around each other, outside our old house. I looked about four years old. I tried to remember the last time we were all huddled up close like that, smiling and laughing.

I practised the cute face from my younger screensaver self on my way to the kitchen.

'Ma?'

Mum and Dad looked up at me from the table where they were sat preparing vegetables for a roast.

'Mm?'

'I was just … I mean, I've been consistent with chores and schoolwork, so I was just wondering … would it be OK to call Alex? Like, just to catch up, say hi?'

Mum and Dad looked at each other. Dad shrugged. Mum sighed.

'You know I'm not the biggest fan …'

'She's my best friend, Mum. *Please.*'

'I don't want to find out that she put you up to all that nonsense.'

'No one put me up to it. I was stupid. And … and I'm sorry.'

A small glance between Mum and Dad. They weren't expecting that one.

Mum nodded and went to collect the portable phone from its cradle next to the bread bin. She held it out to me with her eyebrows raised. I smiled and went to grab it, but she whipped it out of my reach and held it to her chest.

'Ten minutes. *One call only.* OK?'

'Yep.'

She held out the phone for me again.

'Thanks, Mum,' I said, already tapping in Alex's mobile number as I walked to my room. It took every inch of my self-control not to break into a run.

Alex answered as my flustered body bounced on to my bed.

'Hello?'

'Al, it's me!'

'Who is this?'

'It's Car, you donut!'

'Car! Jeez, I thought you were dead. What is this number?'

'My home phone.'

'Gross. You've got about seventy texts, ninety memes and like a hundred funny videos waiting for you when you get yours back!'

'Al, we need—'

'There's one with this cat who sees himself in the mirror and he's all like *Grrrrr mmmrrrow! Mrow!* Right? And his owner walks in but—'

'Alex!' I actually sort of shouted a bit, then looked to the door, spun my head back and lowered my voice to a whisper.

'We need to take that video down.'

'What? Why?'

'What if people actually see it and share it?'

'I thought that was the plan! Go viral. Get famous. Get rich. All the expensive trainers we can eat …'

'I'm serious. What if kids at our school share it, then the teachers catch on? I'd be permanently excluded for sure. Then grounded for life. The next time you'd see me we'd be adults.'

Silence.

'Al. Al, you still there?'

'Yeah.'

'What?'

'No, it's just … I dunno.'

'What?'

'I mean, we were trying to make it go viral, right, so I sent it to as many kids as possible. In our year, at least.'

'But it's only got, like, four views.'

'Have you seen my mash-up version though?'

'Mash-up?'

'I realised pretty quick no one can actually be bothered to watch eight minutes. So I made a sixty-second version with some of my favourite quotes – "The best school day of the week is Saturday", "Six Cruel Hours Of Our Lives", your Dad dis, your French dis … the "Goodnight, Wainbridge" mic drop, crowd reaction … It's cool.'

That did sound kind of cool. I *knew* it. *I'm kind of cool.*

'Are there … comments?'

'Yeah, a few. Err … *He's in my class, brooooo!* with like five *Os* … Um … *Legendary … Hashtag Car4Prez* … Er…. *I heard about this, madness!* One just says *Dead.* I mean, it's all positive stuff.'

Positive. I felt the crack of a smile, then knocked it off my face with a sharp shake of the head. Just one question I had to know the answer to though …

'How many views?'

'Hold on … er … Four hundred and seventy-two. Decent!'

That is *decent*, I thought …

'And trust me – *everyone* is talking about that night still! Like, *IRL!*'

Everyone … Maybe we could … No.

NO.

'Take it down.'

'What?'

'Delete it, Al, *please*, before Mr French or someone sees it!'

'OK, OK, I'll delete it.'

'Like, now.'

'OK, Jeez.'

Is it done?'

'Hold on … Lemme just … Yeah. OK. Done. Happy?'

'Not really.'

'What?'

'It's hard to be happy sat here. In this … this *limbo*. Like … when's the punishing over, exactly? When do I go back to school? *Can* I go back to school? When do I get my phone back?'

'Hmm, yeah. I mean, in a weird way, *now* would actually be a good time to come back. You're kind of famous. In Year Eight at least.'

'Yeah,' I said gloomily, 'but *infamous* with the staff.'

'Ha! Yeah, totally, totally … What does *infamous* actually mean? And why is it suddenly like *"Fummus"* instead of *in-fay-mous*?'

'I dunno about that but, meaning-wise … I think it's, like, *famous*, but evil.'

'Cool.'

'Or, I guess more like, famous for all the wrong reasons.'

CHAPTER 30

A New Normal

And that, really, was that.

A month ago I'd been a funny, popular, slightly frustrated kid. I'd been a kid who needed to find a platform for his talents and blow off some steam. Then I'd been onstage and even on video – on that platform.

And now it was all over?

It felt like a massive amount had happened but nothing had really changed.

It made me wonder if, as much as I'd always felt Carmichael Taylor was potentially *Da Man* (except perhaps when he talked about himself in the third person), maybe there was some change that he – sorry, *I* – still wanted to see in himself. Myself. You know what I mean.

* * *

It was Thursday. I was coming to the end of the second week of my suspension and things in the flat had calmed down a lot. Malky had been back at school since Monday, I carried on with my chores, finished all my comics, my last novel and all of a magazine about films from Dad's Sunday newspaper. I was bored out of my ginger-Afro-covered mind, but – like some dude hanging on to the edge of a coastal cliff by a branch – I clung desperately on to little things to keep from falling.

I was living in anticipation of three things:

1. **Mum Softening.** I could feel this happening. And my instinct told me to keep my trap shut and let it continue.
2. **A Call from School.** By now, my future must have been discussed with the Head, Mrs Craig. The whole Talent Night thing was *so* last fortnight, I figured they'd probably ease off all that *permanent exclusion* talk. I mean, the last kid to get permanently excluded was Rashad Tilbrook, and he'd set a sizeable chunk of the Science Block on fire. A few bad jokes were small fry, surely? A bunch of detentions, or redoing Year 7, or making lunch for the staff every day or something would be plenty, no? Come on …
3. **3.48 p.m., Daily.** This was a crucial time

because it was just *after* Alex got home from school but *before* Malky, who always got in around 4.30 p.m., thanks to dilly-dallying with TJ and Dane. It was also before Dad got back from his jog, so I would have a small window when I could sneak in a phone call to Al if needed.

On this particular afternoon, my 3.48 call really lifted my spirits. Al had all three Moes over for a FIFA tournament, so I'd had the whole crew on speakerphone, updating me on all things Wainbridge.

Mo had nearly got in a fight with Tosun, the textbook meathead who we all wished would get his comeuppance.

'It was a close call. I'm telling you, man, if we weren't split up ... I nearly had him!'

Nothing new there – Mo always nearly did amazing stuff. He'd *nearly* won a competition, *nearly* gone to Japan, *nearly* scored a hat-trick. He never seemed to actually achieve the ultimate goal, but his ability to make himself sound like the hero in any retelling was kind of impressive.

Tyler had had his first kiss. When we'd established the girl in question was the pretty, smart and cool Natalie Drummond, the roars of approval distorted the tinny phone speakers.

'Anyone needs romantic advice, come see the Don,' Tyler crowed.

Mehmet, meanwhile, had been making the most of his attachment to me, telling anyone at school who would listen that he was one of my main inspirations for my performance at the Talent Night.

'I just told 'em the facts– I taught the guy everything he knows!'

Finally, Alex assured me that I was still big news at Wainbridge, that when I stepped through the gates I would be mobbed by fans and well-wishers.

'Not people who throw pennies down wells. People who, like, y'know …'

'I get it, Al. Ah, snap, I gotta go!'

I heard the front door open and close, two pairs of feet heading up the steps to our flat. I flew from my room to the kitchen, returning the portable phone to its cradle.

Two voices emanated from the hallway. Malky and Mum had arrived together – Mum must've been on an early shift.

As the pair approached, deep in conversation, I fished in the cupboard for some rice cakes, making it seem like all I'd been doing was innocently making a snack.

'I hear you,' Mum was saying. 'Oh, hey, Car. You OK?'

'Mm-hm.' I nodded.

'I haven't slacked, I've been on it.'

'You've stuck to your task, Malk, I can't say you haven't.'

'You talking about the chores?' I chipped in. 'I've done my bit as well.'

Mum sighed, turned to face me, but looked at the floor mid-sigh, which I have to say seemed a way of hiding the tiniest of smiles. *A smile!*

'Yes, Car, you have. I've been impressed by the way *both* of you boys have grafted.'

I beamed at them. Malky turned on some tentative charm.

'Sooo, back to standard chores this weekend … *maybe?*'

'*Maybe,*' Mum offered. 'And just *maybe* back to school for both of you on Monday.'

Was it just me or were things looking up?

Ping.

Her phone beeped and she gave it a cursory glance, then a double take and her whole demeanour shifted.

'Speak of the devil. *Email.* From Wainbridge.'

My mouth went dry. Malky jumped into the silent space.

'What's the verdict?'

Mum took a deep breath.

'I'll open it when Dad gets back.'

She slid the phone into her back pocket.

CHAPTER 31

What's the Story in Purgatory?

*P*urgatory.

One of the few words that stuck with me from Religious Studies. Roman Catholics considered it to be a place between Heaven and Hell, a kind of waiting room for the soul, immediately after death. It was a place that could be either brutally painful or enlightening, but always mercifully temporary – *soon you would discover your eternal fate.* A bit like being sat in a dentist's waiting room, wondering whether you're going to get a soft polish and a superhero sticker or a canyon drilled into your face.

For thirty-seven minutes I sat silently in my purgatory, on the sofa, staring at the ceiling. I glanced across the room at my brother, flicking through a football magazine without a care in the world.

For Malky, it would be business as usual when that

email was opened. My whole life could change in seconds.

For the first time, the enormity really hit me.

I really, really didn't want to get expelled. To have the parents of all my friends keep me away from them. To be alone. To be labelled as a problem child. To have to find a new school. Maybe a special school for bad kids.

I wasn't a bad kid. Was I?

No, I was a good kid who did something stupid. They'll see it was a moment of madness. They'll see I regret it, I've apologised and I'm not revelling in my own bad behaviour. They'll also see that I take no pleasure in other kids celebrating it. No pleasure whatsoever.

OK, some pleasure. But they didn't need to know that.

The point was, I'd finally realised how much I had to lose and maybe for the first time in my life, it really was no joke.

Maybe for the first time in my life, my parents were right!

Ewww.

I bolted upright on the sofa as I heard a breathless Dad stagger in from his jog. Both Malky and I hurried to the hallway.

Moment of truth.

Dad, red-faced and sweaty and still insisting on

those Lycra jeggings, stretched out his calves, pushing both hands against the hallway wall.

'Gents.'

'Hey, Dad,' said Malky.

'The school emailed,' I said quietly.

'What's the damage?'

'We were waiting for you.'

The four of us sat around the table.

Mum took a deep breath, then pulled out her phone. Dad guzzled water from his sports bottle.

'*Dear Mr and Mrs Taylor,*' she read. '*All of us here at Wainbridge would very much like to see Carmichael return to school this Monday …*' She raised her eyebrows in a satisfactory smile and Dad exhaled with relief. Then she scrolled down and, even though it's not technically possible for a black person, her face seemed to drain of all colour.

'*However, as you can imagine, I was deeply shocked and disappointed to be told that footage of Carmichael's antics at the Talent Show has been uploaded to a public forum.*'

WHAT? Wait … But Al, you said …

'*I watched the footage this morning and, whilst I appreciate this may well not have been Carmichael's doing, the celebratory comments by many of his peers frankly fly in the face of his apology and make a mockery of any remorse he might have displayed.'*

This morning? You promised me you deleted it, there and then.

'I am currently investigating who was responsible for filming and posting the footage, but I must warn you that should we find any collusion in this act from Carmichael, he will be permanently excluded with immediate effect. I would like to meet with Carmichael and one or both of you tomorrow at a convenient time. Regards, Michael French, Head of Year Eight.'

You said you'd deleted it. How … ?

Mum looked up at me, a tiny shake of the head that weighed a ton.

'A *video*, Car?'

Air left my body like a popped balloon. I was speechless.

'Oh, Car,' my dad said tragically.

How?

'It … It can't – there must be a mistake.'

Mum shoved her chair back and stood.

'Get up.'

I rose sheepishly as she stomped to the computer in the hallway. I looked at Dad and Malky, who actually both looked a little worried for me.

'Get over here!'

I shuffled over to join her. She had opened a fresh Google page, its empty, patient search box innocent of the potential nightmare it could provide me. Mum hovered over the keyboard.

'What am I looking for?'

'This doesn't make any sense!'

'*Car.*' Mum shot me a look.

Stop.

'Tell me what the video's called?'

'*War of Wainbridge,*' I mumbled, and turned away.

If it was still there, I didn't want to see it. I didn't want to hear another word.

'Oh, Car,' Mum said, as the unmistakeable atmosphere of a packed Wainbridge Gym crackled through the computer speakers.

How … ?

She closed the page.

'Look at me.'

I couldn't.

'Turn around and look at me.'

I did.

'What the hell were you thinking, Car?'

I balked.

'*I* didn't put it up there!'

'Then who did?'

I fell silent. Realisation dawned on Mum's face.

'Don't protect her, Car.'

I looked down to the ground.

'Car. This is serious.'

How ... ?

I shook my head.

'Have you seriously got nothing to say?'

I looked away bitterly. My mum exhaled deeply and threw her hands up.

'Get out of my sight, Car. Just – go to your room, I need a minute.'

I spun on my heels, stomped off and slammed my door behind me.

How ... How could you, Al?

For the next twenty minutes or so I sat on the edge of my bed, fists clenched, my head swimming.

There was a knock on my door.

'Car?'

'Go away, Dad.'

'I'll be back.'

You lied to me.

All these years. We'd had petty squabbles and disagreements. But we shared *everything*. We knew everything about each other. The truth was never in question. We *were* each other's truths.

And you lied to me.

In my silence, when Mum confronted me, I lied for *you.*
But you lied to me.

I tried to settle my anger enough to think strategic-ally. What was the best ploy? If I kept her out of it, I could avoid snitching and handle my story alone. *I don't know who uploaded it, but I had nothing to do with it.*

Or: I drop her in it, deny my involvement. Maybe *she* gets expelled. At least suspended. But then there's the danger of her telling the truth, that I *knew* there was a video, that I *couldn't wait* to see it uploaded and make me a star …

No.

The only option was the truth. But the whole truth.

I wanted it deleted, *you* kept it up.

I wanted to do the right thing. That meant some-thing, didn't it?

We meant something.
Didn't we?

CHAPTER 32

Judgement Day

'I wanted it deleted, she kept it up.'

I finished my sorrowful and genuinely remorseful story as Mr French and Mrs Craig listened intently from the other side of the Head Teacher's desk.

'That's got to count for something, hasn't it?' Mum chipped in.

'Surely,' Dad added for good measure.

'Hmm,' Mr French offered.

'Hmm'? I just spill my guts, snitch on my best friend, and all you can say is 'Hmm'? I've just changed the course of my friendship forever. She lied to me. I don't know which hurts more. I can feel the pain etched all over my face, I know it is, and all you can do is sit there in your stupid spinny chair, scratch your idiotic moustache and go, 'Hmm'? Do you know how much I hate you, French?

Mrs Craig elaborated. 'I'm afraid I don't see how that changes the situation. We wanted to know if you were a part of this video, and you've just admitted you were.' She turned to my parents. 'I'm sorry but we must stick to our principles here and permanently exclude your son.'

Mum's body twisted in her seat.

'But you can't—'

'You'll have the right to an appeal. We'll send you all the information by the end of the day. In the meantime, Car, could you please remove any belongings from your locker on the way out and hand your key into reception. I'm sorry.'

'Oh, I'll be appealing, don't worry about that!'

'I'm sorry, Mrs Taylor, I truly am. I wish you all the best. Mr French will see you out.'

Mum, Dad and I rose to our feet, shell-shocked. Mr French jogged to the door and opened it. I swear there was a little spring in his step. My parents stepped out ahead of me, but I stopped in front of Mr French. My voice was small, fragile.

'What's gonna happen to Alex?'

'Well. After a long phone call with your mother last night we thought it would be wise to meet *both* families today. We contacted the Kembers this morning and –' he checked his watch – 'should be seeing them shortly actually, so we'll get to the bottom of this.'

'She should be expelled too!' Mum said indignantly.

'I'm not at liberty to discuss other pupils with you, Mrs Taylor,' said Mr French awkwardly and closed the door, leaving us alone in the hallway. We headed for reception, with Mum cursing most of the way. It was a strange sort of respite because now she was angry at general injustice, rather than specifically at me.

As Dad signed us out, I was reminded of my last duty.

'I forgot to get my stuff from the locker.'

Dad glanced nervously at Mum, who looked set to explode all over again.

'We'll meet you in the car,' he said, which was code for: 'WE NEED TO GET THE HECK OUT OF HERE BEFORE SHE BREAKS SOMETHING.'

I headed towards the common room. At my locker I heaved a huge sigh. How had it come to this? I opened the door and pulled out a few old books, an empty lunch box, spare tie and a calculator. All that remained were my old stickers, plus remnants of the stickers of former owners, and a few photos I'd stuck up of my friends goofing about and gurning for the camera. Some I was in, some not. The only constant was Alex, warm and smiley in every single shot. I lingered, then looked down the empty hallway. No two ways about it, I was alone. I turned back to the locker and ripped the pictures down.

The bell went for first break and kids suddenly poured out from every doorway. I froze, the only one not in school uniform. And with no break to go to, I suddenly felt even lonelier.

The spell broke as the Three Moes and others swarmed around me.

'Hero!'

'Yo! You seeing the Head today?'

'What's happening, you coming back?'

'That vid is nuts, bro!'

'How come Alex ain't in this morning, though? She get catch?'

'You're a legend, y'know.'

'Natalie dumped Tyler!'

'What's the deal?'

I looked around the circle. Pretty much every friend I had. I looked down at the sorry pile of belongings under my arm and pushed past them.

There was an awkward pause, then the horde hurried after me, still barking excited questions. Some were already drawing their own conclusions. They followed me back to reception and watched as I silently dumped my locker key at the desk.

I pushed through the doors and stomped out to the playground, my ears ringing.

Then time stopped.

The voices behind me, and the shrill chaos of the school at play ahead of me, all faded away.

Marching towards the reception were two deeply concerned-looking adults, and trailing behind them, her face ghostly white and her mouth in a position I'd never seen, was their daughter.

Alex.

CHAPTER 33

Showdown

On seeing me, Alex slowed to a halt behind her parents.

'Ma, I'm just gonna go toilet, meet you inside,' she called, throwing a thumb over her shoulder towards the Bathroom Block.

Her mum nodded, and walked on. I turned my back on the Kembers and motioned the burgeoning crowd of kids towards me conspiratorially.

'You lot wanna know what really happened?' I asked.

A chorus of approval. The Three Moes, Natalie, Hani, Bahir, even Tosun Kendall were practically squished against my face.

'I got expelled,' I said, staring straight at Alex.

The kids around me roared their disapproval:

'Nah!'

'What?'

'Peak!'

'No way, man!'

'Yeah, *someone* left some footage up online way too long, for some reason.'

'Hold on, Car …' Alex began.

'You said you deleted it! I begged you to, Al, and you said you'd done it. *Now* look!'

The crowd of ten or so had now become at least thirty-strong. The odd *Ooh!* and *Whoa!* or *Nah, that's cold!*

'I did delete it!'

'And now you're even lying to my face! It's embarrassing, Al. It's embarrassing for you. But you know what? It's worse for me! What're you gonna get? A week's suspension?'

'Car, listen to me—'

'One week. Maybe two? What am I gonna do, man? You've basically ruined my life. And for what? To get some more views on your little video?'

'I deleted it!'

'You know what one of the craziest parts is? My mum was actually right about you. You're not a good person for me to be around. But thanks to you I won't be around any more anyway. So congratulations. Have a nice life.'

I felt that juddery, distorted breath rise up from my

chest to my throat – a sure-fire sign that I might cry, and there was NO WAY that was gonna happen in front of this crowd.

I started for the car park, but as I passed Alex, her hand reached out and grabbed my shoulder. Her eyes were glossy and red.

'Car! *I deleted that video.* Remember the mash-up I made? I just forgot to delete the long version. I had no idea it was still up.'

'You *forgot* about the original video?'

She nodded desperately. 'I just forgot.'

'Wow.' I looked around the playground, blind fury coursing through my veins. My head felt hot.

The crowd fell silent with anticipation.

'Then you're an even bigger idiot than I thought.'

Kids exploded behind me.

'OOOOOH!'

'NAH!'

'HE WENT THERE!'

'COLD!'

I spun away and pretty much ran towards the car as my lips trembled. By the time I got there, my face was soaked. My body heaved up and down, creating uncontrollable fountains of tears. I opened the back door and jumped in, trying to hide my face, to no avail.

'Hey!' Dad said. 'Hey … Come on, we'll work this out.'

'That's right,' said Mum, 'we're gonna appeal, and we're gonna win. Get you back in, OK?'

No. No, it's not OK. Nothing is 'OK' and we're not just gonna 'work this out'!

Mum squeezed my arm. 'Car. I know it's a mess. But we'll clean it up together. As a family. You're not alone.'

But I'd never felt lonelier. My breath disjointed, my chest and throat contracting repeatedly without warning, there was no way to respond with words even if I wanted to. It was probably for the best, because I'm not sure I'd have been able to explain to them that I wasn't crying about the loss of a school.

CHAPTER 34

A Long, Hard Look

A week passed.

I sat at the little desk in my bedroom with a pen in my hand and a blank sheet of paper in front of me.

Mum had already begun the appeals process, sending a letter from her and Dad, and convincing Miss Miller to write a character reference – basically a couple of pages about how much great work I did and what a loss my leaving would be to the school.

Now it was my turn to express remorse, but also highlight my attributes, what I could bring to Wainbridge, should I return.

I didn't feel like a legend.

I didn't feel like I had anything positive to say about myself at all.

I stared at the blank page like it was a mirror,

disgusted at my own reflection. It looked just like I felt: empty.

I'd spoken to Mehmet on the phone the night before, asking about Alex without asking about Alex. Vague yet pointed questions like, *What's the latest?* Alex had been suspended for two weeks – Mrs Craig accepted that she had made an honest attempt to take the video down.

It made me angrier – at myself, at Alex again and at the world. It just didn't seem fair that she'd got away with suspension, and here I was with a life sentence. I ran a bunch of my previous offences through my mind, telling myself Alex had always been at least a partner in crime, rather than a simple sidekick.

The Year 1 Sand Incident: already referenced.

Hmm.

Al loved every minute, but that was all my idea.

The Year 3 Pedalo Incident: pedalos are NOT bumper cars, the water of Regent's Park boating lake IS actually gross, DON'T shout 'shark' when someone is already quite scared. I know all these things *now*.

I mean ...

Al was in my boat, but I was steering.

The Year 6 Picket-Line Incident: I'm not sure what I hoped to gain by starting a protest against SATS exams on the basis that they were in breach of my human rights, but nonetheless I'd made an actual sign ('*PANTS TO SATS*', with the sign shaped like a pair of pants – genius) and Alex collected actual signatures from kids outside the school gates. We were shut down abruptly by the IT teacher Mr Yates, who took my sign as I screamed, '*See?* This is the oppression of the system! You're all witnesses!'

To be honest …

Al was a loyal campaign member, but I was President.

Naturally, Mum saw our estrangement as a good thing. To her it was a sign that I was serious about turning over a new leaf. I let her go on believing it.

When you feel bad about something, it's really, really hard to focus properly on other stuff.

I filled those first few days of permanent exclusion with reading, chores and a few phone calls, but everything I did felt like a distraction from something more important, something I didn't know how to fix.

It was Thursday, late afternoon. I looked at my clock, exhaled deeply and headed to the house phone. Lan picked up after the fourth ring.

'Yallo?'

'Hey.'

'Carm?'

'Yeah.'

'How you holding up?'

'I dunno.'

'Hang in there, man, things will sort themselves out, they always do.'

'Mm. Hey ...'

'What?'

'No, I was just ... It's Thursday so I was thinking ...'

'Backgammon club? Alex texted. She's on lockdown.'

'Cool, cool, yeah. Of course.'

'You wanna come over anyway?'

'Huh? Nah. I'm good. I better go.'

'OK ... Y'know, she feels pretty bad.'

'I gotta go.'

This was excruciating. I needed a way out, a back door to escape these feelings. I needed some lifeline to grab on to, to drag me out of the choppy waters in my head. I wanted to be somewhere, *anywhere* that wasn't right here, right now.

I returned to my bedroom, screwed up my blank piece of paper and prayed for a miracle.

CHAPTER 35

Praise Be

My phone was still confiscated, but Mum had shown some leniency since I'd been formally excluded. Her sense of injustice at the whole mess meant I was now allowed to use the internet during the day – principally to do these really boring online classes Dad had found to keep me up to speed with schoolwork and give my days some sort of structure.

The program delivered daily assignments to my email account and I had set times to complete and submit them. My parents received daily notifications that the work was done. It was tedious, but Miss Choudhary and Miss Miller had said it would 'show willing', another positive they could add to the appeals process.

But today, the assignments for Science and Geography sat unopened in the first two emails.

It was the third unread message that had caught my eye. From someone called George Lacey.

SUBJECT: Your Video

What the heck?

FROM: georgelacey@themissyshow.com
TO: cardaman2006@me.com
Hi there!
My name's George Lacey. I'm the producer of *The Missy Show*. We L O V E D your video and would absolutely LOVE to talk to you about featuring on the segment 'Those Crazy Kids'. Please let me know the best way to contact your parents or guardians.
Many thanks
George

I read the short message again. Then a third time. I noted the little banner at the bottom of the email with a picture of Missy herself, superimposed over the shiny *Missy Show* logo. I studied the contact details for George Lacey, a studio address in New York and an international phone number.

This was real. This was definitely real.

They'd seen the video and tracked me down somehow. But how? *No, this was a fake. Someone's punking me.*

Then I thought some more.

Wait a minute …

I logged on to my Instagram account. Without a phone I hadn't checked it for weeks. And there it was. If you clicked the MESSAGE button on my page it gave you my email address, not that anyone ever emailed me. *Until now.* They must've scoured social media for Carmichael Taylor.

These guys were serious!

My heart started bouncing around like a basketball. *Millions of people around the world watched that show.* My mind raced ahead – *I was going on* The Missy Show! I was going to be an overnight sensation. I was going to move to Hollywood. I was going to be rich! Where I was going, there were no broken friendships, no grey and lonely days. There were no online assignments, no desperate appeal letters.

That was my old life – I didn't need any of it, or anyone.

Well, apart from parental consent.

Damn it. How the heck was I going to get my parents' consent to drop everything and go to the States?

'Hey, Ma – I know I got expelled and ruined my life and destroyed a lifelong friendship and lied and cheated

and betrayed your trust and insulted you and Dad and brought shame upon our family, but do you mind if I just nip off to New York and become famous real quick? Cheers, Ma, you da best.'

Unlikely.

I reread the email.

Hang on.

'Parents or *guardians'?*

I pushed my chair back and headed to the kitchen.

'You're out of your tiny mind,' Lan scoffed on the other end of the line as I sat in front of the open email with the phone to my ear.

'Maybe, but if – *if* – I could convince her, would you think about it?'

'Hey, if she says *yes*, I'll fly you there myself, wearing a mankini.'

'A what?'

'Google it.'

I laughed, we both said our goodbyes and hung up. A second later the phone rang.

'Hello?'

'*Don't* google it.'

CHAPTER 36

New Word Alert

I don't really want to, but I'm gonna talk about the word *hubris*.

I don't want to, but I need to.

It's an ancient Greek word, which is already annoying, because they seem to come up with almost everything. Like, when you say *Hey, where does that weird word or concept or game or philosophy come from?*, some nerd always says, 'Ancient Greece.' They were basically a race of Smart Alecs and Gods With Issues.

Anyway.

Hubris popped up a lot in their tragedies, usually when there was a hero who thought they were a hero, then realised they weren't as much of a hero as they first thought. I guess it's basically *cockiness*. Like that dude Icarus whose dad built him wings thinking he was one of the Marvel Avengers or something, but then he flew too close to the sun, burned his butt – and said wings – and fell to his inevitable death. Or Achilles, more of a DC guy, who thought he was as indestructible as Superman but overlooked the fact that he had one rubbish heel and someone shot it and now we all have a bit of leg named after him.

The ancient Greeks saw *hubris* as a dangerous character flaw. I guess even the fact that I don't want to talk about it is kind of a result of it.

It was Friday afternoon and my family would start appearing one by one over the next few hours. I'd managed to get my assignments done, but I couldn't stop reading and rereading that email. I was itching to reply.

Tempted as I was to write a joyful message like *'Hey there, George, the Taylors are IN! Here's my mum's number! Or should I say "mom"? Ha-ha!'*, there was no way of making this thing work without me convincing my folks first.

But time was of the essence. *They have a different kid on that show every week*, I reasoned to myself. *Soon enough they'd just move on to the next one.*

I needed to be the next one. The only one. I needed to be Da Man.

And if that was gonna happen? The Taylors were gonna have to have a bit of a chat. A chat to end all chats. The chat of the century. And it needed to happen fast.

I went to close the email window, but paused as a new message appeared … *From Miss Miller?* I clicked.

Dear Car
Just to let you know how upset I was to hear about your exclusion. I'm not sure if your parents have mentioned it but – as much as we can't condone what you did – Miss Choudhary and I will do everything we can to support your appeals process.
I just feel that what happened at Talent Night wasn't really you.
All the best
Miss Miller

I closed the window and shut down the computer.

She's right, I thought, *it wasn't me. Not the Me you knew.*

The new Me is a Star.

And all you ancient Greeks can pucker up and kiss my butt, cos I'm gonna prove it.

CHAPTER 37

Best-Laid Plans

'That you, Car? Someone's keen!'

I heard Mum's surprised reaction from outside the bathroom door and almost smiled through the toothpaste.

6 a.m. and I was already up.

The slight confusion on Mum's face as I trotted by her extended as she took in the fact that I was also fully dressed.

'Morning, Ma,' I said humbly, and she followed me down the hall in her nightie. Her features tightened with more unspoken questions as she was stopped in her tracks by a spotless – and I mean *spotless* – kitchen.

I reached into the oven and pulled out a plate of warming scrambled eggs and toast, pre-prepared with a sprig of what I hoped was parsley.

I pulled out a chair and Mum's face switched immediately from confusion to suspicion.

'Car, what *is* this?'

I lifted a *'not yet'* finger, pulled a steaming mug of tea out from under a tea towel and placed it neatly next to the plate.

'Wait for Dad. I'll explain.'

I trotted out with a smile and did a light tap on Dad's and Malky's doors.

'Mu-um,' whined Malky, 'I thought I was done with the early starts!'

Dad hobbled in, scratching his belly, closely followed by a disgruntled Malky. I pulled out two more pre-prepared breakfasts and teas.

'Father's Day's next weekend, isn't it?'

'Dunno.' I smiled and shrugged. Malky sniffed at his plate.

'Are there mice droppings in this? What's the catch?'

'There's a catch.' Mum nodded. 'Maybe not mice droppings –' she locked eyes with me – 'but it definitely stinks.'

I leaned on the fourth, empty chair at the dining table, hoping me being the only one standing might lend this speech a little more authority. I took a deep breath.

'Breakfast is the most important meal of the day, so I figured it would go well with my news.'

'Dad's sending you to that Scottish boot camp!'

I chuckled.

'Good one, Malk.' I stood back upright and played it as political as I could muster. 'As you know, an act of stupidity got me expelled. But that same stupid act has also been seen – *and enjoyed* – by the producers of a TV show in America and they want to meet me.'

Complete silence. *OK … Not that good, or bad. I'll take it …*

The silence was broken by Malky exploding into laughter. He stopped abruptly when he saw my face hadn't changed.

'Wait, you're serious?'

I nodded. Mum's face hadn't changed. She just stared at me, her eyes fixed with suspicion. Dad was scanning the ceiling like a kid looking for the North Star or the Big Dipper.

I picked up Dad's work laptop from the kitchen counter and raised my eyebrows innocently. 'May I?'

'Uh, OK …'

I opened it up and logged into my email account, selected the message from George Lacey, then spun the laptop around dramatically. The three of them leaned forward.

'What's *The Missy Show*?' Dad asked.

Malky's eyes widened.

'*The Missy Show*! Bro! That's, like, massive! Wow. You have to say – they really know how to find an idiot.'

I gave him a sarcastic smile. 'Eat your eggs.' Switching back to humble family chef, I turned to Mum. 'Ma?'

Mum did one of those scoffs through the nose, clasped her hands together with her elbows on the table and dropped her head to face her plate. After what felt like an age, she pushed her chair back, stood, turned to the sink and looked out of the window.

'Ma? What do you think?'

She spun around.

'What do I think?' She gave a mirthless laugh, then gritted her teeth. Her mouth twitched like a tiger embarking on a hunt. 'I think someone who disrespected his school, this house, his *family*, is suddenly expecting to get rewarded for it. Expecting some scrambled eggs to sweeten the deal, expecting to have it all his way like he's suddenly the boss of this place.'

Abort Plan A! Execute Plan B: Calm Justification Mode.

'Mum, I've said sorry, I've done my chores, I've been punished. This is an opportunity to—'

'*To what?*' She exploded. 'Celebrate your stupidity? Go on TV and say, *Hey, look how funny it is I ruined my life? Embarrassed my parents?*'

My turn to explode. Not part of Plan B, to be honest.

'Oh yeah, don't let me embarrass *you*! That would be the worst! If only I was like Malky and always made you feel like a success – that's what's most important!'

'Ha!' Malky snorted.

'How dare you!' Mum snarled at me.

I clenched my fist, my cheeks burning.

'How *dare* I do something with my life? *Be* somebody? You're always saying *Focus, find something you enjoy, work at it*. Maybe this is it! Maybe this is the start of something!'

Mum laughed again, hollow, disbelieving.

'Stuart? Wanna chip in at any point?'

'Uh …'

Boxing gloves removed, brakes fully off, I echoed Mum's body language and rounded on my father. Malky leaned back in his chair; the only thing missing from his smug demeanour was a big box of popcorn.

'Yeah, Dad, what's *your* opinion? Lemme guess, *your mother's right.*'

'She *is* right,' he said quietly, firmly. 'You're way out of line here, Car.'

I smiled a mean smile.

'He agrees with his master! *What a surprise!*'

Mum shook her head in disgust.

'OK, I need some space. Go to your room, Car! *Now!*'

'I will. Trust me, I'm on my way.'

And I was.

Of the many things I had prepared since receiving that email, one was a bulging rucksack. I stormed off to my room, hoisted it up on to my shoulder and stomped back out, across the hall and out of the front door.

'Car? *Car!*'

Code Red.

Execute Plan C.

CHAPTER 38

Plan C

I watched London buzz with early weekend promise through the windows of the 274. I was still breathing heavily and my eyes were stinging with salty water. But I wasn't angry any more. Honestly. I just felt determined. *The universe had finally simplified.* I had one singular goal and I was going to make it happen.

But when my uncle opened the door, my confidence bolted like a dog off a lead. Lan was hunched over in an oversized baggy white vest and white boxers, dreadlocks hanging over his bleary, unprepared eyes. He yawned and shook his head lightly.

'Sorry, man, late gig last night … Hey!'

When he saw the tears, his body suddenly straightened and he swept his hair from his face.

'Carm?'

My shoulders rocked, my head fell. He enveloped me in a hug and ushered me inside.

'Whoa,' Lan said simply, after I'd brought him up to speed on the latest developments. 'Pretty heavy.'

I nodded, sniffed, shuddered, and sipped from the mug of tea he'd given me. He got up, put a hand on my shoulder, then walked towards his bedroom.

'Y'know, I ignored like three calls whilst I was in bed. I think I can guess who they were from.'

He returned with his mobile phone and turned the screen to face me: *MISSED CALLS (3) Taylor Home.*

'Don't call back yet.'

'Carm, they need to know you're safe.'

'I know just ... five minutes?'

'Carm ...'

'*One* minute. I need to ask you something first.'

Lan sighed and held his palms out, upturned, as if to say, *Go on.*

'Can I stay here for a bit?'

He looked down at his feet. I pushed.

'Just for a few days. *Please*, Lan?'

He looked up at me, picked up his phone and dialled.

'Joss? Yeah, yeah – hey ... No ... No, it's OK, he's OK ... I know. Yeah, he told me ... I don't ... I mean that's not my … Joss, listen for a sec … *Joss!* Hold on a second … He wants to stay here for a while … I dunno, a few days … No, I'm not trying to interfere, I'm …'

He paused, then paused some more. Then some more. I didn't need to hear the other end of the line to know Mum was on full throttle. To be fair, I was impressed by how many words Lan had got in so far. He nodded a few times and managed to squeeze in the occasional 'Yep'. Then:

'So we let him cool off … Uh-huh … Exactly. But yeah, I'll make sure – I'll make sure he does … Yeah … OK. I will … Hey! Joss, I will! I promise … OK. OK, bye.'

He dropped his phone and exhaled sharply, widening his eyes as they met mine.

'You gotta do your work assignments every day you're here.'

I smiled. 'Course!'

'No easy rides – I'm basically your mum's eyes and ears, right? No corner-cutting. I promised.'

'I promise, too.'

'OK then.'

He offered his hand and I shook it.

'So,' I began tentatively, 'you're like, my *guardian* now.'

'Huh?'

'My guardian.'

'I mean … Yeah, I guess so.'

It was already nearly 9 p.m.

Time seemed to move a lot quicker at Lan's flat. Perhaps it was the lack of tension. Maybe it was the company. With my assignments for the week already completed back home, I got to relax and watch my uncle go about his day. At any given time he'd be drawing or writing or singing, or on the phone to his bandmates. *So content*, I thought, even though I knew my presence put him ever so slightly on edge. I was pretty sure Mum didn't fully trust him ... and *that*?

Well, *that* was going to make Plan C all the harder to execute.

Lan had a battered old laptop he let me use. He didn't technically have WiFi, but he lived close enough to a coffee shop that did, and he always made sure he was up on the latest password.

'MochaBlock1, capital *M*, capital *B*, all one word,' he called from his bedroom, where he was scribbling away.

Dear George
This is Carmichael! My friends call me Car. I just wanted to say I'd be super hyped to be on the show. My guardian's details are below.
Landonbenjaminplays@me.com
Can't wait to hear from you!

Thanks
Car Taylor

I paused, looked to Lan's room, pressed SEND. I closed
the laptop and lay back on the sofa, my stuffed rucksack
operating as a temporary pillow.

Through the material in the bag's front pocket, I
could feel the reassuring outline of my passport.

CHAPTER 39

Big Mouth

'Wicked! Blueberry and vanilla, yeah?'

'Yup,' I said on my return from the cafe the next morning with Lan's favourite muffin in tow. He flipped the kettle and we both sat up on the counter in Lan's minuscule kitchen. There was a kind of table, but it was more like a large chopping board on hinges attached to the wall – definitely a one-man party.

Perched with one arm leaning on the dripping tap, Lan nibbled away happily and I took my chance.

'Lan. You've always stuck up for me …'

'Uh-oh.' His muffin-muffled voice winced.

I hopped off the counter and stood facing him. He frowned.

'What?'

'I emailed the producer of *The Missy Show*. Said you'd be my guardian.'

'What!?'

There've been very few times I've seen Lan truly panicked, but this time I definitely saw a bit of blueberry fly past my right ear.

'I mean, you are technically my guardian now.'

'Carm, I can't make your mum and dad's decisions. I wouldn't want to. And even if I did want to, she'd kill me.'

'But what if it was for something good? To make things better.'

'For who?'

'OK, yeah, mainly for me, but Lan – what if this is my big break, man? What if I come back from America a star? I could go home and give Mum the money to pay for me to go to some posh private school if that's what she wants. What if—'

'Sounds like a lot of *What ifs*.'

'How do you chase a dream without a *What if*? How did you do it?'

'I tried not to upset anybody on the way.'

'What about Grandma?'

Lan gave a soft chuckle and a conceding nod. 'True.'

'Certain people might just have to be upset for a while, but it'll all make sense in the end.'

'Really?' Lan shrugged, unconvinced.

I looked around the chaos of Lan's flat. 'Everyone on your side of the family, everyone on Dad's side – Mum and Dad especially – they all think you're mad for living how you live.'

I watched a flicker of hurt zip through my uncle's eyes, in the shape not of new information, but a reminder. I didn't let up.

'But what none of them see is that you're *happy*. *You like your life*. You made a choice that worked for *you*.'

I paused.

'Lan.'

I paused again.

'Tell me I'm wrong. Tell me I'm wrong and we'll forget all about it.'

We stared at each other.

Then he laughed and shook his head.

'Bwoy …' He chuckled. 'You got a big mouth.'

'So they say,' I said, smiling. 'Don't you wanna find out how big it could be?'

'What time is it over in New York?'

I looked at the old alarm clock perched precariously on top of a stack of cassettes that looked ready for some Jenga action.

'Four thirty p.m.?'

'Perfect.'

We sat on the sofa eating pizza in front of the laptop while Lan typed. When he'd finished, he paused and looked at me.

'You sure about this?'

I reached over and clicked on SEND.

'Hey!'

I shrugged.

'I'm sure.'

He shook his head.

'Well, I guess I'm not the one you have to convince.'

CHAPTER 40

Winds of Change

It had been dry and warm for at least two weeks. If you're not from the UK, you probably wouldn't appreciate what a miracle that was. But as Lan and I stood outside my house the following evening, the heavens opened and in seconds we were wiping biblical amounts of rain from our foreheads and shoulders.

'Seems about right,' I said nervously.

'Yup.' He nodded.

The door opened and Dad appeared. Three of us stood in silence for what felt like an age.

'Kinda wet out here,' Lan offered.

Dad gave a slight nod.

'I don't think you'll find it much less stormy inside.'

Straight away, the vibe in the kitchen was off. We were all there: Malky pulled a comical scared face at me.

Mum sat at the table with an air of eerie silent calm around her. I broke it first.

'Hey.'

She looked like a newsreader. All business, no emotion.

'I'm gonna make this short and very, very clear,' she said. *Oh God, she even sounded like a newsreader.* I felt my heart thumping in that way it does after a sudden jolt of exercise.

'Ma ...'

She held up her hand to stop me and I did.

'Your father and I have formally lodged an appeal to get you back into school. I have to be honest, Car. I'd been starting to think that maybe you didn't actually deserve a place back there ...'

Need a 'but' here. Come on, a nice big 'but'?

Still frighteningly calm, she stood up, leaned forward with her fingertips stretched out on the tabletop like a sprinter in the blocks and locked eyes with me.

'But ...'

Yes!

'Now I think I know what you really wanted to do on that stage. And I know what you have the potential to do. I'm not happy about how you showed your talent, but I get that it *is* a talent. Of some kind. I've spoken with the Head and you have this week and next while they look at the appeal, so here's the deal.'

This was it. She was gonna kick me out and I'd have to live with Lan forever, become his sidekick, grow some ginger dreads. Maybe be a roadie for his band, carrying instruments and getting meal deals from supermarkets for the musicians. I could wear gloves with no fingers and denim jackets with no sleeves …

'It's a once-in-a-lifetime thing and travelling is always an education. So … your dad and I will give authorisation for you to go to America and perform.'

… vacuum the band's dressing room, put petrol in their van, go back to Lan's flat and eat baked beans out of cans and—

Wait, what?

'If …'

Lan and I looked at each other, gobsmacked. Mum could see us both getting excited. She straightened up and raised a finger and, for the first time, her voice.

'*If* … you can get there and back by the end of next week, after which you'll hopefully be starting school again …'

Easy.

'*If* you can manage not to insult everybody …'

Hmm …

'And *if* … you promise to stop seeing Alex.'

Already done, so …

'No lunchtimes, no after-schools, no phone calls, no emails, no texts … No nothing.'

I nodded slowly, partly to myself. Alex didn't want to speak to me anyway and I didn't have anything to say to her. She hadn't tried to contact me, so why would I contact her?

No. Times had changed.

I needed to look out for *me*.

I looked at Lan, who raised his eyebrows and shrugged.

Malky shoved me playfully. 'Hollywood, bruv! Don't be an idiot.'

'New York,' I corrected him, still a little dazed.

'So?' Mum looked from her brother to me. 'Do we have a deal?'

I pushed Alex's face from my mind.

'One hundred per cent, Mum, One hundred per cent.'

Lan spoke for the first time, at pace.

'Honestly I think it's a good call, Joss. I'll keep an eye on him, call you every day we're out there. I can—'

'What?' Mum scoffed.

'I – I was just saying, I'll keep an eye—'

'*You're* not taking him.'

I looked from Lan to Mum and back again. Lan's face crumpled in confusion.

'Oh. I thought … with the hospital, you wouldn't be able to get time off so—'

'I can't,' said Mum, as if the solution were obvious. 'I don't have that kind of flexibility. But Stuart does.'

Dad smiled. My face fell.

'Oh,' said Lan. 'Yeah, I mean. It's your call, of course.'

'Yes, it is.'

'Just … the producers kinda have me down as Carm's guardian, and …'

Mum shot her brother a look so sharp I thought it might slice a graze along his forehead.

'Why would that be?'

'Uh …'

I jumped in as Lan flailed.

'It was me, Mum. I emailed and—'

'Great, then you can give me the address and we can clarify, can't we?'

'Joss—'

'I think you've done *enough*, Lan, don't you? His dad'll take him. Right, Stu?'

Dad stepped forward cheerily and nodded.

'What she said.'

CHAPTER 41

A Lotta Maybes

Technically, it was a win, I thought to myself two days later. Mum had given her permission to George Lacey, and Dad had sent over our passport details. In return, Lacey had emailed over boarding passes and hotel details for a three-day, two-night stay in New York City. *I'd made it happen, somehow. Technically a win.*

So why didn't it feel that way?

After one night back at home I'd stayed at Lan's the rest of the week – neither me nor Mum was quite ready for a full reunion. Plus Malky wasn't taking my 'reward for bad behaviour' too well, and I didn't feel like another three days of that. But mainly, the way Lan's face had dropped when he realised he wouldn't be the one taking me to New York made me feel like I owed him some more *uncle–nephew* time.

'Everything you asked for.' Lan smiled as I packed my stuff.

'I guess.' I shrugged.

'Or maybe it isn't.' Lan raised his eyebrows.

'Huh?'

'Remember what I said a couple of weeks back? You either *know* what it is you wanna do, or you *try* stuff so you know what you *don't* wanna do.' He grinned. 'You can't lose.'

'Y'see? That's why I need *you* backstage! *Dad* wouldn't have an opinion like that. He wouldn't have an *opinion* at all.'

'How do you know?'

'Cos he never does! On anything!'

'Maybe he does, but doesn't know how to tell you. Maybe you don't know how to ask the right questions.'

'I do all the asking!'

Lan shrugged.

'Then maybe it's a listening thing. What do I know? I'm just the crazy uncle.'

He tossed a T-shirt into my chest, wrapped an arm around my neck in a playful headlock and tousled my hair.

I hoisted my rucksack straps on to both shoulders.

'I wish you were coming, Lan.'

He waved a dismissive palm.

'There'll be other times. Maybe we'll both be travel-ling entertainers after this. Never know! You need me, you call. Simple. Oh, and I'll … let you know if there's a backgammon session while you're out there.'

I looked sheepish, doubly so at the fact he didn't even mention her name. I was grateful for the omission – hearing it felt awkward.

I nodded. We hugged and Lan opened his front door. As I stepped out, I had the strongest feeling that the next time I saw him, things wouldn't be the same.

The 274 was always a good creative thinking space.

Buses tend to be encased in glass and slow moving, so there's a lot to see at a leisurely pace. It's good pondering time, and I had a lot to ponder. Including the fact that I'd started wondering about pondering and the difference between a ponder and a wonder. I mean, you could *have* a ponder but could you *have* a wonder? You could definitely have a *wander*. You could ponder some-thing and you could wonder something, but whilst you could happily stare at something *in wonder*, I'm pretty sure you couldn't stare at that same thing *in ponder*.

I'd look it up later.

For now, I was ignoring all the blond kids who flashed past on the pavement, all looking like Alex in different ways, and focusing on my task. George Lacey had asked me to think about funny things to say in an interview with Missy and – more dauntingly – some fresh ideas for a short performance on the *Missy* stage. Now I was trying to separate out the ones that didn't ridicule actual humans from the ones that did.

But as I scribbled words and phrases down in the little pad Lan had given me, like '*School uniform is just a freaky miniature suit*', '*Why chalk and cheese?*' and '*Temporary signs that say Temporary Sign*', what really made me chuckle was thinking of pigeons flying into teachers' faces, brothers who think the Poet Laureate is a lady called *Lorriette* who writes rhymes, or cling film used as a heat conductor.

Cue another blond kid at the zebra crossing ahead. Not even a girl. Haunting me.

Home felt different. Having technically moved out, I suddenly felt like a visitor, or perhaps a lodger. Like I should shake hands with Mum and Dad and Malky, and say, *Hey, I'm Car, I like books and words and saying dumb stuff for my own entertainment. I'm not stopping long, off to New York tomorrow for a work thing.*

That evening, in the kitchen, there was a large suitcase splayed open on the table. Dad was sat staring at its contents, and Mum was stood over it, hands on hips.

'One pair of shorts will do it, Stu. It's three days – on

how many of those are you gonna hit the beach?' She held up four pairs of swim shorts. 'I'm thinking less than four.' She separated one pair from the pile, returned it to the suitcase and dumped the extra three on the table. 'You always do this. You're an over-packer.'

Dad shrugged. 'I just like to be prepared. Any eventuality.'

'There's no beaches in Manhattan, Stuart.'

'Hey,' I said from the doorway.

My parents both stopped.

'Hey, Car,' said Dad. 'You ready for this?'

I nodded. 'Yeah.'

Dad rolled his eyes.

'Don't look too excited.'

'Car, get me the small suitcase, please,' Mum said, shaking her head at Dad's jumbo choice. 'He's not gonna need this.'

As I pulled open the door to the storage cupboard, Malky popped out of his bedroom.

'*The World's Greatest Entertainer* returns!'

'Not for long.'

I leaned into the cupboard to retrieve the case. Malky moved a few steps closer and lowered his voice.

'Just remember, when you're up there in the flashing lights, getting your meals on the plane, taking pictures of the Statue of Liberty … none of this is right.'

I pulled out the case and turned to face him.

'None of it,' he growled.

We held each other's gaze for a moment. I smiled with only my mouth.

'Maybe not for you.'

'Car!' Mum called from the kitchen. 'Where's that case?'

I cut my eyes and brushed past him.

'That's better,' Mum said as she streamlined Dad's packing. 'Car, you have your passport?'

I nodded.

'Enough clean clothes?'

'Uh-huh.'

She zipped up the smaller suitcase, plonked it on the floor and sat.

'OK. Sit down.'

I sat, forming a triangle around the table. Dad folded his arms and did his best *'I'm also serious'* face. I was close now. *This was real.* I could practically smell my in-flight meal.

'This trip is an exercise in trust, Car. Dad'll be my eyes and ears, so I don't have to worry, do I?'

I stared. Mum leaned in towards me.

'Do I?'

'No.'

'You go, you be safe, you get back, you start school,

we start thinking about GCSEs. The rest of your life. *Seriously.*'

I nodded.

'It'll be fun, Car,' Dad offered, and Mum shot him a look. 'I mean – not ... too much fun, an enjoyable ... I mean *educational* experience.' He looked at Mum. 'Right?'

She raised an eyebrow and looked at me.

'Any questions?'

'Actually, yeah. Can I say thank you?'

The tiniest hint of a smile.

'You can.'

'Thanks, Mum.'

Smooth.

For the first time in what felt like ages, a tingling sensation tickled its way through me. Excitement. First thing tomorrow morning, I'd be above the clouds.

CHAPTER 42

Arrival

In between the aeroplane movies and Dad's incessant snoring, I'd begun scribbling ideas down in my little notebook. It was mainly just subject titles to add detail to later, like *'Freakishly Tall Men in Tiny Seats Somehow Sleeping Like Babies'*.

But I snapped it shut as I saw the lights of New York City shining up at me through the window, like a million fireworks, magically frozen in time. It was an awesome sight. I stayed in that trance-like awe right up until I stepped out of a tunnel into the expanse of the airport itself.

For one of the most iconic cities on the planet, John F. Kennedy International Airport looked like a cross between an underfunded school gym and an old shopping centre. And not even a good shopping centre with, like, an Apple Store and bottomless ice cream.

What lit it up for me – as we edged through passport control – were all the police. Sorry – the *cops*.

'Move it along now, folks!'

'Hey buddy, get in line!'

'Sir! This way please! Sir? SIR!'

When I slowed down to appreciate them, a stern policewoman called directly to me, 'Pick up the pace, kid, let's go already!' I practically swooned. *Those voices. These characters with words like lines from movies ... The aggressive politeness.* I sincerely doubted any British person could make the words *'Please'* and *'Sir'* sound quite so much like *'Now'* and *'Idiot'*. It was a joy to behold.

While we waited for our luggage, Dad and I made a video call home. Mum was her usual firm self, but not unpleasant – there was no hiding the satisfaction a mum felt from knowing her family was safe. Malky wouldn't come to the phone. Still jealous, I guessed.

Our luggage collected, Dad and I scanned the fore-court where a sea of drivers held signs with names on them.

'There!' Dad pointed to a guy who looked how Dad might look if you were able to squish him down like Play-Doh, paint him brown and make him bald but with a ponytail. He was shorter than Mum, even, but as wide as he was tall, kind of like a human grapefruit. He had dark glasses and was chatting away in Spanish on a hands-free microphone plugged into his ear, holding up a sign that said CARMICHAEL TAYLOR.

Dad gave him a big cheesy smile. Grapefruit Guy raised an eyebrow that popped out above his shades.

'Hi. I'm, well – I'm … not Carmichael Taylor but—'

'Then you gots to keep it moving, homie, I'm waiting for Carmichael.'

'I'm Carmichael,' I said, ending the awkwardness my dad had an uncanny knack for creating. 'You can call me Car.'

Grapefruit Guy took off his shades, wiped my name off his mini whiteboard sign and put on a whole new demeanour, but with that same thick Spanish/English/New York drawl.

'And I'm-a call you *a* car.' He smiled. 'Manhattan, right? *Missy Show*?'

'Uh – yes please,' Dad said.

'I'm Manny,' the driver said. 'I'll be your driver.' He turned to me and lowered his voice like we were sharing a secret. 'Who dis guy? He your bodyguard or sumthin'? He don't look dangerous. He look kinda *English*.'

I laughed.

'That's my dad.'

'Stuart,' said Dad. 'And I'm … Scottish. Originally.'

'Oh snap!' Manny laughed. 'Like *Braveheart*? Them

Scottish dudes be *crazy*, son! I take it back. Y'all people know how to train a dragon and stuff. I ain't messing with that! A'ight, follow me.'

By the time we got outside, thrust into a melee of boisterous commuters, airport staff and other taxi drivers, I was already in love. The heat of the city smacked me in the face. This was like Camden on steroids. I laughed again – *This was a home from home.*

'Let's hit the city!' Manny sang as he swung what looked like a jeep the size of a small house out of the airport grounds. I looked through the window and wondered where that giant microchip I saw from the plane had disappeared to.

'This ... isn't ... ?'

Manny laughed from the driver's seat. Dad and I looked at each other.

'This *Queens*, son! Ain't nuthin' in Queens!' He thought for a second. ''Cept my brother-in-law Hector and his annoying kids.'

'Your ... *nieces and nephews*?' Dad clarified. Manny nodded.

'Two boys. SO annoying, man. I shoulda NEVER got 'em them super soakers. Nah, the *City* is *Manhattan*, that's where it all go down. The bright lights and the fancy pants ... You'll see.'

We hit a red light and Manny turned and stared at me, as if analysing me for the first time.

'You be like me, huh, li'l man?'

'Huh?'

Manny wiggled his fingers like he was performing a magic spell.

'Li'l special mixture from the paint pots. Limited edition multi-flavour ice cream, am I right? Ha ha, yeah. My family mostly Dominican. But I got *Jamaican*, *African*, *Spanish* … Wooo! *Esta loca!* It's crazy. I'm a *tapestry*, yo. That's New York tho, baby. Whatchoo got?'

I have to say, I loved this directness. Back home this would've felt like super awkward. But here it felt right.

'My mum's from Grenada …'

'That the Caribbean?'

The way he said *Caribbean* put all the emphasis on the '*ribb*', like 'Cuh-*RIBB*ian'.

'The Caribbean,' Dad confirmed, in the way we say it, with all the emphasis on the 'be-an'.

'That's what I said,' said Manny, then turned to me and pointed to my dad. 'So Professor McGonagall over here be the reason you got the carrot top!'

We both laughed.

'Yeah,' I said. Dad rolled his eyes.

The lights turned green and he pulled away, shaking his head.

'Wild! I love it! Ohhhh *snap*! Hold up, *hoooold up*! *Préndelo!*'

A song came on the radio and Manny turned it up to ear-splitting levels while Dad winced.

'Woooo!' Manny screamed and started rapping along. He hit a button and all the windows simultaneously slid down and locked open, the wind from the freeway swirling in. Any tiredness from the flight evaporated as the hot breeze massaged my cheeks. Dad tried to do his window up but couldn't, and I chuckled away, then nearly choked as I caught the sight up ahead.

On the horizon, block after block, skyscraper after skyscraper, were rising up into view. It was like watching plants on those nature programmes where they use the time-lapse cameras. I blinked once, twice, three times. *Whoa. Manhattan. This is really happening.* Manny whooped and hollered through the open window on his side.

'WELCOME TO NEW YORK CITY!'

CHAPTER 43

So Fresh

What a welcome it was. Half an hour later the traffic slowed and we were weaving at a snail's pace through the grids of the microchip at ground level. My eyes darted about at lightning speed, hungrily gobbling up every store front, every pedestrian, every residence. I couldn't wait to get out and look up.

'How much further, Manny?' I called from the back seat.

'Oh, five minutes, tops. Your hotel is just a couple – EY! *HEY!* What are ya, tryin'a get yourself *killed*, bro? Keep your bummy five-dollar sneakers on the sidewalk, fool!'

A guy in a suit had stepped out in front of Manny and the pair exchanged various offensive hand and finger gestures until the flustered pedestrian gave up and went about his day.

'Jaywalkers,' Dad said.

'What's that?' I asked.

'It's what Americans call people who cross the road like that.'

'Well, *this* American would like to have called him something else but I got customers in the car. A'ight, boom next block.'

'I'm'a wait right here for George. Parking po-lice be *trippin'*,' said Manny as we pulled up outside the Courtyard Hotel.

As I closed the door on my side, I did a slow-motion three-sixty on the spot, looking up at the perfectly aligned buildings, criss-crossed with tic-tac-toe boards of streets and avenues. Everything seemed so ordered, so modern, so opposite to the higgledy-piggledy mess of lanes and high roads back home. Whilst I felt like I was stepping back into scenes from my favourite movies, I also felt like I'd stepped forward into a near future. I took a deep breath in, as if I could suck a portion of the city's soul into my lungs. Manny's voice snapped me out of it.

'A'ight, you boys have fun now.'

'Thanks, Manny.'

'You got it.'

'Yeah, thanks,' said Dad, and Manny rolled his eyes as we passed him towards the hotel entrance.

'OK then,' he said, leaning his elbow on the open door frame.

Something felt off, then I remembered something. I pulled out the crumpled ten-dollar note Lan had given me, spun round and handed it to Manny.

'Sorry, it's all I've got.'

Manny beamed.

'You keep it, little man, ain't your job anyways. Plus it's the thought that counts, ain't that right, McGonagall?' He shouted the last bit pointedly to my dad.

'I – uh, I still need to change up some cash and uh, I …'

He tailed off.

'Mm-hm. See y'all on the flipside.'

'Yeah,' said Dad awkwardly, and walked in through a set of revolving doors in which, much to Manny's amusement, he promptly got stuck.

In the hotel reception, a slim man around my dad's age whipped off a pair of expensive-looking sunglasses, bounced off a sofa and skipped towards us.

'Carmichael Taylor, as I live and breathe!' he exclaimed in an attempt at an English accent. 'George Lacey.' He shook my hand with a vice-like grip, then looked up a few feet at the beanpole by my side. 'And you must be Dad.'

'Nice to meet you,' Dad offered.

'Believe me, the pleasure is all mine.'

George Lacey looked *new*. Kind of like a Ken doll, fresh out of the box. His blue eyes sparkled with zero bags underneath, his teeth aligned like piano keys, reflecting the light with some intensity. To call both him and my dad 'white guys' was an insult to his bronzed skin, no doubt the result of some holiday we would never go on. His blond, product-heavy hair looked like a brand-new cap, placed with precision on the top of his head; the peak was a slicked-up quiff, every strand obedient and deliberate. He even smelt good. Like a freshly talcumed baby. The white bits on his Converse were still white, the singular crease down the centre of each trouser leg looked like they'd been ironed in, seconds before we entered. His T-shirt was designed to look faded and worn but still looked like it might have the price tag hanging off the back of the collar.

'Welcome to New York, let's get you guys settled in.'

As we stood at the reception desk waiting for our room keys, George Lacey spoke a mile a minute.

'Tomorrow morning Manny will scoop you up out front and run you to our studios in Chelsea. Few blocks away. We'll do a full rehearsal and you see the space, meet the crew. Saturday we'll record the show fully live,

Saturday night we fly you back to your fans in sunny England! Sound like a plan?'

'Uh, yeah,' I said. 'Totally!'

He nudged me playfully.

'Alrighty then, you keep working on those gags, buddy, I can't wait to see what you've got in store for us!' He did a fake whisper to my dad, loud enough for me to hear. 'Gotcha self a live wire, hey, pal? Don't tell anybody, but he's gonna be a *star!*'

The receptionist pulled out two key cards. George took them, peeked at the numbers and handed one to each of us.

'You guys are up on the fourth floor. Great views. Enjoy!' He turned to leave.

'Wait – what do we do till tomorrow?'

He stopped at the revolving door and spun round to face us.

'This is *New York City*, gentlemen. Whatever your heart desires.'

CHAPTER 44

Like Father, Not Son

If this was a movie, we'd cut straight from George grinning and saying 'Whatever your heart desires' to a snappy, joyous montage of me and Dad, wide-eyed, flying around New York's hotspots, posing for photos with hot dogs, a catchy guitar-riff soundtrack playing underneath.

Instead, there's just a lot of basically walking and standing and walking again.

After dropping our bags at reception we walked the length of this thing called the High Line, which used to be an overground train track and was now like a long, skinny park on a never-ending bridge. After that we walked to the harbour and tried to spot the Statue of Liberty but realised we were on the wrong side. I stared out across the water. Just the fact that Manhattan was an island city seemed magical to me, like it was tropical but with no trees.

Then we spent twenty minutes wandering up and

down crowded streets to the wrong subway entrances, followed by twenty more minutes mopping our sweaty brows, stuffed into people's armpits on a packed train, missing our stop for the second time and feeling like we'd travelled halfway across the world just to experience an ever so slightly different version of the London Underground at rush hour.

'Dad, can't we do the museum tomorrow?'

'I'm sure it's the next stop.'

'I don't understand why we can't just get a yellow cab.'

'Cos I'm not a sucker. Those things will cost five times as much.'

'But also maybe get us where we wanna go,' I muttered.

'What's that?'

'Nothing.'

I was desperate to be above ground. I didn't care where we went particularly, I just wanted to wander, wonder and ponder. Soak it all in.

Truth be told, we were both tired and irritable. We'd lost track of what time it was for our British bodies, but we knew if we were back home it'd be past bedtime. With such a short trip to a place we may never come back to though, Dad was determined to see as much as he could.

My belly was rumbling. It became painfully clear that hunger plus tiredness equalled impatience. We passed a tiny diner selling pizza by the slice, Dad leading the way, me lagging behind, dragging my heels.

'Dad, can we stop a second?'

'We're too close now.'

'I'm hungry!'

'So am I.'

'So let's stop.'

'This is a once-in-a-lifetime thing, Car. We're not stopping.'

He marched on and I slumped behind him, the smell of melted cheese and pepperoni disappearing behind me like a helium-filled balloon lost by a toddler.

'Maybe I don't care about the Googletime.'

'*Guggenheim*. And you *do* care. Everyone does, you just don't know it yet.'

'Since when did you feel so strongly about anything?' I muttered.

'What?' Dad spun to face me as we rounded a corner and an admittedly amazing, bulbous building that looked like a gigantic cup of tea on a humungous saucer suddenly loomed over us. 'Stop muttering. Look at that.'

He pointed up to the museum.

'That, my friend, is a feat of structural engineering.' He smiled. 'And the inside ain't bad either. Come on.'

With a new pep in his step, Dad trotted to the entrance.

A huge security guard stepped into his path.

'Folks, just to let you know, we close at seven, last admission is in fifteen minutes.'

Dad slumped.

'How long would you recommend to see everything?'

'Everything? Three or four hours.'

Dad frowned.

'OK, so we could still do forty-five minutes … We could have—'

'We ask visitors to begin making their way out at six forty-five.'

Dad looked at me and I shrugged, really thinking more about pizza at this stage. He sighed, admitting defeat.

'Fine. You win, Car.'

'What do I win?'

He shook his head, exasperated.

'Let's go.'

'Can we get pizza now?'

Ten minutes later we were having a romantic meal for two: a slice and a can of soda, sat on a kerb next to a homeless guy outside a pharmacy called Duane Reade. *Who calls a pharmacy Duane?* I wondered, and would have written that down, but I was too hungry to stop eating.

It was only after we'd chucked our greasy napkins and empty cans in the trash that we noticed how close we were to Central Park. It looked huge and beautiful in the early evening sun, dappled light bouncing off a gigantic silver lake in its centre. Couples, friends and families were dotted around on the grass or benches, joggers trailed up and down happily.

We stood at the outer wall looking down on it all, sluggish in both mind and body because of the criminal amounts of melted cheese. I nodded down at the vast green oasis of calm.

'That might've been a nicer place to eat.'

Dad sighed and shook his head. He scrolled through some information on his phone.

'There's an exhibition on the history of bridge making at the New York Hall of Science. Maybe we could catch that after the rehearsal tomorrow.' He walked down towards an entrance to the park. 'Come on.'

Bridge making.

I'm not even going to put a question mark there. Or an exclamation mark, for that matter. Heck, I'm not even using *italics*. I'll just leave you with those two words and a full stop to chew on.

Bridge making.

A happy thought struck me as we got out of Penn Station (wrong exit): *The hotel*. I loved hotels. The breakfasts, the disposable flip-flops, the end of the toilet roll mysteriously folded into a little triangle …

When George gave us our key cards, we'd been so excited we'd just gone directly out to explore the city.

So it was with some anticipation that we took the elevator up to the fourth floor, wheeling our little cases behind us.

The elevator doors parted and Dad pulled out his key card.

'Four-one-four,' he read, and trundled along, checking the doors as he went. 'What are you?'

Dad stopped at the matching number and I paused alongside him. I looked down at my card.

'Four-one … four.'

'What?'

'Oh.'

'Looks like we're sharing.'

'Cool.' I winced.

'Cool.' Dad shrugged.

Cool.

He tapped his card and opened the door on to what was, to be fair, a pretty nice room: spacious, little fridge, big bathroom, huge window with admittedly great views …

And *one double bed.*

Cooooool.

CHAPTER 45

Reality Bites

'I'm so sorry for the inconvenience, sir. We'll get you guys into a twin room right away.'

'Thank you,' Dad said to the receptionist the following morning. The staff were falling over themselves with apologies and willingness to help. Dad and I had been gearing up for an awkward complaint situation, but the whole exchange was so quick and easy I headed to the restaurant thinking we probably should've said something to them last night and avoided the … unnecessary unpleasantness. *Ever had your father's naked feet on your cheek? For all that is sacred in this world, I hope not.*

As we reached the breakfast buffet I offered, 'Y'know, maybe we should have said—'

But Dad interrupted me and just said, 'I know.'

And in a nutshell that's pretty much how men discuss feelings.

* * *

Side Note: When you're in a hotel, what's the point of sitting at a table before getting your breakfast? It's not a restaurant. It's a hotel eating area. It might be like a restaurant at night, with proper waiters and stuff, but at breakfast, it's a place you serve yourself everything you need, then sit anywhere you want. *It didn't make any sense*, I thought, as Dad and I sat at a table for five seconds, then got back up and went to the buffet we'd walked past five seconds ago.

Yes, I was feeling a little frustrated that morning.

The reality of my situation was starting to creep in. This wasn't a family holiday. It wasn't even necessarily a dream ticket to superstardom. This was a real, bona fide challenge. *I had work to do.* This was a high-pressure situation, one I had lost my best friend and perhaps my school place to be in. Tomorrow I was going to entertain a large portion OF THE ENTIRE WORLD. I was embarking on something extraordinary, but also pretty scary, and my only support was a guy I struggled to talk to on a *normal* day.

What made it all temporarily better was bacon.

And sugary cereal. And waffles. And muffins. And pancakes. And little cocktail sausages and fried potato slices and watermelon and yogurts on ice and eggs of all styles and granola and smoothies. And sliced cheese (for some reason).

'You done now?' Dad shook his head at the carnage in front of me. I held up a *'one moment'* finger and guzzled down the last of a strawberry-and-banana smoothie that a nice lady had made for me on my fourth trip back to the buffet. I exhaled with gusto and slammed the glass down.

'Yup.'

Dad checked his watch.

'Manny'll be outside by now. Come on.'

He got up and turned from the table. I stacked up my collection of plates (thoughtful) and followed behind.

'*¿Cómo estás hombres?!* We ready to rock this?'

'Hey, Manny.'

He held out a fist and I reciprocated with a bump.

'Morning,' said Dad, and got straight in the car.

'Oh, I've got a good one actually,' I said to Manny, and showed him the handshake Lan taught me: a fist bump, two slaps and a ripple of the fingers.

'On a wave.' I smiled.

'Say whaaaat! That's dope, *hermano!*' Manny laughed as we both climbed into the car. He repeated the finger ripple. '*On a wave.* I like that.'

The studio was less than ten minutes' drive, so I felt a touch of the VIP treatment making such a small trip in such a massive car, then having the door opened for me by a guy with a walkie-talkie who only looked a couple of years older than me.

'Morning!' he said brightly, and smiled. 'How was your trip?'

'Uh … short?'

Dad and I looked at the building we'd stopped outside. It was just like the clips Alex had showed me online: a corner building, the bottom floor an L-shape made entirely of tinted glass so you could see right into where they filmed the show. On TV you could see the general public outside, right where we were stood, pressed up against the glass, watching, waving, cheering.

We could see the shiny studio floor, brightly coloured walls, a small rake of around a hundred or so audience seats, tons of lights angled off rigging hanging from the ceiling, a small stage, a backdrop with the show's logo, mini palm trees, a sofa and Missy's famous chair. Studio staff buzzed back and forth in a hive of activity. I looked at Dad and he looked back at me with the expression I'm sure was on my face: *This is real now*.

'That's an arrival on talent,' the young guy said into a little remote microphone clipped on his shirt, wired into his walkie-talkie. Then he turned back to me and said, 'This way please.' I looked around for The Talent and then realised it was me.

'Go get 'em, li'l bro!' Manny called from the driver's seat.

'Here he is!'

George Lacey turned away from a group of people wearing *The Missy Show* T-shirts and did a little exaggerated jog across the reception area to where Dad and I waited in increasing wonder at the scale of this operation. George put both hands on my shoulders and leaned down to me, grinning with teeth so bright I had to squint a little bit.

'You OK?'

'Yeah.'

'Good night's sleep?'

'Not really.'

'Bummer! That jet lag's a doozy, huh!'

Dad and I exchanged a glance.

'Yeah,' I said. No one needed to know any more than that.

George lowered his voice like he was letting me into a secret.

'*Shall we make some magic?*'

He turned to the team behind him and shouted, 'Shall we make some *Missy* magic?!' The group all cheered and whooped, I guess because – America.

'Follow me,' he said, and pushed through the double

doors into the studio, then clapped his hands and called out, 'OK, everybody. This is Carmichael. He's our special guest this week. Say hello! Car, this is everybody.'

'Hi,' I said. George turned to Dad.

'Dad, you wanna watch from the audience? Pick your spot!' He called Dad 'Dad' in that way nursery teachers do to parents instead of using their actual names. Dad picked a seat halfway up the rake.

'OK,' said George, and pointed to the sofa. 'Let's do it.'

I flopped down into the plush cushions and George perched on Missy's chair.

'Where's Missy?'

'She likes to keep her powder dry for the live show.'

'What does that mean?'

'She prefers to be in the moment, meet her guests on the day so the conversation is fresh and genuine.'

'Oh, that's cool,' I said, trying and failing to hide my slight disappointment at the delay in meeting a genuine superstar.

'Yeah, she's … *eccentric* like that. Anyway. Let's run through the show. You've seen it before, right?' I nodded. 'Great, so you know how it goes. We'll have a big singer, a commercial break, a big actor, a break, some crowd interaction, another break and then boom. Everyone's favourite part of the show – kids doing crazy stuff, right?'

'Right.' I chuckled.

'So Missy'll ask you a few questions, where you're from, what you're into, bit of background. Be natural, but try and throw some funny observations in there.'

'Observations?'

'Stuff you've seen or done that's funny, y'know?'

'Right. OK.'

'Let's try it. I'll be Missy, you be you – ready?'

'Mm-hm.'

'Alrighty, here we go.' He spun round to face a camera that was sat unmanned in front of the front row of audience seats. He suddenly sat bolt upright and put on a weird presenter-type voice.

'Welcome back, and we are joined all the way from London, England, by the razor-tongued comical prodigy, Carmichael Taylor! Carmichael, how are you?'

'You can call me *Car*. And I'm good.'

'Good, good, so hey, what's London like, Car?'

'Rains every day. And everyone talks about it. And when it doesn't rain, everyone talks about it.'

'Ha-ha, I hear ya. What kinda stuff?'

'What?'

'What kinds of things do these *idiots* say?'

I glanced up at Dad, who had leaned forward in his seat, frowning.

'Uh … Y'know, just … moaning.'

George slouched, stopped smiling and started nodding

slowly, watching me. Then the big smile came back, but without the presenter voice and demeanour. He leaned towards me and patted my knee.

'Doing great, Car, real great. Let's get that energy fizzing, huh? Awesome though, buddy.'

He leaned back in Missy's chair, switching again to presenter mode. 'So hey, who's the *Moaning Minnie* in your family?'

'Oh, definitely my mum. She's one of those hardcore Army General-type mums. Like, I'll spill a drink and she'll be, like—'

I sensed Dad shifting in his seat again.

George looked out to the audience, then back to me. 'Go on.'

'That's just … how she is sometimes.'

'Hmm.' George looked disappointed. Then within seconds he was all smiles again, 'All right, OK, no worries, we can finesse that, we'll get a spark going …'

'Yeah,' I muttered. I couldn't hide my uncertainty, and I could feel George picking up on it too. Mum's warning rang in my head, making me feel as if I wasn't just sat in my seat, but strapped to it too.

When the chat was over, George looked out, shielding his eyes from the bright lights above, and called, 'Bryan! Bry, can we move into live state with the lighting? Siddiq, can we get cameras up? We'll try rehearsing the move from couch to performance. OK, let's get moving, people!'

About twenty people suddenly started rushing around, and suddenly cameras on huge tripods and wheels were rolling around with operators sat behind them; ladders were pulled away and theme music was playing, stopping, rewinding, playing again. Then everything went black for a moment. Then pink. Then blue. Then red. Then a mixture of colours, then a pool of light focused on us. George was watching over all of this with a careful, authoritative eye. Then he turned his attention to the audience, which was now shrouded in darkness – I could barely see Dad at all.

'How you doing up there, Dad?' he called. 'You still with us?'

'Yep,' Dad's voice called down, with all the trademark lack of enthusiasm. 'It's cool. I'm watching. *Listening.*'

George gave the shadows a thumbs-up and shuffled round to face me.

'So, uh, you managed to get some ideas together for a little performance?'

I pulled my little notebook out of my back pocket and tapped it.

'Actually I've got quite a lot of stuff.'

George beamed back at me.

'*That's* my guy! All right! Marcie! Can we get the show-time sting cued up please?'

An invisible voice came through an invisible speaker. 'Ready to roll, GL!'

George turned back to me.

'OK, so I'm gonna start some applause, Marcie's gonna play in a little music, and that's your cue to get on that podium up there and do your thing. Missy'll give you the big intro tomorrow but we'll just run through it anyway, get a feel for it, OK?'

'Sure,' I said, a word meaning *certainly* delivered with zero certainty. George raised an exaggerated eyebrow.

'OK?'

I forced a chuckle and nodded.

'OK!'

George jumped up and punched the air. 'All right! Positive energy!'

I looked at the circle of light on the little raised platform. A man checked the batteries in a microphone, blew into it and placed it into a stand in the middle of the circle, on top of a tiny *x* made of coloured sticky tape – there was a sticky-tape guy for that. There was a man or woman for every tiny thing going on around me. I suddenly felt an overwhelming sense of responsibility, and this was just a rehearsal. *But just a rehearsal*, I told myself, *a practice run of being a big mouth in front of people – your speciality. This is what you were built for.*

I took a deep breath.

'Ready?'

'Ready.'

'OK, gang, let's get cameras up. Dana, the floor's yours.'

A woman with *1AD* printed large on her walkie-talkie appeared from the darkness and started barking instructions like a sergeant major at boot camp. Everyone took their positions, then she called out, 'End of intro and applause in five, four, three ...'

When she passed *three* she mouthed *two* and *one* silently and all the lights on the cameras went red.

Although I couldn't see anyone but George now, the sound of around fifteen mouths and pairs of hands whooped and clapped.

'Car Taylor, ladies and gents!'

George stood and stretched his left arm out, his palm presenting a path to the podium. I got up from the sofa and ambled over to the microphone, trying to add a little swagger to my approach. The lights on Missy's chair and sofa lowered. Under the intense spotlight, George disappeared and I now couldn't see anything at all. The applause died down and I pulled the microphone out from its stand. Knowing all eyes were on me, but pretending they weren't, I started to feel a little burst of confidence.

'Hey, I'm Carmichael Taylor, because in England, everyone is named after old-timey castle owners.'

A few chuckles came out of the darkness, including my dad's. I felt calm. I figured I was never going to get the laughs I got on Talent Night until I had a proper audience. So instead of pausing and worrying, I just took another big breath in and didn't stop.

'I don't know if any of you have been to England, but we all share one ancient and sacred religion ... It's called *tea*. We believe very strongly in its healing powers and are willing to kill those who prepare it badly ... Hey, I flew over here in Economy Class, think you guys call it *Coach*? I think we should all come to a universal agreement across the globe and call it the *Loser Section*, cos that's kind of how you feel after you have to walk past people getting foot massages in four-poster beds, right? I noticed you guys give a lot of tips here and tell people to *keep the change* and stuff. Back home the only reason we might tip a driver is if they somehow saved our life on the journey. Even then we probably wouldn't. We'd just say *thanks* and wait for our exact change of, like, twelve pence ...'

I felt odd. Outside of myself, like a guy doing an impression of me.

I checked my pad. *Differences in American and UK English* was next, more little observations that felt funny-*ish*, but gentle and safe and not very ... well, *me*.

I shook off the discomfort and continued, but Dana

and George suddenly started clapping and whooping and everyone joined in.

'House lights!'

The studio was suddenly bright again, automatic blinds whirred upwards and I could see the street. I looked up to the audience and Dad was smiling. He raised his eyebrows in an *'I'm impressed'* expression and gave me a thumbs-up.

'Fantastic, fantastic,' said George, still clapping as he approached the podium. 'I just cut you off cos we only needed a couple minutes, check for lights and sound, make sure you feel at home, y'know? How'd you find it?'

'Yeah,' I said, then quickly added, 'I liked it.'

'Great! You hear that, Dad? He liked it!' he called up to the audience. With his back turned, I swallowed and frowned, a vague sense of confusion nagging me. As he spun back I reinstated an excited smile and his blinding white teeth sparkled at me once more. 'That's great. Really great.' He put both hands on my shoulders and lowered his voice into a gentle, bedtime reading tone. 'Now listen, before Missy brings you out onstage she'll be showing clips from that *insane* Talent Night video – *so awesome* – and talking about how brutal you are with the jokes, right? *Bam*, that guy gets burned, *bam*, this guy gets burned, y'know? So when we actually get to meet you we … we wanna see a bit more of that.'

'Like … when I'm talking about tea or … ?'

'Oh it's beautiful, that stuff is beautiful, I'm just saying … What you are so, *so* good at is picking a target and hitting that bullseye, you know what I mean? No prisoners. *Ruthless.*' He started laughing. 'I mean, what did you call that teacher?' He had another chuckle at the memory. 'Maybe … be *that* Carmichael, know what I mean?'

'No, what *do* you mean?' George and I spun round to see Dad right behind us, arms folded. 'You're saying Car's not being, what? *Mean* enough?'

Surprise, surprise, the Lord of Awkward had masterminded another awkward moment. The two men eyeballed each other for a second, then George looked down, then up again with that tractor-beam smile back in full effect.

'I'm saying your son has a unique talent. I'll show you exactly what I mean. Tonight. I'm taking you guys out to dinner. Boys' night. Whaddaya say?'

'Awesome!' I said.

'OK,' Dad said, less enthusiastically. George put one hand on my shoulder, one on Dad's.

'Beautiful. I'm gonna take you guys somewhere it'll all make sense.'

CHAPTER 46

Travelling at the Speed of Stuff

Before that though, we were headed somewhere that didn't make sense. Not if you only had a couple of days in the coolest city in the world. Yep, I'm talking about the History of Bridge Construction exhibition at the New York Hall of Science.

'O … *kay*,' Manny said, starting the engine with a shrug, 'I mean, everybody got their own thing, right? Saddle up, *amigos*, let's ride out!'

For the first time that day, Dad looked more than a little pleased with himself as Manny spun the steering wheel and pulled his massive car away from the studio.

Five minutes later I looked wistfully through the back window at the Empire State Building, which loomed over me like a massive finger pointing to a fun spot I *could* have visited.

'What did you think?' Dad asked. 'Like, how do you think it went?'

I was slightly taken aback by Dad actually initiating a conversation, so it took an extra second to register.

'Huh? The rehearsal? Yeah. OK.'

'And George?'

'What about him?'

'I dunno.' Dad shrugged. 'I mean, are you happy … doing what he wants?'

'I'm doing what *I* want. That's why we're here,' I said, more than a little snappily, then threw in a mutter for good measure. 'Apart from this little school science trip.'

'Sorry?'

'Nothing.'

Manny whistled. 'Tunnel looks clear for once. This is gonna be a breeze!'

We approached the east side of the island and before I could get a good view of the river, I saw a big green sign for the Queens Midtown Tunnel and we dipped down into a huge concrete tube.

When we re-emerged the sun seemed brighter and the buildings more spread out. We passed a few parks and a big cemetery and finally slowed as we neared a big lake and the Queens Zoo.

'Aw'right y'all, I'm'a drop you right here, you just follow the signs. I'll meet you back here at three, cool?'

'Great, thanks,' said Dad.

'What are you gonna do, Manny?' I asked.

'My brother's family live like ten minutes from here,' he said.

He lifted a huge colourful water gun with a bulbous tank attachment from under the passenger seat and grinned.

'And revenge is a dish best served cold.'

I don't think in numbers. My brain hates calculations and I've never wrapped my head around physics. If Albert Einstein had written a rap saying *Yo it's Big Al, listen – it's all about your vision / The speed of stuff? It just depends on your position*, instead of $E = mc^2$, I might have cared more about the Theory of Relativity. For as long as I can remember, I've always told myself: *Science? No. Maths? No. Geography? Obviously no. English? Unquestionably, indubitably, emphatically affirmative.* That means *yes*.

BUT.

I can't lie, the New York Hall of Science was not lame.

It was one of those museums where you could touch everything. There were illusions and rocket ships and even a golf course that tricked kids like me into learning about gravitational pulls – and I wasn't annoyed by it. I got to sit and read whilst Dad studied right angles and steel rivets. Occasionally I would look up and see him hopping about with excitement at how one iron joint attached to another, and I'd think, *Ah, bless him. He's going to be so tired tonight!*

Afterwards, we sat on a wall at the front of the museum eating ice creams in the grounds of Flushing Meadows Corona Park. But instead of wondering why the park seemed to have three names instead of one – which is what my brain would normally be doing – I found myself enjoying the sun, my lemon sorbet and, surprisingly, the gentle calm of my father's company.

'Hey,' Dad said, 'know what made me laugh?'

'What?'

'That thing you said about not even tipping a taxi driver if they saved your life somehow.'

I chuckled. 'I mean, that was kinda inspired by you.'

'Charming!' Dad said with a smile. Then, '*Inspired by* is good. You don't always need specifics.'

'Dad …'

He held up his palms.

'I'm not telling you how to do your job, I'm just—'

'Giving Mum's orders, I know.'

'Not orders. *Suggestions.*'

'Dad, I'm gonna do what I think is funny, OK? And no humans or animals will be hurt in the making of this show. Cool?'

Dad shrugged. 'Cool.'

The dull thud and boom of drums and bass approached and I hopped off the wall as Manny pulled up, his ponytail dripping wet. He pulled out his water gun and sent a barrage of spray our way.

'Heads up, *hermanos*!'

I turned to Dad, who was mopping ice cream residue from his face.

'Now can we see some *New York*? Like something Wainbridge wouldn't force me to do as an assignment?'

Dad laughed and followed me to the car.

CHAPTER 47

Treat 'Em Mean, Keep 'Em Keen

And we did. Manny dropped us back in the city and we walked to the southern tip of the island where we could get a good view of the Statue of Liberty. Dad explained that she wasn't really green and that, being made of copper, her true colour would have been the dark brown of a penny. Green was simply a result of oxidisation.

I told him to stop ruining moments with learning.

Then we had bagels, filled with what felt like two entire tubs of cream cheese, and worked off the calories with a walk across Brooklyn Bridge. Every turn of my head felt like the opening shot from a movie, and even though the cameras weren't on, I felt like a film star.

All the while I ran lines back and forth in my head for tomorrow's show.

As we headed to the hotel to get changed and meet

George, I was suddenly struck that tomorrow would be our last day here. Sunday morning it'd be back to Camden.

Back to reality.

But first I was going to do something remarkable.

And perhaps I'd be coming home to a *whole new reality – unrecognisable and magical.*

Only time would tell.

'I smell VIP!'

George Lacey stood in a crisp white shirt, unbuttoned at the neck, with his arms outstretched outside a black door with a neon sign above it that read *The Yuck Stop*, which seemed a pretty gross name for a restaurant. Just behind him to his right stood a huge guy with his hands behind his back, surveying the street from the doorstep.

'Hey,' I said as he shook our hands vigorously.

George nudged Dad playfully.

'You been looking after this superstar?'

'Uh, yep.' Dad pointed to the nondescript black entrance. 'Are we … ?'

'Oh! Yeah, follow me!' George widened his eyes and the huge guy pushed the door open.

'Thank you, Malik,' George said, as Malik ushered us underneath one tree-trunk-sized arm.

It looked even less like a restaurant on the inside: a long, thin, gloomy corridor lay before us, and the floor was sticky as if it were covered in a thin layer of drying varnish. The light at the end of this tunnel came from a small glass booth, behind which sat a young woman scrolling through her phone. She looked up as we passed and George paused only to point us out to her.

'My guests.' He beamed.

'Sure,' said the lady.

'Thanks, Lizzie,' said George, as I began to wonder if he knew every New Yorker on a first-name basis.

At the bottom of a dark stairwell, narrow enough for me to question if Malik ever had reason to venture down it and, if so, *how*, the sound of life grew louder. As we hit the last step and turned the corner we were suddenly bathed in lights and action. The light was a dingy red, provided by shaded bulbs sat in lamps on around twenty small circular tables. The noise came from the raucous groups of customers sat around each. The atmosphere was decidedly *unrestauranty*.

But before Dad could address any of this, a skinny man made a beeline for George.

'Lacey! How you doing?'

'Hey, Freddie!'

'Got just the table for ya,' Skinny Freddie said, then

did an exaggerated double take when he spotted me. He turned back to George. 'So this is the guy, huh?'

'Yeah,' George said brightly. 'Still OK if he … ?'

'Hey, any friend of George Lacey's is a friend of mine.' He nudged Dad as if he knew him. 'Just don't remind the cops there's no kids allowed after seven, am I right?'

George and Freddie cracked up, and Dad's face moved from mildly quizzical to concerned.

'Uh, George … What is this place?' he asked as we weaved through the crowd to an empty table in the middle.

'You like ribs? The ribs here are *crazy*.' George pulled out a chair for Dad and jerked a thumb towards the kitchen. 'Alessandro, the guy who preps 'em? *Artist*. Like the Monet of meat.'

We sat, and Freddie plonked three menus and three glasses of ice water down in front of us.

'Eight thirty-five,' Freddie said. 'Jules'll call it.'

George nodded.

'I owe ya one!' he called in Freddie's wake as he headed off to another table. George turned back to our bemused faces. 'Great guy, Freddie, been running this place twelve years.'

I checked my watch. Ten to eight.

'What happens at eight thirty-five?' I asked.

George smiled and – as if on cue – all our lamps went out. In the darkness a booming voice came through the speakers.

'LADIES AND GENTLEMEN, WELCOME TO NEW YORK CITY! IT'S FRIDAY NIGHT, ARE YOU READY FOR SOME YUCKS?'

Everyone whooped and cheered.

'PLEASE GIVE A BIG YUCK STOP WELCOME TO YOUR HOST FOR THIS EVENING … JUUUUUUUULES TORRIO!'

Applause rippled around the room and a spotlight illuminated the far corner where there was a bar stool and a wired microphone on a stand. Into the light jogged a guy about Dad's age with long dark hair, jeans and an open check shirt over an old T-shirt.

'Sup, Yuckers!' he yelled in what sounded like the same voice that had introduced him. 'I'm Jules, your host, we got a bunch of great comics for you tonight, how you feeling about that?'

The crowd hollered their approval. One man down the front seemed less enthusiastic. Jules turned to him immediately.

'What, am I boring you already, Vern? Jeez, can I do a gag first?'

'If you think it'll work,' said Vern, and the crowd oohed and laughed. Jules jerked a thumb at Vern.

'Every week, this guy!' He returned to his target. "Ey, Vern, maybe if your wife hadn't kicked you out you wouldn't have to be in here so often!'

The audience howled. I looked on with the same feeling you might get if you saw a flying saucer hovering outside your bedroom window.

I was in a nightclub.

Wait till Al …

Wait till the Three Moes heard about this.

I must have let out an audible gasp because Dad's head snapped towards mine, his face growing scarlet. He whispered through gritted teeth.

'You shouldn't be here. George, what is this?'

George waved a hand at him dismissively.

'*Sh-sh-sh*. Just watch. We'll talk at the intermission.'

Jules introduced two different acts. The first was a short bald man who told a long story about how he took a sleeping pill on a plane but it only put his legs to sleep. He acted out his journey to the toilet and had us all snorting with laughter.

Apart from Dad.

The second act was a woman called Silver who swore more times than a Year 10 boy at lunch break.

Dad had seen enough. He jumped out of his seat.

'Right, that's it. Come on, Car.'

The commotion distracted Silver, who stopped mid-sentence, shielding her eyes from the spotlight.

"Ey! Carrot Top!' she called. Everyone in the venue – and I mean everyone – turned their heads to face Stuart Taylor. Even in the darkness I could see his pasty face redden. 'You leavin'?'

'Yes, actually I am,' Dad said, spinning to face her, the tips of his hair brushing the low basement ceiling above him.

'Cool, cool ... 'Ey, before you go, you mind just dusting off the ceiling there? Few cobwebs forming ...'

There were chuckles as everyone saw how close Dad's head was to the ceiling, and just how tall he was, *full stop*. Or as the Americans say, *period*.

'Hey, if you don't mind sticking around,' Silver added, 'it'd be great for my friends – they're running late and we could use you as a meeting point.'

The audience bent double with laughter and Dad slumped back down in his chair, out of the line of fire. George patted his arm and shook his head, as if to say, *'Don't worry about it.'* But Dad's cheeks had gone from scarlet to crimson, his body heaving with indignation.

Silver combined her farewell with the mother of all swear words, and Jules returned to the mic to announce a short break.

Dad pushed his chair back.

'OK, Car. Let's go.'

'Whoa, whoa, whoa,' said George. 'At least try the ribs!'

Right on cue, Freddie arrived with a massive rack of ribs and a bowl the size of a cauldron stuffed with French fries. It looked spectacular. I looked pleadingly at Dad and he sighed. It's hard to turn down a free meal, no matter your mood. Plus the look on his face suggested he had a few unanswered questions.

'Mm! Oh, that's unreal,' said George, tearing into a rib. I followed his lead, devouring the soft, meaty, barbecue-sauce-covered goodness.

'George, this place isn't appropriate for kids.'

'Even ones that are smarter than the average adult?' George winked at me. I smiled back, sauce dripping down my chin.

Dad lowered his voice.

'I just … Is this really necessary? I mean, if it's for research purposes, I really think—'

'You know how many people watch *The Missy Show*, Stuart?' It was the first time George had used Dad's actual name. 'Fourteen and a half million. That's just in the States. The YouTube clips and international figures grow so quickly that by the time I gave you a number it would have already doubled. "Those Crazy Kids" is every-one's favourite, no matter what celebrity we have on. People wanna see a star in the making, and if that means adding a drop or two of something provocative, that's what we'll deliver.'

'And what if Car doesn't want to deliver that?'

George looked at me and smiled.

'He already did, right?' He cracked up. 'Show me a kid in the world who doesn't wanna fully *own* their Geography teacher!'

'Which got him expelled!'

'Whoa. That sucks,' said George. 'Albert Einstein got expelled from a bunch of schools, you know that? So did Snoop Dogg.'

'But maybe he doesn't wanna be a rapping astro-physicist!'

'Have you asked him?'

'Excuse me?'

'Just saying. You ever actually asked him what he might like to do with his life?'

I started to feel heat rising in my cheeks. Too many things were happening at once. I'd never heard my dad raise his voice like this, let alone have such strong opin-ions. On top of that, it was as if George were in my head. He wasn't wrong, but I felt super uncomfortable having these two grown-ups speaking for me. It was like being in Mr French's office all over again.

'I can speak for myself,' I said suddenly, and both men's eyes snapped towards me.

'LADIES AND GENTS, PLEASE WELCOME BACK YOUR HOST, JUUUUUULES TORRIO!'

'Yes you can,' smiled George, clapping with the rest of the audience. *Yes. You. Can.*

'OK, George, listen,' Dad started. 'I get that you're trying to produce something memorable. That's your job, but ...'

'Welcome back, Yuckers!' Jules drowned Dad out from the re-illuminated microphone. 'Now listen up, we got something very, very special for you right now. In a few minutes we'll bring out Danny Jam, but first, in our open spot for new talent, please welcome ...'

I put down a greasy rib and wiped my face, looking forward to the next act.

'Aaaaall the way from London, England ...'

Ah, cool – a Brit!

'Carmichael Taylor!'

Whaaa ... ?

My jaw hung open as George began whooping along with the crowd.

'Trust me,' he said. 'Give 'em hell.'

'Wait a minute!' Dad growled.

'Carmichael Taylor!' Jules said again. My heart started doing keepy-ups against my ribcage.

'Dad. Let me try.' I tensed my jaw and clenched my fists.

'But—'

I pushed my chair back and stood. Dad reached out to grab my arm but I shrugged myself clear. George pulled out his mobile phone and followed my movement with it. Heads turned with clear gasps as I shuffled my way through the crowd. I felt a huge surge of adrenalin course through me. It felt like if I lifted my hands they might shoot lightning across the room.

When I reached the stage, there were more shocked murmurs, then the clear sound of laughter as I had to reach up to retrieve the mic, which was well above my head. Just as at the studio, the piercing spotlight meant I couldn't really see anything and, in that moment, that was *exactly* what I needed.

'Yes, I am short for a thirteen-year-old,' I said. 'This is like a flashback to my school play, *Snow White and the Seven Dwarfs*.'

A few chuckles.

'Guess which one I was?'

More than one person shouted 'Dopey!'

'Nope. Wicked Queen.'

Surprised sniggers.

'Cos no one trusts gingers, right?'

Full laughter. Whoa. This was no school Talent Night – these guys had *come* here to *laugh*. And I was gonna deliver. I felt my notepad in my back pocket.

Don't think I'll need you tonight.

'Not too bad for a kid!' Vern shouted. And suddenly I wasn't scared.

'Daddy?' I said. The audience kept rolling, 'Is that you? When are you coming home?' Howls from the room. 'Let me know, and I'll tell Mum's hot new boyfriend to make himself scarce for an hour.'

Actual applause. People whistled and cheered. Someone put Vern in a headlock and frisked his hair, laughing and nudging him.

'Truthfully, the Carrot Top Guy who tried to do a runner in the first half – that's my real dad. I'm serious. I know – we make quite a pair. Now you can go to the authorities and report a sighting of Bigfoot and a Troll all in one night.'

I frizzed my hair up with my free hand for good measure.

'Dude, you look like a *Muppet!*' a young guy in the front shouted.

Big mistake.

'That's a beautiful irony considering you look like a guy who walks around all day with a hand up his butt.'

The room erupted again. I soaked it up until I couldn't feel my feet any more. It felt like I was floating on air, yet built of impenetrable granite. I had no doubt of anything I was about to say.

I was *invincible*.

'You Americans crack me up,' I continued. 'Always surprised at the way we pronounce stuff in the UK. I'll let you into a secret. You know how we pronounce stuff? *Properly.*'

They were loving it. I was insulting them to their faces and they were lapping it up. I forgot everything in my little pad and went with the wave.

'Properly! You should try it some time. We're not all smart though. I mean, you wonder why *I'm* a clown? My dad's a walking circus attraction, my mum is shorter than me – I'm serious, imagine being raised by Gargamel *and* Smurfette … My uncle is one of those tragic *one-man-band* guys you see on the corner with cymbals strapped to his knees, and I got this one friend at school? She's so dumb she once tried to start a fire using the sun and a strip of plastic wrap. She once moulded a mug out of chocolate cos she thought it would make her cocoa taste richer. It's actually a great ego boost – having a friend like that will make you feel like a genius! Then there's my brother … Oh Jeez, my brother – he's an Olympic-level Jellyhead. I mean, he thinks an acorn is called an acorn cos it's a seed for corn. He thought *Star Wars* was based on a true story, and Abraham Lincoln was a fictional character. So yeah, I guess I didn't have much of a chance, right? You either laugh or cry.'

I pointed down to a man who was slapping the Muppet Guy on the back, wiping away joyous tears at his friend getting burned by a kid.

'Or do both, like this guy!'

Jules appeared to the side of me and tapped his watch with a nod and a smile.

'I guess that's my time,' I said, and applause began to ripple. 'I'd say thank you but you guys should probably thank me, right? Kinda made your lives better so ... you're welcome!'

Meaty claps merged with whoops and cheers and Jules took my place.

'Holy moly, you ever seen anything like that before? Give it up for the kid, Carmichael Taylor! I want what he's having!'

As I returned to our table I felt pats on the backs and shouts of 'Amazing', 'Slayed 'em' and 'Killed it, kid'. For a short guy, I felt ten feet tall. And speaking of ten-footers, there was one missing from the chair opposite George, who was doing a slow clap with a huge grin.

'I knew it. We got ourselves a champ.' He waved his phone. 'Missy's gonna spew *chunks* when she sees this. In a good way.'

'Not bad, right?'

'Not bad? *Not bad!?*' George put both hands on my shoulders. 'Listen to me, little man. *You.* You have the ability to do anything. I'm telling you, kid, it's all up to you. The world is your oyster.'

I smiled. 'I hate oysters.'

George cracked up.

'This guy! Never off, are ya? Now look, I get that your dad is a little … old-fashioned, but you gotta follow your instincts here, buddy. This is *your* superpower, not his.'

I looked around.

'Where is he?'

'Who?'

'My dad.'

'Uh, I … think he went to the bathroom.'

I turned to find the toilets, but George stopped me.

'Kid.'

'Hm?'

'This business. You can't have anyone else making your decisions for you, you understand? *You're* the star, *you* call the shots. Right?'

'Right.' *Right. Damn right!* 'Can you email me that video?'

'Sure, kid. Hey – what a warm-up, huh?'

'What a warm-up.' I smiled, and headed for the Gents.

CHAPTER 48

Sad, Mad, Bad and Dad

Dad wasn't in the toilets. There were a couple of young guys washing their hands and discussing the night so far. I turned to leave and one of them spotted me.

'Oh snap, Clark – check it out!'

'Whoa,' said the one called Clark, shaking his hands over the sink and wiping them on his jeans. 'Dude, you were hilarious!'

'Thanks. I, er – I have to go.'

'Can we get a selfie, bro? Jay, get your phone, man, quick.'

'Sure.'

The pair stood either side of me, against the romantic backdrop of two urinals and a toilet with the seat up. Jay pulled goofy faces and sighed with awe.

'Was it, like, your first gig and stuff?'

'Uh, kinda.'

'Wow. So I get to say I saw the Ruthless Kid Who Kills Everybody at his first ever show? That's dope.'

Jay put the phone away and Clark high-fived me.

'Don't worry, they're clean! Hey, what was your name again?'

'Car. Carmichael Taylor.'

'Cool. Stay funny, little man.'

They pushed through the swinging door.

'*Ruthless*,' Jay said again, shaking his head as the door swung back behind them.

I stood at the sink and stared at my reflection in the grubby mirror.

This little guy with the freckles and the Afro really just did that?

I really did. George was right. I had the power. I didn't need anyone telling me what to say or do. I was in America, on the cusp of greatness, for one reason: me. I did this.

I shook back into my body and remembered who I was looking for in a public toilet.

Back in the club, Jules was telling a story and all eyes were on him. It was dark, but I was sure Dad wasn't there. In the gloom I could see George craning his head towards me. I held up a finger then made for the stairs, jumping them two at a time.

At the main door, the warm night air hit my face and everything felt foreign and strange again. Massive Malik turned and looked down the length of his man-mountain stature to me, then jutted his chin across the street where Stuart Taylor was sat on a wall outside a corner store, looking more than a little tragic – like a little kid waiting for his dad to pick him up.

He looked up as I crossed the street, no change to his defeated demeanour.

'Why'd you leave?' I asked.

'Why'd you stay?'

'Didn't you see what happened in there?'

'Yeah, I did.' He hopped off the wall. 'You broke your promise.' He started walking towards the nearest subway. I jogged to keep up with his endless legs.

'Wait a minute, what did you expect me to do? Are you trying to tell me that wasn't a unique situation? I wasn't gonna go up there and talk about tea for five minutes! Did you see how rowdy that crowd was?'

Dad stopped as we reached the subway.

'So maybe you should've just insulted them, instead of the people that care about you, who weren't there to defend themselves.'

He trotted down the stairs. I stomped after him.

'What? I was *improvising*, Dad. It's called comedy!'

'Long as you think it works for you, then.' He spoke

calmly, which only made me angrier.

'It worked for everybody!' I screwed my face up, feeling my temperature rise. 'What would you know, anyway? *I'm* the one with the talent. It's *my* superpower. The world is my oyster!'

'Sounds like something George Lacey would say.'

'Of course you'd have a problem with him, wouldn't you?'

'What does that mean?'

'Come on, Dad. He's like your age but he's cool, he's rich—'

'Oh, please. You should have heard what he said to me in there. He's not a—'

'He's successful. And he believes in me. Unlike you.'

'Is that really what you think?'

'No, it's what I *know*.'

'And you think he's got your best interests at heart. You're all that matters to him?'

'I don't know, Dad. Why, is that how *you* feel about me?'

'Of course it is!'

'Is it?'

'Yes!'

'Really,' I said flatly.

'Really.'

'Fine.'

289

'Fine?'

'Fine!'

We both paused in stubborn silence, then Dad softened.

'OK, Car.'

'What?'

Dad sighed, still calm. '*OK*,' he said, in a way that sounded like nothing was OK.

We climbed on to a subway carriage and fell silent for four of the five stops on the short journey. I was quietly fuming as we sat side by side, not looking at each other. Then I caught his reflection in the window opposite as he gave another small sigh and a shake of the head.

And I snapped.

'You *hate* it that I've found something I'm really good at.'

'What?' Dad scoffed.

'Or Mum does, and whatever Mum does, you just agree with it anyway. Cos you don't have any opinions of your own!'

A few other passengers looked up and I felt my face redden. Dad lowered his voice, still irritatingly calm.

'OK.'

'Stop saying "OK"! What does that even mean? You're not saying anything! You never *say* anything!'

'This is our stop.'

I laughed bitterly.

'Great.'

We stomped up to street level in silence, but being out in the hustle and bustle made me less self-conscious.

'Lan would've found it funny.'

'You think? You think he would've appreciated that? Alex too?'

'At least they would have understood that someone on*stage* in a *comedy* club might, just *might* be joking!'

We reached the spinning doors of the hotel's reception. Dad turned to me.

'Whatever makes you feel better about yourself, Car.'

AAAAAAARGH!

Dad went to the elevator, but instead of following him, I made a beeline for the reception seating area, where they had hot drinks and public computers. Dad turned as he reached the elevators.

'Where are you going?'

'Getting a hot chocolate,' I said without looking back. 'I'll be up in a minute.' All the adrenalin I had was still bouncing around inside me, but now it was mixed with real rage, an explosive *kiss-my-butt* cocktail.

Why couldn't he just be happy for me?

Lan would've been whooping and cheering.

Alex would've wet herself with laughter.

I'll show him, I thought. *I'll show them all.*

At one of the computers, I logged into my email account and smiled as I saw the unopened message at the top of my inbox, sent only twenty minutes ago.

FROM: georgelacey@themissyshow.com
Hey buddy. Holy smokes what a night! Didn't get to say goodbye. Here's the vid as promised. Save some of that fire for tomorrow, cowboy!
G

I knew I hadn't imagined it. I killed that show. I mean, I destroyed that room.

I looked around the quiet, gentrified reception. *Man, if I had some earphones I'd watch it back in all its glory right now.* I added Lan's email address, typed *'Guess who!'* and pressed FORWARD. I checked my watch. Five hours ahead back home. He might be fast asleep right now, but he'd wake up to something special.

I made my hot chocolate and jumped in the elevator. All four walls were mirrored, giving the effect of infinite Me's, and I was back in my own movie again. It didn't matter if Mum and Dad didn't get it. I was a force of nature now.

You rode with me, or got rolled over.

When I opened the door to our room, Dad was laid on his bed, reading a book. He didn't acknowledge me and I didn't acknowledge him. I put my drink on the bedside table and began flicking through the cosy little observations in my notebook, but all I could think about was how much I didn't need them any more. I didn't need notes, or my parents, their approval, or anything or anyone else.

My instinct had got me all the way to New York City. My instinct had nailed that gig. There was no point in over-thinking it. I mean, it's *instinct*, not *thinkstinct* – right, guys?

Guys?

CHAPTER 49

Whatever

*B*ellicose, *pugnacious* and *truculent*. They all sound like words you might find in a cookbook, maybe because *bellicose* appears to have 'belly' in it, *pugnacious* seems to suggest a stinky but delicious dish, and *truculent* rhymes with 'succulent'. But actually they all just describe my state of mind when I woke up that Saturday morning:

Ready for war and willing to start one if necessary.

I lay in bed, staring at the ceiling.

Last night proved that the promises I'd made to Mum shouldn't have been asked of me in the first place. I should've believed in myself from the start.

Then I realised there was no snoring from the adjacent bed.

'Dad?'

I got up and checked the bathroom. Empty. Then

I saw a piece of hotel headed paper in front of the television – a note.

Gone jogging, back at 10. Dad.

I checked my watch: 9.23 a.m. Quick maths told me that meant it was 2.23 p.m. back home, on a Saturday – *perfect*. I had enough time to check my emails downstairs and see what Lan thought.

I pulled on a T-shirt and shorts, then – *Wait ... Is that ... ?*

I sat down on Dad's bed and shifted his book from his bedside table.

Yup.

Dad's phone. Now I wouldn't need to wait for an email response at all!

I poked my head out into the corridor, just to make sure Dad wasn't headed back early, then rushed back to my bed and called Uncle Lan.

'Stuart?'

'Hey, no, it's Car! I'm on my dad's phone.'

'Carm? How's it going out there, man?'

It was good to hear my uncle's voice.

'Oh man, it's incredible. You see the vid I sent?'

'I did. I did. Spoke to your mum about it already.'

'You showed her?'

'No, your dad told her about it and she called me this morning. Not the happiest.'

'She just doesn't get it.'

'I think it's more that she thought you two had a deal. Y'know, no insults ...'

'But if she got it, she would've known I could never promise that. You saw what that club was like, right?'

'Yeah, and I do get it, Carm, I get why you said those things about me.'

Funny things. *Jokes.*

I mean, what hilarious story ever began with '*So there's this really lovely and amazing dude who only ever did lovely and amazing stuff and he was lovely and amazing every day, always and forever more*'? What kind of guy even bothers to tell that story? I'll tell you who: the type of guy who's never tried any other flavoured crisps because of his lifelong love of Lightly Salted. Not even fully Salted. *Lightly* Salted.

'That was just—'

'You don't have to explain it, just listen for a sec. Everyone is inspired by their own experience. No one just imagines stuff completely out of the blue, so it's only natural you're gonna talk about what you know or think you know.'

'Exactly!'

'But that comes with responsibility, Carm. Not everyone has a platform to tell their story on. I could go and sing a song about you, but what about your ma? Your dad? Think of all the mean things Malky's ever said about you, then picture him telling the world. The world wouldn't know *you*, but *he'd* be the guy on the platform so the world would take his word for it, right?'

'I wouldn't care!'

'Wouldn't you?'

'People like me get what's funny – what's a joke and what isn't!'

'People like you.'

'Yeah.'

'So people like … Alex?'

My turn to go quiet.

I felt a prickling under my skin. I'd made all these strangers cry with laughter, and not one person I knew could say, *Well done*. The prickling sensation rose up my neck and into my cheeks. I spoke quietly but I felt like I was out of breath.

'I told Dad *you'd* get it.'

'I do get it, Carm, and I love the way you love me, I'd never wanna change that. But there's a lot more people who put a lot more time into you than I do.'

'What's that supposed to mean?'

'You think Alex is happy not talking to you?'

'I don't know. She probably doesn't care what I'm doing.'

'I doubt that. I mean she's the reason you're there.'

I scoffed.

'She put a video on YouTube. Hardly a mastermind.'

'No, she—'

'Ugh. God, it's like no one I know even wants me to succeed, to do anything good!'

'Carm, hold on a sec, man, you're not listening.'

And now, my turn to get the last word.

'I need to prepare for the show, Lan, I gotta go.'

'Carm!'

'If you wanna watch it, it'll be eight p.m. for you, but, whatever.'

I hung up and stared at the phone.

Jealous.

They're all jealous.

Lan would *love* to be on TV instead of busking or performing in some rubbish arts centre.

And Alex …

Maybe Alex thinks she should've been invited to New York, just because she shot the video. Sorry, but pressing RECORD on a phone doesn't make you a movie director.

Just jealous.

Like Malky. It's sad. He *wishes* he could go to the States. Who wouldn't wanna be in my shoes right now?

That's why they're all against me.

My chest heaved as if I'd just finished a sprint; my

eyes darted around the room. I suddenly had no idea what to do with my body. I threw Dad's phone on to the bed and picked up my little notebook, flicking through the pages but not taking anything in. I flicked faster and harder, ripping a couple of pages – at first by accident, then on purpose. In a blur I began yanking and tearing like crazy, until I was sat at the edge of the bed, shreds of paper like confetti at my feet.

The sound of the door unlocking made me jump to my feet. Without thinking I pulled my shoes on just as Dad entered, red-faced and sweaty.

'I'm going for a walk,' I said, brushing past him.

'Wait – Manny is picking us up in an hour,' Dad called after me as I strode down the hall. I didn't even turn around.

'Then I'll see you in an hour.'

CHAPTER 50

International Man of Mystery

I climbed the steps to the High Line. It was busy and I plonked myself down on a bench to watch the tourists, happy families and couples pass me by, laughing, kissing, taking photos. I wanted to get onstage and dis them all.

They don't know who I am, I thought. *None of these people has the slightest idea what I can do. What I'm capable of.*

'Excuse me,' a lady with what sounded like a German accent said. I looked up. Wide-eyed and friendly-faced, she held out her phone. 'Would you please take a photo of us?'

I sighed and nodded. The woman joined a man of similar age and three kids, leaning against the barrier opposite me, a classic New York City vista of yellow cabs and grey buildings framed behind them.

'Käsekuchen!' said the dad.

Ugh. They looked so damn happy I wanted to throw the phone over the edge. The woman beamed gratefully.

'Thank you so much! Very kind!'

'*Ja*, we thought you guys were supposed to be rude!' the dad joked, assuming I was an actual New Yorker.

I forced a smile.

Nah.

They don't know who I am.

I wandered, wondered and pondered down half the length of the old railway, and found myself at the edge of the city, staring out at the Hudson River from Pier 62. An old carousel with creepy wooden animals turned round and round slowly behind me.

A young couple stopped nearby, laughing and canoodling, sharing a paper cup stuffed with churros. The woman fed one to her partner and he paused with it hanging out of his mouth like a cigar. She laughed and stepped back, motioning for him to pose as she got out her phone to take a picture. From nowhere a seagull swooped and snapped a churro from the cup in her free hand, causing her to scream and him to choke on his sugary cinnamon stick.

'Did you get that?!' I heard the man call. They laughed, kissed and tried to take a selfie, but the woman dropped the whole cup, causing a small pigeon riot on the ground. It was one of those romantic moments they'd hark back to in years to come.

It moved me about as much as watching a man paint a fence.

I turned away in disgust and saw a man filming his toddler on the carousel, waving every time the little girl reappeared at his vantage point. He watched the entirety of this magical moment through the tiny screen on his phone, recording a memory he never physically had that he would most likely never even watch back. Or worse, perhaps he'd send it to various members of his family and friend group, and *those* poor suckers would have to watch it instead.

Yup, I concluded as I left the pier and headed back to the hotel. *People are big, empty, goofy, needy idiots.*

It's my duty to destroy them all.

CHAPTER 51

The Carm Before the Storm

'Thought you was gonna chicken out there for a second, *hombre!*'

Manny was leaning against his gigantic car out front of our hotel, chewing on a toothpick. I swaggered over, shaking my head.

'Who, me? I'm from Camden Town, bro, we don't chicken out of anything!'

'Ha! *My guy!*' Manny laughed and we did the *Uncle Lan* handshake.

The back window rolled down and Dad poked his head out.

'Where have you been? We should've left ten minutes ago.'

'I'm here now,' I said and walked round to the other side of the car.

Music played as Manny drove, but Dad and I sat in

uncomfortable silence for at least five minutes before he turned to me and said, 'Car, listen, I—'

I held up my hand. 'Can we talk after the show?'

'That might be a very different conversation.'

'Whatever. I need to concentrate.'

Dad shook his head and we went back to silence.

Outside the studio, a small number of Missy fans were already gathering by the famous window on to the set, and were being herded patiently by security guards with *The Missy Show* logo embroidered on to the backs of their high-visibility vests.

'Show time!' Manny sang as we stepped out into the midday sun. Dad looked over to me, but I turned to a young security guy.

'I'm ready,' I said. He nodded and relayed my arrival over his walkie-talkie.

'See you on the other side,' Manny called after me. 'Knock 'em dead, killer!'

I strode past the twenty or so fans, eager in their earliness with packed lunches and Thermos flasks and home-made signs that somehow smacked of both huge effort and huge lack of quality. I pitied the severe lack of excitement in the rest of their lives. They looked like nerdy kids on a trip to the zoo, vying for positions to see the Great Apes.

Wait till they get a load of King Kong, I thought.

*　*　*

'Uh-oh! Take cover!'

George Lacey ducked down when he saw me enter reception, as if he were being shot at.

'Ace marksman in the house! Security? We got a trained sniper on the loose in here!'

He cracked up at his own joke and I smiled as he headed over to meet us.

'Hey, George.'

'How's it hanging, buddy? Hey!' George turned to my father. 'Still got goose pimples from last night! Right, Dad?'

'Something like that,' Dad said.

George nudged him like they were sharing the same inside joke.

'So! Dump your stuff, we'll have a quick walk through for lights and camera, do make-up, break for a bite, then go live, baby! How you feeling?'

That was actually a question I realised I couldn't answer, so I just said, 'Good.'

'Beautiful,' said George, then turned to my dad. 'Now, Dad, I was thinking – the show is live, it's quite intense, plus there's a lotta competition for those audience seats, so if you were gonna be in the studio for the show you'd have to be stood in the wings, and I know that ain't the most comfortable. Cables, cameras brushing past you. So we got a beautiful green room, you can watch the

305

whole thing live from the comfort of the couch – food, drink. Katie here will getcha whatever you need.'

A voice piped up from behind us.

'So he's gonna fly halfway across the globe to see his son perform on a *screen*?'

The four of us turned.

There, behind me, was Missy herself. Only inches above me in height, her pale green eyes sparkled with warmth underneath her trademark short-cropped pink-dyed shock of heavily gelled hair. She wore an outrageously loud, multicoloured blouse, the collar of which was being temporarily protected from make-up by a kind of wrap-around paper bib. It looked a bit like a flattened Shakespearean ruff and, combined with her diminutive size, reminded me of a court jester.

Showy as it all was, though, none of it seemed like a show. She looked comfortable and she made me feel comfortable too. She looked up the long ladder of my Dad's lanky frame.

'Mr Taylor, is it?'

'Uh, Stuart,' Dad said a little uncertainly. Missy shook his hand.

'Missy Green, pleasure. So, Stuart …' Missy smiled. 'Where would you like to watch the show from?'

'Oh. Er, I mean … Obviously it'd be great to actually see it in the flesh, but—'

306

Missy held up a hand to stop him. She turned to George.

'Then we get a seat for Stuart, cool?'

George nodded and smiled, his lips tightening slightly.

'Reserve a back row seat for Dad please, Katie,' he muttered to his assistant, and started texting frantically on his phone.

Missy turned her attention to me.

'Now *you* I don't need an introduction to. Carmichael, right?'

'Car.'

'George showed me the videos. Should I be worried over here, Car?' She laughed, playing scared.

'No.' I chuckled.

'But everybody else should be, huh?'

'Uh …'

'Ah, I'm just yanking your chain. You go out there and enjoy yourself. That's all that matters. People see you enjoying yourself, they enjoy it even more. Best advice I ever got? *Love whatcha do, they love you too.*'

'Exactly what I said to him.' George beamed.

'And I'm sure he woulda also told you I don't like to talk too much to my guests beforehand. Keep the convo fresh on the day, y'know.'

'He *did* say *that*,' Dad said. George looked up briefly,

then buried his head back in his smart device. Missy nudged me playfully.

'OK then, I will see you out there, my friend!'

She hopped back down the hall to a door marked *MAKE-UP* and I found myself smiling in her wake.

While George continued texting, Katie pointed to a room at the end of the hall where I could make out a big bowl of fresh fruit and some mirrors through the open door.

'That's the green room, you guys can dump your stuff in there, that's yours for the day. Anything you need just holler!'

'It looks white,' Dad said.

'Sorry?'

'Why's it called a green room?'

The King of Awkwardness returns!

'Uh, I'll find that out for you,' Katie said with a smile as she ushered us out of reception. As if she was genuinely going to find out the origins of the term.

(Being the Word Nerd I am, I've done that research and I can tell you she will never know – because *no one knows*. It's just one of those English language oddities that has a hundred and one theories behind its birth, from as boring as a room in the medieval Blackfriars Theatre happening to be green, to the much more fun East End Cockneys nicknaming the stage 'The Greengage', the result of something called *rhyming slang*, which I like the sound of.)

As soon as Katie closed the door on us in the un-green green room, Dad picked up where he'd left off.

'So … you had a think about what you might do today?'

I sighed theatrically.

'Yes, Dad. I think I'm going to get up, do some jokes, then leave.'

'You know what I mean.'

'And you know I don't care.'

'Car …'

'No, Dad, it's my mouth, my brain, my opportunity.'

Dad just looked at me.

'What?'

'I think you should have a word with Mum.'

'I'm not gonna do that.'

'Just say hello.' He pulled out his phone.

'No, Dad.'

'Come on … Here.' He scrolled to Mum's name and selected a video call.

'Dad!'

'Five minutes.'

'I said no!'

Ugh. Why did every single adult in my life feel like they had the right to tell me what to do? And worse – tell me what to feel? *I'm a thirteen-year-old boy, not a three-month-old puppy. And I don't feel like heeling!*

So I didn't heel. I spun on my hind legs and bounded outside.

'You done already, *hombre*?'

Manny was by his car playing a game on his phone. I shook my head.

'Just … Needed some air.'

Manny jutted his chin out towards the studio, still one eye on his game.

'Stuffy in there?'

'Yeah, you could say that.'

He nodded knowingly.

'You and your dad, huh?' Manny's phone emitted a comical explosion and a few notes of sad music. 'Oh come on, man! I was close to killing the evil donkey that time.' He turned the screen to show me the multicoloured pixels.

'That's a dragon.'

He looked back at the screen, 'Nah, man, thassa mean *burro*. Donkey.'

'With wings?'

Manny took off his shades and squinted at the screen. He shrugged and put the phone away. I looked out at the growing crowd of fans at the window, then to the small queue forming by the entrance.

'You know, *my* dad, he just walked out, bro.' Manny's demeanour shifted. 'Yeah. I musta been four, five. Just left. I dunno where he went, but my mama to this day, she say *"Buen viaje a la basura mala,"* like, er ... *Good riddance to bad garbage*, y'know? So maybe it was for the best. And she always been there for me, my brother too. Even his annoying kids. The thing that always bugged me? I couldn't ask my dad why he left. I couldn't tell him I was angry. Couldn't even say "Good riddance" to him, you feel me? He never gave me the chance. So I was mad, y'know? Like no one cared how I felt, no one lost what I lost, no one understood me, right?'

I nodded slowly, not sure why he was telling me this. He smiled as if he heard my thoughts.

'Instead-a focusing on what I don't got, I focus on what I *do* got. 'S'why I ain't mad no more.'

I spun on my heels as a voice called my name from the front door: Walkie-Talkie Guy.

'Car? Ready for you on set.'

I turned back to Manny. He smiled, put his shades back on, held out his fist and we did the handshake.

'On a wave!' Manny sang joyously.

'Nailed it,' I said.

'Just like *you* gonna do, little man.'

CHAPTER 52

Countdown

'That's lunch, guys!'

The lights went up in the studio and everyone darted off in different directions. The dress rehearsal was finished and now I knew where to stand, sit, wait and perform. An assistant had sat in place of the famous actor I'd never heard of – I guess they were way too famous to rehearse. A country singer called Big Wes did a sound check with his band, and one of the *Missy Show* team had offered me a bunch of different shirts. I told them I'd stick with my favourite hoodie from Talent Night.

The most important thing was that I'd avoided Dad throughout the whole procedure. I preferred it that way, because every time his freckly face was illuminated in the back row it looked sad and needy. Frankly, it was really starting to annoy me. I mean, it was an annoying face on a normal day. But today? I just really didn't need it.

Ninety minutes until the real thing.

When I got back to the green room, Dad was already there, picking food from a menu with Katie.

'Car?' Katie offered me a menu. 'Anything for you?'

'I'm good. Not hungry.'

I wasn't saying it to be difficult or moody. I mean I *was* feeling difficult and moody, but I genuinely wasn't hungry. My stomach felt knotty and my mind was racing. Like at Talent Night, but with less excitement. Katie left to order the food and I found I couldn't sit, so I shifted awkwardly on the spot until my dad said my name.

'Car, listen …'

'Dad, I really need to focus now. I need to practise – I need to get ready.'

Dad held up his hands.

'OK, OK. Hey. I'm not here.' He pulled his finger and thumb in a pantomime *zip* across his lips, reached for his book and turned away.

'But could you really not be here?' Dad looked up at me. Like, '*Seriously?*' 'Please.'

'OK.' He shrugged. 'I'll eat in the canteen.'

He got up, picked up my hoodie from where I'd dumped it on the sofa and hung it carefully on a rail at the back of the room.

'Don't want it getting creased.'

He walked past me and stopped at the door.

'See you after the show,' I said.

'Yeah,' he said, and walked out.

I still couldn't sit.

I paced and shuffled like an avatar in a video game who you can't manoeuvre out of a dungeon – you just keep bouncing him off insurmountable platforms and locked doors while he paces as if on a treadmill with his forehead grazing various walls. My thoughts were totally shot to pieces. I ran funny lines through my head, then forgot them immediately, or couldn't work out how they related to each other. My brain had become a half-set jelly in a string bag.

What was going on with me? Last night, when I had exactly ZERO preparation, I had jumped onstage in front of a bunch of aggressive adults and the words flowed like a river bursting through a dam. Now I had time, silence, even encouragement from Missy herself, and I could barely remember how to say my own name.

I couldn't stop checking my watch.

Do you ever struggle to sleep, then check the time and get really angry that it keeps moving forward, ever closer to the moment you'll have to get up and go to school? It's only funny afterwards, when you're up and over it all, that you were ever angry at *time moving forward*.

Nevertheless, I was furious at how time seemed to be ebbing away faster than normal, not so much edging me closer to show time as shoving me in the back, blindfolded, to the edge of the cliff. And – made worse by the fact that I'd torn up my old notebook with stuff in it and had a new notebook in my hoodie pocket that had no stuff in it – I genuinely, suddenly felt like I had nothing to say.

Fifteen minutes to go.

Fifteen. FLIP! Where the flip did the flipping time go?

A knock on the door. Katie popped her head in.

'Fifteen minutes, Car.'

'Is it? *Great*,' I returned, as if I was just so damn bright and breezy I hadn't even noticed.

Another knock at the door.

'Come in.'

The door opened a crack and George's satisfied voice sang through theatrically.

'I'm coming in, unarmed – don't shoot!'

He eased in with his arms up in mock surrender, laughing at his own line, then put one hand on my shoulder.

'This is it, champ. Katie and I will come and get you just before the curtain goes up. We'll watch from the floor for the first three parts, then get you in position in the final ad break, just like we walked through. You good?'

'Yeah,' I mumbled.

'What are you, *nervous*? *The Camden Town Killer*? You punking me right now?'

'No, I'm – I'm good. I'm ready.'

'Listen to me. That crowd out there? They're a bunch of bunny rabbits and kittens. Last night you buried a pack of *wolves*. You got this. Like Missy said, just go out there and be you.'

'Be me.'

'Yeah,' said George, striding backwards through the door. '*Brutal.*'

He's right, I thought. *I'm over-thinking. Just destroy them all.*

'Hey, George?'

'Yeah?'

'Is that why you picked my video? I mean, of all the stuff on YouTube, I really stood out that much?'

George's forehead wrinkled slightly.

'Well, kinda. I mean, obviously we don't have time to scroll through the whole of YouTube, right? Ha. That'd be nuts. That's why the submission forms are so useful, y'know?'

'Submission forms?'

'Sure. On the website. People send us their clips

every week, we just pick the best. Like I said to your buddy when he sent it over, *This really is the best.*'

Wait, what?

'Hey. Knock 'em dead, kid.'

He turned to leave. Now it was my turn to wrinkle my forehead.

'My buddy?'

'Hm? Oh, yeah – guy called Alex, I think? Gave us your contact and *poof!* Here we are, makin' magic!'

My ears rang and my toes curled.

I got that cold feeling you get in that moment when you knock your mum's favourite vase off the mantelpiece, just before it hits the floor and smashes into a million unfixable pieces.

'Don't forget to thank him on the other side. Y'know, there's an old showbiz saying – *"Remember those you meet on the way up, cos you'll meet them again on the way down".*'

He laughed wildly and pulled the door open.

'As if you're ever going back down, right?'

'Right.'

'OK, let's do this!'

Ten minutes later I heard George's call from the hallway and Katie entered the green room, where I had just tried and failed to eat a grape.

'Shall we?'

'Yeah.' I grabbed my hoodie from the rack, zipped it up and followed.

Alex had submitted the video.

Her way of squaring things was to make New York happen for me. Lan was right! She *was* the reason I was here. He tried to tell me, and I didn't listen.

In my head, days sped past like a movie on rewind as I tried to pause on what I'd actually said to her the last time we saw each other.

Idiot.

I'd said she was *an even bigger idiot than I thought.*

I trudged behind Katie without any feeling in my feet, fighting the urge to slap myself in the face. The irony!

I mean, how would you describe me, swaggering around New York, assuming an army of Missy's Minions had trawled through YouTube for days, just to find Car Taylor – the greatest thing on the entire internet? *Idiotic* would probably do it. I *almost* laughed.

In the hall, people were bustling back and forth. George was talking to a lady with a shoulder bag full of make-up equipment when he spotted me.

'Show time, cowboy, let's slaughter these critters!'

I followed him, Katie and Make-Up Lady down the hall, through the double doors and into a world of darkness. Inside the studio the audience were shuffling in their seats, a general murmur moving in waves around the group. We stood in a shadowed alcove, shielded from their sight, but with a full view of Missy's chair, the sofa, the little podium stage and the famous window, now steamed up with the breath of the excited young mouths outside, all straining to get a glimpse.

I felt dazed, like I'd just woken up from a dream.

A man came over and held out his hand to me. I shook it limply.

'Hey,' he said. 'I'm Rick. Is it OK to put a mic on you?'

'Huh?'

'A microphone. So people can hear you?'

'Right. Sure.'

'You gonna be wearing the hooded top?'

'Yeah.'

'OK then.' He passed me a tiny little microphone with a tiny little ball of fluff and a clip on it, and showed me how to attach it to the top of my zip, then run the cable down inside my hoodie to a small box that I tucked in the back pocket of my jeans.

'Say a few words for me?'

'Sorry?'

'Uh, a few words? To test?'

I shook my head in disbelief, looking straight past him.

'Sorry, sorry, sorry.'

'O … K … Uh. Great. I'm gonna switch this off until the final commercial break. You're good to go.'

Am I?

My mouth was dry. I felt hot and cold. I couldn't see myself but was suddenly convinced I looked ridiculous.

'Here we go,' said George, and held out his hand for me to shake. As I did, I became aware of the clamminess of my own and winced. 'Break a leg,' he offered, and jogged out in front of the brightly illuminated audience.

'OK, guys, welcome to Midtown Studios, are you ready to have a good time?!'

A small man with a shiny bald head ran up and down the floor along the front row, gesturing wildly and clapping, his eyes wide, encouraging the audience. He seemed a little superfluous, as this lot appeared to be ready to go wild with or without encouragement. They whooped and cheered, and I scanned the back row to find Dad. It was like a really easy game of *Where's Wally?* where you have to find the awkward, bargepole-shaped Scotsman amongst a crowd of overexcited, average-height Americans. I watched as he looked around uncomfortably at the burst of emotion exploding around him. *Was that a funny thing to reference onstage? What even IS funny at this point?* I wasn't sure. I didn't seem to be sure of anything any more. I felt a sudden urge to fast-forward my life a few hours and be in the relative safety of my plane seat home.

A voice boomed through the speakers. 'Cameras up!'

Three camera operators rolled into place, perched on stools attached to wheeled platforms, and a fourth ran back and forth on foot with a camera hoisted on his shoulder, whipping his lens to and fro, catching different members of the audience.

'House lights down!'

The audience *ooh*ed as the lights above them dimmed and a purple-and-pink filter washed over the stage. George spun on his heels and made exaggerated gestures to the crowd out on the street. 'How we doing out there?' They immediately went crazy, which looked surreal when you couldn't hear them. A screen on wheels was pushed in alongside me and suddenly I could see all the camera angles that people would be seeing at home, all over the world. There was even a fifth camera outside amongst the fans at the window. The disembodied voice boomed again.

'Cue music and … we're coming in in ten.'

'Enjoy the show, folks!' George waved to the ecstatic audience – and Dad – and jogged back to where I stood.

'In five, four, three …'

The *Missy* theme music started playing at ear-shredding levels and the little bald man did another lap, whipping up a frenzy like a football mascot with no costume. A new, showy voice came raining down from above.

'Live from New York City, what a way to make your weekend ... *Heeeeeere's MISSY!*'

The music and the cheering went up another few decibels, and there was Missy Green, like a human Tinker Bell, absolutely made for this moment. She waved to the crowd, shook hands and did high fives with the front two rows like they were old friends. This was her house. She flew round to the window and blew kisses to the fans on the street who looked like they might explode with happiness.

'Everybody OK?' she sang when she finally reached centre stage, which started off another round of whooping.

'How about this sunshine – New York, huh?' Another whoop. *Jeez, was there anything these guys didn't whoop at? Maybe I could just go up there and say Hello, then leave.* 'I mean, today's a three-shower day, am I right? But it's not just the sweat. When New York City gets hot, the grime levels rise as well, I'm sure of it. I left the house this morning dressed in all white, got to work in all grey.' Raucous laughter. To what was more a pleasant observation than a cutting satirical master stroke.

As Missy's welcome continued, my nerves took off like a space shuttle, blasting off from the ground up, consuming my whole body – and I was happy to let them. Anything to stop me thinking about ... *everything*.

*　*　*

I tried my best to enjoy the show but nothing would stick. After the first break for adverts, Missy's first guest came out to rapturous applause. He turned out to be Paul Rudd, whom I recognised immediately as Ant-Man from the Marvel movies, I'd just never known his real name. In any other situation it would have been the most thrilling moment of my life, but I couldn't stop thinking how at some point he would stop talking and I'd have to start.

I had no business being here at all.

The show paused for a second commercial break and George came over, a firmness coming over him as he got closer, reading something in my eyes.

'Hey. *Game face.* Don't worry about anybody else. *Ever.* You got this, OK?'

As soon as I nodded, he switched back to Old Smiley George and scampered off towards the stage. As the minutes ticked by, my trust and faith in the natural passage of Time disappeared entirely. Time had become a Year 10 Bully, shoving me further and further down a school corridor towards some horrific form of social homicide, like running face first into a locker or catching my trousers on a coat hook and ripping them off in front of everyone.

Time didn't care about my social status at all.

After the break, Big Wes got the same rapturous response that everyone and everything seemed to get on this show and I was still no closer to knowing whether that was a gift or a curse for me. When Big Wes's dog, who looked about a hundred and five years old, staggered onstage with a red bandana around his neck to howl along with the final chorus, I could actually feel the floor vibrate with the power of a hundred audience members shaking with unbridled joy.

'Big Wes, ladies and gentlemen! OK, we're gonna take one more break and we will be right back *wiiiith* …' Missy paused and Mini Mascot Man threw out his arms, questioning the audience. As one, they all shouted back in unison:

'*THOSE CRAZY KIDS!*'

'Don't go anywhere,' Missy said to the nearest camera, and the music and lights came rushing back on.

My moment of truth hurtled towards me like an avalanche.

And I was the hiker stood frozen stiff at the foot of the mountain, looking up at my inevitable destiny.

CHAPTER 53

Are You There, World?
It's Me, Carmichael

'Three minutes, we'll get you in position. Five minutes, you're live, got it?'

I nodded at George.

'You good?'

I nodded again, words still failing me. Rick changed the batteries in my little microphone box; George yabbered encouragement; Make-Up Lady appeared and started brushing my face with the softest brush I'd ever felt. The three adults buzzed around me and as the brush tickled its way across my cheeks, I closed my eyes.

'Hey!' I heard George saying. 'You hear me, kid? They don't own you. You own them! That crowd? Buncha nobodies. *You're* the man, got it? What they think is *irrelevant* right now, you'll *tell 'em* what to think, got it? They

325

don't know you, not like I do. You're like me – a *winner*. Winners are ruthless.'

I wanted to keep my eyes closed. Just be in darkness with my face lightly brushed for all eternity. George's voice drifted away, as did Rick's and Make-Up Lady's. I stood in blissful silence with only the backs of my eyelids to focus on. I'd stopped Time! *Ha! Take that, Time – you big bully.*

Suddenly, I felt a buzzing vibration in my stomach.

What the heck is that? Butterflies?

Another buzz.

I opened my eyes. The three adults had gone and I was alone. There was also a bright light emanating through my hoodie.

A third buzz.

In my left pocket was a mobile phone. I withdrew it slowly.

Dad's phone.

The studio speakers came alive.

'Four minutes!'

The buzz was an incoming video call from 'Jocelyn'.

Mum. Now? Really?

I stood, dumbly watching the screen. They'd all be watching at home, so they must have known I'd be up next. Fine. I'd just say, *Hi, enjoy the show and goodbye*.

I swiped the screen to answer, and everything changed.

Because it wasn't Mum's face that appeared.

It was Malky's.

'I was about to hang up, bruv!'

'Malky, what are you … You know where I am, right?'

'Course! Everyone's in the living room watching right now.'

George's voice boomed from the stage. 'Coming back from commercials in three and a half!'

'I'm kinda busy here, Malky. What do you want?'

'I, uh – Mum and Dad told me to call and, y'know. Wish you luck.'

I looked to where George was standing – his eyes widened as he saw my face illuminated by the phone screen. He tapped his watch and glared. I felt my heart beat a little faster. Didn't he understand the roller coaster I was on in that moment?

'Oh, so good luck from them, but not from you?'

'Why you always gotta do that?'

'Ugh. Malky, I haven't got time for—'

'For what? The truth? I think you have, bro.'

'No, I haven't!'

'Just listen for a sec!'

'Mal—'

'No, listen! You always think I'm sucking up to Mum and Dad, doing what they say, playing perfect.' The speakers piped up again.

'THREE MINUTES, FOLKS!'

I gave a thumbs-up to George. I wanted to hang up on Malky, but I just couldn't let his comment go.

'You are!'

'Maybe I am, but you ever ask yourself why?'

I shrugged and sighed theatrically. 'You're already their favourite so I dunno why you even bother. Enjoy the show, I'm hanging up now.'

'Wait! Listen to yourself. Then look around you. You got expelled and *still got to go to New York*, bruv. You're all we talk about. We're watching you right now. When was the last time you even came to watch me race? I'll wait.'

I briefly thought I had something to say, but didn't. George began stomping over towards me. I held up one finger and his face screwed into a question as he approached, his arms out in frustration. The speakers blared once more.

'WE'RE BACK IN TWO!'

'Malk, seriously, I need—'

'No, you need to hear this. You wanna know why I try to be perfect for them when I'm not? Because of *you*, man. I've been fighting for their attention since the day you were born. But you get it all cos you got the big mouth. *Uh-oh, Car's done this, Car's done that*. There ain't no favourites, man, but in terms of their time? Their worries? Nah, you get all o' that, bro …'

'Oh, please! It's *Prince Malcolm* they're interested in!'

George and Katie stood over me.

'Wrap it up, kid. We're on.'

'One second.'

'*Now*,' George said with his hands on his hips.

'Look. I know I'm a butthead to you sometimes ...'

'Sometimes!'

'Sometimes. I know, I am. But the difference between you and me, Car, is you don't even know *when you're being one.*'

The speakers came alive again.

'*SIXTY SECONDS, PEOPLE! CAMERAS UP!*'

George shot me an urgent look.

I looked back down at the screen, speechless.

'Malky, I ...'

'You gotta go, I know. I just wanted to say—'

George snatched the phone out of my hand and passed it to Katie. He gave me a hard stare, then the three of us walked at pace into position at the edge of the stage. Rick reappeared and switched on my microphone. I looked out at the bright lights.

Mini Mascot Man rolled across the front row, a bowling ball of hype, and the crowd went wild. *What did this guy do in his spare time?* I wondered. *How did he even apply for this job, and what was the interview like?*

'*AND WE'RE BACK IN TEN, NINE, EIGHT ...*'

'Focus, Car. OK?'

'*... FOUR, THREE ...*'

The music blared and the tinted spotlight fell on Missy, whose make-up assistant quickly finalised a touch-up on her hair, then pelted back into the shadows. Katie had her hand on my shoulder, silently steadying me. The music stopped and Missy beamed at her audience, all sweetness and light.

'Aaaaand we're back! Now. Every week I promise you I'm gonna find a crazier kid than the week before, right? Well, *Missy's Minions* have been scouring the globe again, and boy have we got a treat for you! When you were at school, you ever just wanna tell everyone exactly how you feel? I mean, really? I bet you did, but I also bet you never did it quite like this little guy. Take a look at this.'

The studio lights dropped and Alex's Talent Night video was projected on to a huge screen behind the sofa. The audience gasped and chuckled in all the right places as this strange English boy, in the same hoodie as me, berated everyone around him.

I looked up at George. He seemed a little frantic.

'Sorry about the phone call, George,' I whispered.

'What?'

'Sorry.'

He turned to me. For the first time on the whole trip, something fell away from the brightness in George

Lacey's face. His lips were curled into the beginnings of a snarl, like a dog sensing an intruder. He whispered through his teeth.

'We got timings for a reason, kid. You got something more important you should be doing?'

'I was just a little nervous.' I feigned an easy-going chuckle. 'Getting some reassurance from my brother—'

'Reassurance? I'll do the reassuring, OK? God knows you ain't gonna get it from your old man. You're carrying a lotta dead weight back home. I told you, you're a winner, kid. Do yourself a favour …'

The video came to an end and Missy reacted along with the surprised crowd. 'I tried to warn ya! Those Crazy Kids, huh?!'

George leaned in a little closer.

'Don't waste your time on *losers*.'

'Ladies and gentlemen, please welcome the kid with the poison tongue, all the way from London, England … *Carmichael Taylor!*'

Music and whoops pierced my eardrums as Katie tapped my shoulder and a floor manager ushered me out.

I looked over my shoulder at George, who was back to his smiley self, clapping along happily with the crowd.

Then a flood of light and heat hit me. Everything looked and felt different to how it did on the sidelines. I was centre stage in New York City, in the USA, *in the world*.

Missy gestured towards the sofa, then we both sat down and the audience cooled.

'Still got the same hoodie on, huh?'

Big laugh. I looked down.

'Yeah, it's kinda my favourite.'

'So tell me this, what made you wanna be a comedian?'

I'd never heard anyone call me that.

'Uh, I didn't. I mean, I wasn't planning to. I just got really mad and … Yeah, it just kinda happened.'

'Like a comedy Hulk.' Missy turned to the audience. *'You wouldn't like him when he's angry!'*

More big laughs. I forced a chuckle.

'Yeah.' *Really conversational, Car.* Offstage, George was rolling both hands, desperately encouraging me to say more.

'So tell me about that night! I mean, you gave a few people what for there! I could relate, I'll tell you that! I think everyone woulda loved to get it all out like that at some point in their lives – I know I did!' She turned to the camera. 'Mom, if you're watching!'

The crowd laughed supportively. 'But come on, how did your teachers react?'

'Uh, not great, if I'm honest.'

A big laugh from the audience.

'But thank your lucky stars it had a happy ending, right? A trip to New York, a shot at the big time … Coulda been a lot worse, no?'

'Yeah …'

I watched George shake his head at another monosyllabic response, disappointment all over his features.

'I mean you coulda been expelled! Imagine that!'

'Imagine …' I forced another chuckle and shifted in my seat, hoping the world wasn't picking up on my discomfort.

'I guess you have a pretty understanding bunch around you, huh? Letting you come out here and do your thing. Impressive.'

'I guess.'

'Comics like you and me, that's all we need, right? A bit of love, a bit of encouragement.' My stomach turned. She turned to the camera again. 'Thanks, Mom. OK, so Car, I hear you've been doing some gigs over here …'

'One gig.'

George rolled his eyes.

'You wanna show us whatcha got?' The audience began their token whoops and Missy responded in kind. 'You guys wanna see him strut his stuff?!'

The whooping became manic again and, accordingly, Mini Mascot Man was flapping his arms like a pelican. Rick came over and turned my little microphone off.

'Get on up to that microphone, my friend! *It's time for ... ?*'

The audience screamed their response. *'THOSE CRAZY KIDS!'*

A short burst of rock guitars rained down and the floor manager hustled me to the podium.

I stole one more glance at George Lacey. He gave a business-like clap along with the audience, watching me with a new indifference I hadn't seen before, as if he were already thinking about next week's Crazy Kid.

Over the crescendo, Missy called, 'Live on *The Missy Show*, it's Caaaaaaarmichael Taaaaylor!'

The spotlight hit the microphone stand and I waited for the audience to quieten. Missy offered me a thumbs-up.

I took a deep breath and the studio fell silent ...

I stood behind the mic, clenched and unclenched my fists ...

As I opened my mouth, Time thought it might be cool to make it seem like it happened in slow motion.

George put his hands on his hips and looked at the floor.

'Hi,' I said, and yet another round of whoops went up, smaller this time.

'Hey, do you guys whoop at everything? Like when your train pulls into the platform on your way home today? *WHOOO!!*' I screamed. 'Or like when the coffee shop guy brings your drink? *WOOHOOO! OH MY GOSH, YES!*'

Polite chuckles ensued, not exactly a gut-buster.

I paused awkwardly. The studio returned to that horrific silence. I looked over to George again and saw him sigh, whispering something to Katie, who nodded.

I sensed a few audience members shifting in their seats. The silence was deafening. I desperately tried to remember some lines, bits, *anything* from my notebook.

'I …'

My lips smacked shut again.

Oh no.

No-no-no-no-no-no-no.

No!

I was freezing up!

Every part of me was stiff and unmoving except for my heart, which felt like it was hopscotching up to my throat and preparing to roll out of my mouth.

Despite the millions of people watching, I thought of Mum and Malky sat in horror, feeling my pain through the screen.

I thought of my teachers, wondering if this might be a more poetic punishment than any detention, suspension or exclusion.

And I thought of Alex.

Alex watching with … with *what*? Satisfaction? *Her former friend, getting his comeuppance.*

I looked up to where I imagined Dad was sat, hoping he could save me. He probably wanted the ground to open up and swallow him, away from this nightmare, like the rest of this audience.

There was nowhere left to turn. Mini Mascot Man was nervously shrugging to some audience members in the front row. Missy looked at me inquisitively. George was now in a panicky exchange with Katie.

Now, I'm no lip-reader.

Even as I write this, I'm not a hundred per cent certain. But at the time it looked to me like George said the word 'Loser'.

LOSER.

He'd said it just before I went onstage and now he was saying it again.

Maybe he was talking about my family again. But it looked more like he was talking about me.

LOSER.

I had no idea how long I'd been standing at that microphone. I had no idea what I was doing any more. The only thing I knew I could trust in, in that moment, was how I *felt*. I rewound to my first two performances. All I did was what I *felt*. In those situations it just *felt* right.

So how do you feel, Carmichael?
Tell them how you really feel.
Tell yourself.
(Third Person alert.)
(Soz.)
How did I FEEL?
Missy already told me.
LIKE A COMEDY HULK.

I inhaled hard, as if I was about to dive twenty feet underwater with no oxygen tank.

'No whooping any more?' I threw the question to the crowd and the sudden break in silence felt shocking, like a slap to the face.

'That's fair enough. I'm not anti-whoop by the way. I like what it says about you guys. *Positive, outgoing.* I guess some Brits think you're arrogant, but arrogance is different. Trust me, I know.'

I swallowed hard, hoping to push my heart back down into my ribcage. Then I looked pointedly over at George, whose face had become one of concerned confusion.

'You know the type. Ice-white shirt, ice-white shoes, ice-white teeth. Permanent orange tan, spends more time on his hair than with his kids. Shakes your hand but looks over your shoulder to see if there's a more important person behind you … Arrogant people think they can say and do anything and there'll be no consequence, right? But the one thing they can't handle is being told the truth about themselves. A few home truths, like being a butthead who becomes successful doesn't suddenly mean you're no longer a butthead. Right? Working in television doesn't make you smarter than my dad and, because you're so orange, when you smile you look like a Halloween pumpkin. *Generally speaking*, of course.'

Yup, I went there.

And for the first time, I didn't feel like I cared about the response. I looked down at my feet and chuckled to myself.

At least I'm *enjoying it*, I thought.

But then something strange happened.

As I raised my head back up, everything had changed. The light around me seemed a warm orange, like I was bathed in the glow of a hot summer sun. The crowd in front of me appeared in a wash of colours and I felt I could see every face.

And every single one of those faces was creased in hysterical laughter. For some reason, I couldn't hear it.

But I could *see* it. Everyone but my dad. Everyone swaying back and forth, slapping each other on the back, illuminated with different shades and moving in what seemed like slow motion. I felt my eyes widen.

Something magical was happening, and I was the wizard.

I turned away from the odd-moving, strangely lit audience and smiled over at George. His jaw was edging closer to the spotless laces of his ice-white shoes.

That's right, Georgie boy.

I'm KILLING it.

I stole a glance at Missy, who had a look of impish curiosity on her face, then I turned back to the multicoloured, Northern Lights-bathed audience and beamed at them.

I pulled the mic out of its clip on the stand and forced as much confidence into my body language as I could. It wasn't easy – in fact it was easily the hardest thing I'd ever done – but now I was on a mission. I guessed I'd lost George and I couldn't see Dad, but everyone else was on board.

I was *gonna say my piece*.

'Hey,' I offered breezily. 'Let's talk about idiots – we all know one or two, right? There are all kinds of idiots in the world, all different shapes and sizes. Take me, for example. Yep. I'll say it loud. *I. Am. An. Idiot.* I realise that now. I mean, it takes a special kind of idiot to stand up here and, well, make a *me* out of myself.'

Another wave of hilarity swept through the audience, their raucous laughter still weirdly blocked from my ears. I found myself pausing briefly to concur with my brain that it was some kind of spiritual moment, an other-worldly experience that performers elevate to when they're in the zone, speaking their truth.

'One of the secrets to being an idiot is *not listening* – that's key. Especially not to sensible people – that could knock your idiotic levels down, like, fifty per cent, easy. You gotta be careful of that. But also not listening to bigger idiots. One thing I won't stand for is a bigger, better-dressed idiot telling me how to go about my idiocy, even if he does have a nice car and perfect teeth.'

The crowd morphed into one big, ecstatic mouth, gasping for breath between hysterical fits.

I stole another glance at Lacey. *Can't stop me now, Georgio.*

'No, I do all my best idiot work alone. You see, being in the idiot business is tricky. You can't just barge in and be a *bit* of an idiot – no. If you wanna be like me, you've gotta be a *massive* one. Think of yourself as an idiotic chef. Sprinkle in a bit of arrogance, a spoonful of ego, a pinch of cockiness and *mwah –*' I kissed my fingers with a flourish – 'you got yourself *a huge, nutritious idiot stew.* My mum, my dad, my brother, my uncle – they all tried to warn me off making that stew, but I ignored them. That's family, right? There's no one more annoying that cares about you so much.'

The giant mouth returned to a hundred bodies, still laughing. Some of them were even hugging each other or high-fiving. Some were wiping away tears. I nodded knowingly back at them, appreciating the moment.

'I sacrificed a lot to be here. Risked a lot. Lost a lot. But that's idiots for you, I guess. We *lose* stuff. Keys, wallets, phones, pets ... school places ... best friends ...'

I shook my head in disbelief – at this moment, at myself.

'It takes a special kind of idiot to lose the funniest, friendliest, smartest person you know, all because you're so focused on becoming the President of the Idiocy Corporation.'

I looked straight into the camera opposite me.

'And I'm gonna need to get really smart, really quickly, to work out how to win you back. To win everything back.'

George appeared in my eyeline again and started waving the fingers of one hand back and forth across his neck as if to say, *Finish up, asap.* There was no need. I was pretty much done. I turned back to the audience.

'I always believed in words more than people. Loved finding big words that no one knew. One of my favourites, incidentally, is "*Hippopotomonstrosesquippedaliophobia*". It means the fear of long words. *Beautiful*, huh? That's why I say I'm a special kind of idiot. I've never been scared of big words, only little ones. Like "*Sorry*".'

I put the mic back on the stand.

'And … *"Thanks".*'

The spotlight left me and the studio lights came back on. I took one more look at this beautiful, appreciative gang of folks who'd helped me through the most profound five minutes of my life.

And …

Hang on a second …

They weren't crying and hugging.

They weren't laughing.

They weren't even smiling!

The heavenly multicolours snapped away to reveal the stark reality: a hundred strangers, sat in silence, arms folded, faces skewed into frowns, wondering what the hell they'd just sat through.

I'd had a transcendent moment all right.

I'd basically just waffled on about being an idiot, to myself, on national – no, *international* – television. No wonder they'd all looked like happy-clappy cartoon characters for the last five minutes! I'd just seen exactly what I *wanted* to see.

Then in that horrific, torturous silence, I finally saw, heard and felt a very real response. Somewhere in the back row, an enthusiastic, almost manic clap rang out from a single seat. I squinted to see Stuart Taylor jump to his feet, applauding, whooping and screaming 'Yeah!' like a naturalised American. As the rest of the crowd looked on, completely baffled, I smiled up to my dad and nodded. I guess it was like that old saying – *'In the land of the blind, the one-eyed man is king'.*

Well, in the land of the excruciatingly awkward, the Scottish lamp post reigns supreme.

Mini Mascot Man was looking at me like I'd just sprouted a tail or something, then checked himself as if he'd forgotten why he was there and spun round to the audience, encouraging them to go crazy. And of course they did. The delayed reaction told me it was probably more for the weirdness finally being over than anything else.

In amongst the whooping and cheering, I watched Dad shake his head at the mania around him. He caught my eye again and raised his eyebrows as if to say, *'These guys!'*

I laughed and shrugged back at him, took a deep breath and, with what felt like every inch of tension leaving my body, exhaled.

CHAPTER 54

The Car Is Dead, Long Live the Car

The Missy Show theme music pounded back in. Katie practically dragged me off the podium away from the cameras. I guess I had overrun my section by a couple of minutes. Missy was already up and bouncing around, wrapping up the show.

'More *Crazy Kids* next week, folks, make sure you tune in when my guests will be ...'

I turned away, feeling like I'd just done the poo I'd been waiting all day to do.

I felt light – in the feet, in the legs, in the head ... There was still some adrenalin, but it was different to last night. At the Yuck Stop, I'd said what I had to say to them to survive; today I'd said what I had to say to *me* to survive, and to the people that mattered. But I guess the biggest difference was twofold: I had no idea if I was good or not *and* ... I really couldn't care less.

I wandered through the backstage corridors towards the double doors that led to reception and felt a hand on my shoulder. I spun around.

'Car … that was … Mate, that was something else!'

I looked up – all the way up – into my dad's watery eyes and, before I could say anything, he yanked my body into his midriff and hugged me. At first it really freaked me out. Then I smelt that smell. Like hairspray and Marmite. I hadn't smelt it in years, which kind of made sense, because I also couldn't remember the last time we'd hugged. Lame as it sounds? I could have stayed in that hug for a lot longer. But:

'Hey!'

Dad released me and we turned to see George Lacey bounding over, arms spread wide, his face now the redder side of orange.

'You got something you wanna say to me, Car?'

I looked at Dad, then calmly up to George.

'Not any more.'

'Well, I'm glad you had a good time, kid, cos you're finished.'

I smiled politely.

'Thanks for the opportunity.'

Dad put his hand around my shoulder and we turned away, headed for the green room.

'You coulda gone viral!' George shouted. 'Coulda been somebody!'

Dad went to push the double doors. Then:

'Car? Stuart?'

We both turned again.

It was Missy.

'Car, that was … *not* what we booked you for, but I just wanted to say … If I'd known you actually did get expelled, I never woulda made a big thing about it. To be honest, we probably wouldn't even have had you on! I'm sorry.'

'It's not your fault.'

'What you said about family and friends. Jeez, that made me think about my mom. And my sister! They both drove me nuts. You guys are lucky you don't have Thanksgiving. Anyway, look, it was a pleasure, OK? And I hope you get your school place back, truly.'

'Thank you,' said Dad.

'Just promise me one thing,' Missy said, looking serious.

'OK …'

'Keep listening. Keep observing. Keep writing!'

'That's … three things,' I said. 'I mean, maths was never my strongpoint but …'

Missy laughed.

'Keep doing what you're doing.'

'I'll try.'

'See ya round.'

After dealing with more phone calls and text messages in fifteen minutes than we'd had in a year, Dad and I gathered up our things and headed out of the studio.

The fans from the window were being carefully herded out front, split across two sides of the studio entrance, creating a similar feel to the welcoming committees at airports. There was a collective gasp as the doors opened, then an uninterested exhalation as they saw a freckly acorn and a giant stick of ginger celery push out on to the street.

'VIP comin' through, y'all!'

Manny swam his arms through invisible hordes as we approached the car, the three of us laughing all the way.

'What time y'all plane at?'

'Not till nine,' Dad said airily, checking his watch. 'We've still got a couple of hours left.'

'So where you wanna go?'

Dad read an address from his phone.

'Eight-two-eight Broadway and Twelfth Street please, Manny.'

'You got it.'

I looked up at Dad questioningly. He smiled.

'Trust me on this one.'

'This what y'all call fun?' Manny shook his head in disbelief as we pulled up outside a huge storefront with a long
red awning that – to my unbridled delight – read:

STRAND BOOKSTORE … WHERE BOOKS ARE
LOVED … OLD RARE NEW ⸱… 18 MILES OF
BOOKS.

'*Eighteen miles of books?*' Manny said incredulously,
'I'd rather walk eighteen miles up a hill with my nephews.'

'Thanks, Manny!' I said excitedly as Dad and I
jumped out at a red light.

'Whatever floats your English boat.' Manny
shrugged. 'Need me to wait for y'all?'

Dad shook his head.

'We're good from here. Can you pick us up from the
hotel around six?'

'You bet.'

Inside was a maze. Endless aisles of promise from
multicoloured spines as far as the eye could see, and at
least two hours to kill. Not everyone's idea of fun maybe,
but if I'd learned anything that day, it was that while
I definitely needed to start worrying about how I make
other people feel, I could also care less about what other
people thought of me. I was a Word Nerd and proud
of it.

I have to say, the one thing neither of my parents

ever put a spending limit on for me was books. Dad and I went half and half on two graphic novels, a non-fiction hardback on space exploration, two detective stories and an oversized photographic history of New York. Dad whistled as he flicked through the last of my haul.

'Some incredible bridges in here!'

We laughed, bagged the books and headed out, then Dad bought us two hot dogs from a nearby kiosk. We munched them in Union Square, watching a squad of teenage boys and girls doing acrobatic street dance on a big square of rubber.

Dad swallowed his last bite and wiped his mouth, looking at one of the boys who was being egged on wildly as he spun on his head.

'Glad I came,' he said simply. 'Really glad.'

I kept my gaze the same direction as his. I guess we were still men and not quite ready for all out mushy.

'Me too.'

Instead of riding the subway, we walked back to the hotel to soak up our last moments in the city. Everything felt fresh and new and other-worldly. The lightness in my legs made me feel I could have walked for hours, but we were running out of time.

'Let's get moving, *hombres*! You gonna miss your only chance to get back to Middle Earth!'

Manny pulled our cases out from the back of his mammoth automobile as Dad took a few snaps of the airport from the outside.

'Dad, that is gonna be such a boring photo.'

'For you maybe.'

I shook my head.

'Great to meet you, Manny,' Dad said.

'Y'know everybody says that? My biggest sadness in life is that I'll never experience how great it is to meet me.'

We all laughed and I went to do the handshake.

'Whoa, whoa,' said Manny. 'Let's break this sucker down three ways.'

He gestured to my dad and we made a hopeless attempt at a three-way handshake. Manny cracked up.

'OK, maybe not – can't win 'em all! Nice going, *Braveheart*. 'Ey, y'all take care now.'

'Bye, Manny.' I paused and looked at this funny grapefruit of a man one more time, remembering his words to me before the show. 'Thanks.'

He smiled.

'Get outta here already.'

So we did.

CHAPTER 55

Afterword

Word to the wise: If you're ever such a butthead that you need to apologise to numerous people at the same time, try to get yourself on an internationally renowned television show and do them all at once. It really saves a lot of time and awkwardness. Plus they can always watch it back and remind themselves that you're a legend.

It was nice not to have to say too much when I got home. It's hard to explain, but it was all said in the eyes and the hugs when Mum, Lan and Malky met us in Arrivals. There'd be plenty of time to talk the following day, when we went to the Kembers' house to discuss a strategy on getting me and Alex back into school.

'Hey,' I said tentatively to Al when we came face to face for the first time in what felt like years rather than days.

'Hey yourself,' she said.

'Al. My mum was wrong. *I* was wrong. You're not bad for me. And you're not an idiot.'

'All true. Although, if I was an idiot, how would I know?'

'I knew I was.'

'You musta been one of those smart idiots.'

I smiled.

'I guess so.'

An awkward moment of silence.

'Al, I really am so—'

'I know,' she interrupted, sparing me.

She held up my peace offering. It was one of the graphic novels I'd bought in New York that I knew Alex would love (about a snail with a phenomenal IQ who very slowly takes over the world).

'Thanks for this.'

I nodded gratefully.

'No, thank you,' I said. 'For everything.'

Alex put on her goofy American Movie Narrator voice.

'*And at that moment I knew. Nothing was ever gonna be the same in our little town again.*'

'I take it back, you *are* an idiot.'

We both laughed this time and bumped fists.

* * *

After that, Mum apologised too, and both families rolled into action. I emailed Miss Miller and asked if she could organise a meeting. I also attached a long letter Mum helped me write for Miss Miller to forward to the Head, detailing what school, and being a part of it, meant to me (basically me talking about how much I loved English, and Mum making me add 'also Geography' or 'I feel the same way about Science and Maths' or 'which is similar to how much I respect all teachers' at the end of each paragraph). I added a link to the latest *Missy Show* episode for good measure.

'Now, *that's* the Car I know!' she emailed back enthusiastically. 'Oh, and *Hippopotomonstrosesquippedaliophobia!??!!* *clap emoji, clap emoji, clap emoji*.'

In her office on Monday afternoon, the Head, Mrs Craig, spun her computer screen to face us and played the last few lines of my *Missy* performance. Mr French stood behind her chair, arms crossed. She stopped the video, removed her reading glasses and stared at me for what seemed like an age, her expression unreadable. Mum, Dad, Miss Miller, Alex and the Kembers waited for her to break the tension.

'I shan't pretend that this isn't a unique situation, Carmichael,' she began. 'And that being the case, my belief is that this problem requires a more unique solution.

I have discussed this at length with Mr French and we are in agreement.'

Mum's eyes widened.

'You'll let him back in?!'

Mrs Craig held up a finger.

'On one strict condition. Carmichael will need to provide a community service for what's left of the school year and the whole of the next. He'll pay his debt with additional work.'

Alex and I exchanged quizzical glances.

'Our Sixth-Form-led peer-to-peer Drama Club has ended due to lack of uptake and we need something to replace it. Something different. I suggest, Carmichael, that you and Miss Kember here prepare a plan to organise and run a comedy club for students. A sort of "*How to*", in place of Drama Club, every Tuesday after school. No free rides, Mr Taylor. You'll *earn* your place back at Wainbridge.'

Mum nodded enthusiastically.

'He'll do it,' she said hurriedly.

'Uh – I'm not sure I'd know exactly how to run a—'

'This is non-negotiable, Carmichael. From what Miss Miller tells me, you are clearly smart enough to find a way. And I'm certain Alexandra will be tireless in her assistance – will you not?'

'Huh? Oh, absolutely, miss.' Alex beamed. 'When do we start?'

'I would suggest immediately!'

'Could I ask if we can start *next* Tuesday instead of tomorrow? Just to give us a bit of time to prepare and, like … promote it?'

Mrs Craig looked to Mr French and gave a small nod.

'I'd like to see your business plan and at least fifteen participants signed up by the end of this week.'

Alex snapped her fingers. 'We'll get you thirty!'

I shot Alex a look. *Thirty?* Jeez. Well, it could be worse. At least I'd kept this first Tuesday free after school.

I had an engagement I couldn't miss.

'GO ON, MALKY!'

Lan and I leaped up, swept away by the excitement of watching my brother wipe the floor with seven competitors in a two-hundred-metre sprint at his athletics meet on the track in nearby Gospel Oak the following afternoon. A huge cheer came from behind us as Mum, off call from the hospital for the day, and Dad ('working from home') returned from the nearby ice-cream van holding a pair of 99s each.

'Thanks, guys,' I said and dived in for a huge mouthful. Mum smiled as she wiped a splodge of white from my nose.

'That boy is a *whippet!*' Lan laughed as we clapped and cheered along with the rest of the small crowd on the sidelines.

'He kicks the competition like Car kicks chickens,' said Dad, and even Mum joined in the laughter.

'He's actually incredible,' I agreed, and gave a thumbs-up to Malky when he looked our way, hands on his hips and breathing heavily. 'If anyone tells him I said that, I'll kill 'em.'

We watched Malky get mobbed by the other athletes, patting him on the back. He looked like the kind of star I'd thought I might have been, walking back into Wainbridge that morning.

But I'll be honest with you – it really wasn't like that. Some kids had seen my performance, some hadn't. A lot of kids talked about it, some were impressed that I'd been to New York, some were amazed I was actually on *The Missy Show* at all, but very few were that fussed by what I'd said.

The video had a respectable number of views online, mostly from being posted on Missy's official YouTube page and cutting all the references to George Lacey. But it paled in comparison with the kid the week before who'd trained her cats to complete obstacle courses.

And I was more than cool with that. In fact, as the weeks passed, the video disappeared completely. Taken down swiftly by George, I suspected. I really wasn't bothered.

I had a new project.

Alex and I met every day after school that first week back, coming up with ideas for an hour-long comedy club. The Three Moes promised to be regulars and make sure others were too (Mehmet also offered to act as 'security' on the door). I would lead on joke writing, and Alex would lead on clowning – physical comedy. And although not all her ideas hit the mark ('*Lesson Seven: establishing the best surfaces to slip on, from oil to vomit*'), she was never short of them. True to her word, by Friday, we'd convinced thirty-four kids to join the Alcar Kemtay Comedy Club, despite the terrible name she'd insisted on.

I was all ready for a new adventure.

And you know what? Even though it was literally going to be *about* jokes, unlike most adventures in my life, I had a feeling this one might not be just another joke to me.

THE END

Alone, with Everyone

Same old street
Same old bus
You.
Me.
This is us.
Everyone together yet everybody alone
Millions of people and still you're on your own
Use the time to wonder
Use the time to think
Would somebody catch me if I'd fallen off the brink?
Everyone's connected it just feels like we're not
You feel good for now
Tomorrow I might have that spot
You feel bad today
Tomorrow it might be my turn

Pain and happiness, the ups and downs
are what we earn,
Same old street
Same old bus
You.
Me.
This is us.
And every now and then you'll feel like no one
understands
But we can't read your mind, your hopes, your
fears, your dreams, your plans
Speak the spoken word to let you know I feel alone
Could be face to face or just at home or on
the phone
Sharing out a problem
Can be hard but there's no shame
Cos half the time
You'll be surprised
They'll say 'i've felt the same'

So on that bus
Or on that street
Although we'll maybe never meet
Just know I'm not as far away
As you might think your feel today.

Same old street
Same old bus
You.
Me.
This
Is
Us.

About the Author

Ben Bailey Smith began his career as a rapper known as Doc Brown before diversifying and moving into mainstream TV and film acting, stand-up comedy, screenwriting and children's books. He has a host of notable television performances under his belt, as well as creating the BAFTA Award-winning Children's BBC TV show *4 O'Clock Club*.